McCallister Bounty Hunters

GEM SIVAD

WOLF'S TENDER
McCallister Bounty Hunters
Copyright © 2015 Gem Sivad

ISBN 978-1-62622910-5
Published by Gem Sivad LLC

Manufactured in the United States of America.

COVER DESIGN
SelfPubBookCovers.com/Robert

CONTENTS

DEDICATION

To my husband, the inspiration for all my heroes.

CHAPTER ONE

Miss Naomi Parker, deportment instructor at the Sparrow Creek Young Ladies Academy, stood between the Flat Rock Sheriff's Office and the town saloon. In spite of the heated day, she shivered.

Earlier that morning outlaws had attacked her school, carrying eight of her students with them when they rode away. Naomi had remained free during the raid because she'd jumped out the open window and hidden.

Even after the outlaws had gone, she'd huddled in the crawl space under the building, afraid to come out lest the kidnappers return for her too. Had she grown a backbone sooner, the caretaker might have lived. She'd found him dying by the barn when she'd finally emerged from hiding.

"Miss Naomi," he'd wheezed, barely able to speak. She'd lifted him, trying to stop the wound with the fabric from her dress, but nothing slowed the blood as it leaked into the dust around them.

"Go to Flat Rock. Tell the sheriff—Comancheros."

Though dying, he'd had more wits about him than Naomi. Once he'd taken his last breath, she'd followed his direction and ridden to town.

Alternately crying, mumbling aloud and slumping lifeless on Patrick's mule, she'd finally reached the sheriff's office, ready to hand the nightmare over to someone else.

"No ma'am, though that's a sorry thing that happened, first off, you didn't get hit by Comancheros. They rounded that bunch up a few years back and we don't get bothered by them no more. But, it makes no difference who it was. If outlaws are stealing females from hereabouts and took them girls, we can't be leaving our own womenfolk unprotected." Gene Stanton, the Flat Rock Sheriff, adamantly opposed doing anything.

"But they'll get away. My students will be lost if you wait. If you follow them now..." She'd tried to reason with him.

"I'll wire the U.S. Marshal, but I won't be asking the Flat Rock citizens to chase down and fight them devils." Stanton had cut through her attempts at persuasion. According to the sheriff, it would take days for the law to put together trackers and a posse of men, weeks before there was any hope of catching the outlaws.

"Sheriff Stanton, it's your job to catch criminals." She'd tried to sound reasonable but had only gotten more hysterical as he'd shaken his head, denying her his help.

"You're not protecting anyone sitting in this office.

You can start right now and go after them." Perhaps her words had been tart, but lives were at stake.

"It's my job to see to the well-being of Flat Rock," he'd snarled at her belligerently, any measure of civility he'd accorded her before disappearing. "Seems kind of funny you got away. How come you're not ridin' an outlaw horse right now?"

Shame that she'd hidden while her students had been abducted rendered her mute. Before she gathered enough wits to respond, they were interrupted. The deputy, who'd been lounging outside, poked his head in the door.

"The McCallisters are bringin' in a string of horses with carcasses tied on back." It appeared to be the escape the sheriff desired.

"I've got business now. Get my deputy, Sumner Sikes, to point you toward the hotel. You look like hell. You can't run around town with blood on you. It'll upset folks." The sheriff had motioned at the open door, expecting her to leave. Evidently, dealing with the men riding into town was much more important than handling her students' kidnapping.

Clean up? She looked down at her dress where patches of sweat and blood darkened the fabric. Gazing at the material stained by Patrick's death jolted her, reminding her why she needed to act and not tarry. Her students' lives would be lost next. If the sheriff's priority was her appearance rather than the kidnapping of young Texas women, it seemed evident to Naomi their rescue was up to her.

In spite of the day's heat, her shivering continued. A white fichu at her neck, once crisp and cool, threatened to choke her as it reminded her of her duties as a teacher.

I have to do something! She remained in the alley watching the three men riding down the main street.

"Who are the McCallisters?" Naomi asked Deputy Sikes.

"Meanest dammed bounty hunters in the country," he answered. "The big redhead is Deacon. He used to be a preacher. Dumbest thing the outlaws ever did was kill his wife. He strapped on a gun, caught and executed the murderers, and then kept a huntin'."

Naomi studied Deacon McCallister. He wore his hat pulled low over ragged red hair, his features disguised by a heavy beard. One hand held his reins and in the other arm he cradled a rifle. He glanced around the street and rubbed his jaw.

"First thing I need is a bath and a shave." His words carried clearly to her and she wondered if he expected the local hotel to hurry and prepare a tub of water. Frowning, she glanced at the next man in line.

"That's Sam McCallister. The outlaws call him Snake 'cause he can crawl up on a man and slit his throat without makin' a sound. He's a bad 'un for sure." Deputy Sikes lowered his mumble to barely a whisper as the first two riders drew abreast of the alley.

"We need the tender attentions of women, Deak—

after that, a card game and maybe a meal." As if performing for an unseen audience hidden behind closed doors, Sam's slow drawl grew louder.

Naomi studied this McCallister. Dark whiskers outlined his square jaw, contrasting with the light-colored hair trimmed short and barely showing under his hat. Below his holster, one hand rested on his thigh next to the knife strapped there.

Snake McCallister turned his head, meeting her gaze. His eyes were glacier blue and she froze as he appraised her before riding past where she stood in the alley.

The first two bounty hunters led the evidence of their success behind them—live prisoners cuffed and leg-shackled, walking beside the cargo of wrapped bundles loaded on pack animals.

The odor of ripe bodies—Naomi suspected both dead and alive—accompanied the caravan behind the McCallisters. One of the shackled prisoners whined a complaint.

"You damned McCallisters starve a man to death if you don't kill him first. Ma Phillips cooks for the Flat Rock jail. I'm gonna have biscuits and honey or maybe her brown gravy slathered over potatoes."

Naomi stepped back, her stomach rebelling at the suggestion of food as swarms of flies accompanied the caravan, invaded the narrow alley, and buzzed around her. The deputy flinched, batting at the insects and moving toward the boardwalk.

The town had been busy earlier in the day, Flat Rock's citizens scurrying from one business to another. But as the trio rode down the street, people had disappeared behind shut doors, avoiding the three bounty hunters cloaked in arrogance and brutality.

Naomi knew the service the hunters provided was this land's version of rough justice but remembering Patrick in death, it made her stomach clench. The bounty hunters seemed more like the killers who had attacked the school than like honorable citizens doing a needed task.

"What about the third man? Who's he?" Naomi asked after Sam and Deacon McCallister rode past the alley.

"The breed's Charlie Wolf." The deputy didn't elaborate, shrugging away further questions, and keeping his gaze on the ground, not looking at the man at the end of the string of horses. As the third man drew near, Deputy Sikes scuttled up on the boardwalk, leaving Naomi standing alone in the alley.

When the man named Charlie Wolf reached the space where Naomi stood, his horse snorted and pranced sideways. Turning the huge beast to face her, the bounty hunter drew rein.

How odd his eyes are—such a light shade of gray against his copper skin. Naomi stared at him, trying to think of what to say but the savagery of his appearance drove important thoughts from her mind.

A sleeveless leather vest displaying bronze arms as sleekly muscled as the horse he rode covered his upper torso. But for the two braids framing his face, he wore his blue-black hair loose, cascading over his shoulders from beneath his broad-brimmed black hat.

He is actually quite magnificent. As if waiting for her to speak, he leaned on his pommel, seemingly indifferent to everything else in the street. She doubted that his casual posture was anything more than a ruse. He was a predator, searching for danger behind her in the alley before raking her with his glance. Naomi struggled to find convincing words with which to petition him. But she couldn't force any sound through her constricted throat as his fierce gaze measured her for threat and, finding none, dismissed her.

When she said nothing, Charlie Wolf's eyes narrowed to slits and he turned away, riding to the front of the sheriff's office. Naomi followed him with her gaze. When he'd sufficiently moved toward the others, she edged closer to the sheriff's deputy so she could hear the discussion taking place.

Sikes stared horrified at the wrapped bundles of tarp stacked on the back of the pack animals before he began unloading them.

"Dammit, this pile of stink is smellin' up the whole town. Next time just bring in their gear." Sikes' complaints were muffled since he wore his bandanna wrapped around his face, blocking the odor.

"Nope. Tried that. The sheriff didn't want to pay on our word last time. Remember?" Snake McCallister shoved his hat high on his forehead as he mopped his face with a handkerchief. Ragged blond hair and rough beard didn't disguise his handsome features. He laughed but the humor didn't touch his eyes.

"Well, Sam, the sheriff sure as hell ain't the one out here dealin' with rotten corpses. Maybe you could take 'em on over to the undertakers," the deputy suggested hopefully.

Naomi could see that as unpleasant as it might be, it was the deputy's task to give each body a quick once-over and confirm its identity. But wrapped as each bundle was, he had to wrestle the dead on the ground in order to peek at each face.

"The poster says 'Wanted Dead or Alive'. They're dead—job's done." Deacon scratched his heavy red beard and settled wearily in his saddle. When the deputy glowered and spat, acting on his disgust, the red-haired bounty hunter sat up straight, his demeanor a warning. "Stop bitching and get a move on."

"I'm hurrying as fast as this mess allows, Deacon." The deputy quickened his pace, comparing the stack of wanted flyers with the corpses he'd unloaded, ticking them off one by one. "Crawford Bank Robbery—one thousand dollars for the capture of the thieves and one thousand dollars for the recovery of the gold coin." Then he looked up at the bound prisoners. "You got both of the bastards. I don't suppose they told you where they stashed the money?"

The dark-skinned bounty hunter caught Naomi's attention again when he drew a heavy pouch from his saddlebags and tossed it at the feet of the deputy.

"Charlie Wolf," the lawman muttered and flinched, acknowledging the receipt without offering insult by inspecting the content. He kicked the bag of money over to the office door and moved on to the six decaying corpses inside the heavy canvas wrappings.

"Henry Loco Miller, Thomas Wright, Juarez Sutter—payout for these is…" The deputy went down the line, reading off names and bounty rewards in amounts that boggled Naomi's mind.

"Damn sonovabitch," the deputy cursed after he unwrapped the next body. "I hope this one suffered before he died. He shot and killed the Austin bank president's wife during the holdup. The Texas Bank Association put up the money." Deputy Sikes kicked the carcass one last time and moved on, giving the last two bodies a cursory glance before replacing the tarp.

"Alsgood boys, five hundred each. They weren't worth much alive and won't fetch much dead."

Listening to the tally rise as the hunters collected more money per outlaw than she could earn in years of teaching, Naomi's depression increased. When the count was finished, the deputy pushed the live prisoners through the sheriff's door and Sam and Deacon followed to get their reward money.

Charlie Wolf remained a silent, dark outline against the sun, facing the near end of the street, ignoring the caterwauling of the deputy. His gaze flicked to where she stood and moved on again.

Muscles rippling beneath the dark bay coat, his horse pawed the dirt, making its own protest at the stench permeating the air.

"Eyaia Oyamossa," the dark rider said, speaking a guttural language Naomi didn't recognize as he patted the animal's neck. But the horse understood and quieted.

Naomi tucked herself into the shadows as the Indian again glanced her way. Feverishly, she tried to think of ways to ask the man to rescue her students. When the door to the sheriff's office banged open and the other two men emerged, the sound jarred her into action. She gathered her courage, ready to approach the one named Charlie Wolf.

But she was too late. Without a backward look, the men headed across the street, leading the string of horses now empty of their ghoulish burden. They left behind the dead bodies wrapped in tarp. The deputy continued to curse as the undertaker's wagon creaked to a halt in front of him.

"The McCallisters work for hire?" Naomi stepped on the boardwalk.

"Yep," Sikes answered, hoisting a body onto the

wagon. "Deacon does most of the thinkin', Sam does the killin', and the half-breed..." His expression showed reluctant admiration. "Charlie Wolf can track a man to hell and back." He scowled, finishing with his advice, "Pay the devils enough and they'll find your students for you."

Naomi watched the McCallisters cross the street to a tiny building with a sign declaring it the biggest bank around. Charlie Wolf waited with the horses while the other two went inside. In a short time they returned and stood on the sidewalk counting currency.

They're dividing their blood money up, offering bait to outlaws stupid enough to try to steal from them. Naomi frowned at them grimly. Sam mounted his horse and handed Charlie Wolf a wad of greenbacks.

"Give you any trouble?" Charlie asked, stuffing the bills in his saddlebag.

"Figured on making us cool our heels until the U.S. Marshal wired his approval. We discussed the situation and the banker changed his mind." Deacon spoke mildly as he settled into his saddle.

When they started down the street toward Wallace's stock barn, Naomi paced on the boardwalk parallel to them. She hoped they would ask what she wanted, saving her the need to approach them. But they ignored her, more interested in their destination. Their conversation floated to her as they led the string of horses to the stable.

"I think we'll get a pretty penny for that roan and the

buckskin, maybe a couple more," Sam predicted.

Naomi marked the two in the string he'd identified. Most of the horses they led appeared to be old, sway-backed or lame. As the men traveled, the street was eerily quiet, as though the entire town strained to hear the bounty hunters' plans.

"You'd think outlaws would be smart enough to get themselves a good getaway mount," Sam observed loudly.

"I don't believe intelligence and criminals fit together naturally, brother," Deacon answered.

Seemingly oblivious to the talk between his companions, Charlie Wolf rode behind the other two, checking the street, store tops, and shadowed recesses for danger. From beneath the broad-brimmed hat, black hair fell below his shoulders.

He is named well—Wolf—feral as though he's a wild beast in human clothes. Naomi swallowed nervously as she gazed at the man. Strong legs hugging the sides of his mount were encased in deerskin leggings. His body swayed as though part of the horse, one animal flowing into another.

When they reached the stable, he dismounted facing the street, removing his hat to beat the dust from his pants before he settled it back in place. He turned his dark gaze on her and she stopped. When he said nothing and resumed his progress toward the barn, she stepped into an alley and stood in the shadows berating herself for not approaching him.

CHAPTER TWO

IF CHARLIE WOLF ASSIGNED flavors to places, he'd name Flat Rock a bitter brew. The people of the town didn't like Indians and that made a half-Kiowa bounty hunter less than a mongrel dog as far as they were concerned.

Bath, food, women? He'd followed behind the others, listening to even the prisoners anticipate the end of the hunt and a night in Flat Rock. Charlie didn't. *I reckon I'll be spending the night in Wallace's barn.*

Charlie's horse, Old Mossy, didn't like this place either. The big animal had sidestepped, snorting in alarm when they'd approached the alley next to the sheriff's office. A woman had been standing between two buildings, peering at his cousins as they'd passed.

He'd waited for her to speak to Deak or Sam, but it had been him she'd kept staring at. As near as he could tell, she was a respectable woman, which made Charlie question her purpose even more, since white women tended to shy away from knowing him.

He'd given her a chance to say what she wanted more than once, but each time she'd remained mute. It puzzled him the way she'd tagged along, paralleling their progress as they'd ridden toward the barn. Once there, he'd expected her to state her business but she'd maintained her silence though he'd felt her gaze on his back when he entered the stable.

Wonder if she's outlaw kin. It was possible. Most of the men they brought in didn't have anyone who'd waste a bullet on revenge, but there was always a first. He dismissed that idea, considering her appearance. She was a tall, spare woman dressed like a lady with no buttons or bows to adorn her apparel. The dress had been soiled, something that didn't go with the rest of her look.

"I'm gonna find a woman and ride her all night long," Sam called out what was on all their minds.

Regretfully Charlie thought about the trade he had been negotiating for a Kiowa female to make his squaw. He'd almost worked out the bargain. It did no good now though, as Sam's words stirred want in his loins.

"Ain't no use in the Indian going over to Jake's Saloon. He don't serve 'em," Wallace, the owner of the barn, imparted his knowledge to the white McCallisters as though Charlie Wolf were deaf and invisible. "Redskins, I mean. Jake lost a brother and sister to the '72 Comanche raids. He holds on to his hate tight."

"I'll expect that trough over there half-filled with hot water when I get back," Charlie said, standing in front of the old bastard, forcing him to meet his gaze. Old eyes blinked rapidly before the stable owner answered.

"You're a half-breed—can tell from your light eyes. I 'spect I can wait on the American part of you. But it'll cost ya. That trough holds a lot of water." Wallace grabbed a bucket and headed toward the pump.

Satisfied that at least he'd have a hot bath waiting upon his return, Charlie followed his cousins out of the barn. As the three McCallisters walked down the street, he scanned the area, looking for the woman. She'd returned to her original spot, loitering in the alley between the law office and saloon. Her continued presence intrigued him even more since he could see from her clothes she wasn't a whore.

He caught her gaze, considering asking her what she wanted, but she shrank back into the shadows.

To hell with it. He shrugged away his curiosity, entering the saloon with his cousins, more than ready to have a drink before they hit the trail again in the morning.

"I don't serve Injuns," Jake said as soon as Deak, Sam and Charlie bellied up to the counter. Since the beefy man not only acted as bartender but also owned the place, Wallace seemed right about Charlie's chances of getting served.

"Now you do." Charlie peeled some bills from the wad of cash he carried, grabbed the bottle off the counter, and threw the money at Jake. His challenge sent stools scooting away as those in the room anticipated a brawl.

Sam laughed, Deacon scowled and the three bounty hunters made themselves comfortable at a back table with a good view of the ins-and-outs of the place. The original big room of the saloon had been divided. A set of steps separated the area into kitchen and bar. A side door accessed both rooms. Charlie gazed at the area opening up above.

At the top of the steps, the saloon owner had built a narrow walkway fronting three openings. He'd rigged a bell above each doorless space. Bell pulls led from the back of the bar to the rooms, enabling Jake to ring the bell when he deemed the customer had enjoyed enough time with the prostitute.

Jake's rough wood counter stopped just short of the alcove under the stairs where he'd stacked cases of liquor and supplies. It wasn't a fancy layout, but it was efficient.

"Food first," Charlie told the other two, his stomach rumbling as the smell of fried eggs reached them from the kitchen.

"Yep," Deacon said and walked to the kitchen area. In a loud voice, he ordered. "Fix three plates. We want steak, eggs over-easy, fried potatoes, and stacks of toast."

"Told you I don't serve redskins," Jake yelled, wiping the counter with the dirty cloth he held.

"I'm extra hungry," Deak answered, returning to the

table. His words, though spoken softly, carried to the suddenly quiet room.

Charlie's lips twitched and he held back his laugh when Jake scowled, turning away to yank on one of the bells above.

"Hell, I just got started on her," a male voice bellowed.

"Finish up fast or it'll cost you more," Jake yelled back.

Charlie figured Jake needed to bully someone and finding the McCallisters too scary to challenge, he vented his wrath on the poor bastard trying to buy a fuck upstairs. When the side door opened, Charlie's attention returned to the kitchen area.

Well I'll be damned. His female stalker edged into the room and disappeared in the kitchen. He stared at the access door under the steps. Within moments, it opened. The little mouse ducked in, parking her skinny frame, and peering out from a hidey-hole between boxes.

"Get your ass moving, Molly. I don't pay you to sit around," Jake snarled at a saloon girl who'd eased onto one of the high barstools. It seemed plain that the owner vented his anger on the girl for lack of courage in following through on his *we don't serve redskin* declaration. But that didn't help the whore any.

"Bring one of those crates over to me." The fat bastard pointed at the boxes of whiskey under the steps.

"Molly, come here," Charlie called, deliberately

goading Jake in order to distract the saloon owner from the spy's hiding place.

Molly frowned. She knew Charlie. He'd fucked her in an Abilene alley. That was where and how he got most of his needs taken care of—dark corners and hidden places.

From the look on her face, Molly hadn't forgotten his double payment either. Hesitantly, she answered Charlie's summons, slowing her pace to a crawl, waiting for the bartender to intercede. He didn't. When mincing steps brought her to the table, Charlie pulled her onto his lap, fondling her breast as he fumbled one hand under her skirt.

"Who said you got first dibs?" Deacon drawled, laying his gun on the table. The room's inhabitants were left to decide whether the gun was to deter Charlie or them. Since Deak didn't fuck with whores, Charlie wasn't worried.

"Why don't we flip for it?" Sam asked, tossing a coin on the table, watching it roll around before it flopped on its side.

Flaunting his Indian ancestry always made Charlie's blood do a war dance. For the white woman crouched under the stairs, he put on a real show. He mouthed the sweaty material of Molly's dress, capturing the nipple underneath, and sucking hard enough to give the huckleberries in the room something to chew on. But it was the blue-eyed Peeping Tom who irritated Charlie the most.

He knew what whites saw when they looked at him. He was as tall as his cousins but his skin was copper-colored, his blue-black hair fell down his back, and his high, slanting cheekbones proclaimed him Indian. His nose, once a straight blade, had been broken too many times and was now a misshapen lump. Stitch marks bisecting his right eyebrow trailed down his cheek to his jaw. Though faded, the scar was still light against the dark bronze of his face.

Charlie dressed to please his Kiowa side, lacing his high leather moccasins from the top of his feet up to his knees, and wearing a colorful breechcloth hanging from his hips, covering deerskin pants at the groin. But clothes didn't change facts. His white family tied him to their world. Except for his McCallister relatives though, Charlie held most paleskins in contempt.

Anger more heated than usual simmered in his chest. The regular saloon drunks witnessing his insult didn't bother him more than normal, but the woman under the stairway gawking at Charlie infuriated him. He could have grunted out some inarticulate gibberish that would have pleased the spectators, confirming his savagery. Instead, his words were drawled in Texas tones.

"You'll give us a good ride, won't you, sweetheart?" Molly twisted in his grip and, tired of scandalizing his audience, Charlie released his hold. Letting the fancy woman tumble to the floor, he tossed some bills her way as she scrambled to her feet.

"Sorry, mister, I have to make a living. If it got out I let an Indian have a poke, I'd have to lower my price." Hastily, she tucked the money in her dress and backed away. Her fearful glance at the bar owner indicated she'd have to endure more than a drop in wages if she went up the stairs with Charlie.

"My whores don't fuck dirty Injuns. I'm telling you to leave." From behind the counter, the bartender pulled out a shotgun, and aimed it in Charlie's general direction.

"To hell with it," Charlie snarled, sick of the whole game. He grabbed the whiskey from the table and stood, knocking his chair over. The bar owner chambered a round at the same time Charlie threw the bottle, hitting him in the head. Jake dropped like a stone. His shotgun sounded, blasting a hole in the side of the wall next to the McCallisters.

"One of these days, Charlie, you're going to get your ass blown off doing something like that." Sam righted his chair and laughed.

"Hell, Sam," Deacon growled. "One of these days he's going to get *our* asses shot off doing something like that." Both men held their guns in their hands.

"Jake keeps the good stuff here." Sam went behind the bar and reached underneath the counter. He grinned, bringing two bottles up with him.

"Pay the damages out of my share." Charlie headed toward the saloon exit. "I'll see you at first light," he told his cousins.

"Here, take this to keep you company," Deacon passed him a bottle on his way out. "I'll eat your steak and eggs. Like I said, I'm extra hungry."

Charlie resigned himself to beef jerky for supper and maybe coffee if Wallace had any brewing in the barn. The woman interested him more than food though.

Bet we scared the rabbit off. A last look at the place under the saloon steps confirmed his expectation. She'd disappeared from her spyhole, leaving him wondering what she'd wanted.

CHAPTER THREE

NAOMI DECIDED this might be her best opportunity. She backed out of her hiding spot, brushed the cobwebs from her dress, and hurried out the alley door. Her thoughts were centered on the man leaving instead of the two remaining bounty hunters.

She'd been contemplating how to stop the unproductive disagreement between her quarry and the bartender. Mr. Wolf had resolved the issue without her help, raising her respect for his aim but leaving her in doubt of his sense.

He could have gotten himself killed before I find the girls. She knew from overhearing the amount of money the men collected in bounty she couldn't afford to hire all three of them.

"I don't need the one named Deacon to think for me. I can do that," Naomi muttered. "And we have to find the outlaws before any killing can be done, so Sam McCallister isn't of interest.

"Charlie Wolf is a good tracker—according to

Deputy Sikes, the best. He also looks intelligent and very capable of killing with expertise." Heat flooded her loins as she watched the muscles in his shoulders rippling under his bronze skin. "With him, I get all three," she muttered her justification, assuring herself she wasn't indulging in prurient thoughts at this critical moment.

As her choice of bounty hunters walked down the middle of the street toward the livery stable, Naomi followed, pondering how to broach the subject of employment to him.

"Excuse me," she called weakly after his departing back. She stilled her impulse to scamper for cover when he pivoted, turning in the dusty street to study her from steel-gray eyes.

He appeared more predatory up close than he had from a distance. She wet her lips, preparing to begin negotiations, but nothing but a nervous *ahem* escaped her throat. Though she tried as she returned the man's gaze, Naomi couldn't force words from her mouth.

Mr. Wolf shrugged, turned back toward the barn and she watched helplessly as his long strides carried him away.

I cannot waste another night. We must get on the trail of the kidnappers now. She clenched her teeth and hurried forward, placing a detaining hand on his arm. As soon as she touched him, she knew it was a mistake. The muscles she'd admired from afar rippled beneath her fingers. The arm itself felt as hard as a hickory limb.

"Excuse me, sir. I'd like to speak with you if you have the time this evening." Apprehensively, Naomi peered into a face devoid of expression, meeting the man's enigmatic gaze.

Though she was taller than fashionable and accustomed to standing shoulder high to most men, Naomi had to tilt her head. Charlie Wolf stood half a head taller. The sculpted muscles in his arms and chest made him twice as wide as her as well.

He scowled, his lips forming a thin line, signaling his irritation. Rather than meet the piercing gaze, she focused on Mr. Wolf's mouth.

"If you have the time," she repeated in a whisper. Unfortunately, looking at Charlie's lips, she remembered his mouth on the other woman's bosom and heat flooded her face, scalding her senses.

"I don't."

"You don't what?" She blinked stupidly, trying to figure out what he meant.

But he didn't answer her. Instead, he appraised her appearance, his glance roving slowly over a dress torn in several places and stained with Patrick's blood. When she'd rolled under the porch, she'd felt the material give. The thought made her nauseous and jolted her from her malaise. She needed to obtain this man's help. She waited, forcing herself to remain calm beneath his inspection.

She trembled under his glance. He was bigger than

she'd originally thought and his overwhelming maleness frightened her. Evidently in his mind, the two words he'd spoken ended the conversation. He shrugged her hand off, walking away.

Maybe I should wait for federal troops to rescue the girls like Sheriff Stanton suggested. Then she remembered the length of time Stanton had predicted it would take just to get men ready to mount a rescue.

Impossible. We must go now. Naomi straightened her spine, hurrying after Mr. Wolf. When once again she touched his arm seeking his attention, he growled a very rude expletive. Covering her hand, he pulled her along beside him toward the barn entrance and her indecision was no longer relevant. Stopping, he raised the bottle as if to take a drink, then paused, handing it to her first.

"I would like to hire you," she said, declining the drink, returning the bottle, and taking the opportunity to explain her purpose in stopping him.

"You mind drinking with a half-breed?"

Naomi questioned her original assessment of his intelligence when his main concern seemed to be feeding her the spirits. Apparently if she wouldn't drink with him, she had no power to hold his interest.

After he tipped the bottle, drinking deeply, he released her, resuming his trek toward the stables. Hastily she caught up, shaking his arm to get his notice this time. He plowed to a stop, looking at her in astonishment.

"I have need of your services," she announced grimly.

"Likewise," he said, leering at her in a deplorable fashion before he gave a disgusted snort, and resumed his walk to the barn.

"I have no idea how I could be of service to you, Mr. Wolf," she muttered, hurrying to keep up. She touched his arm again reassuringly. "I'm certain we can find common ground."

"Don't worry about it." He peered at her closer, the rock-hard muscle of his lower arm flexing beneath her fingertips. "I'm not looking for work right now, anyway." His stern words brooked no argument.

"But this can't wait. A band of crazed men attacked the school where I'm a teacher. Patrick, our handyman, said they were Comancheros. Sheriff Stanton disagreed with his opinion. Nevertheless, Patrick was killed attempting to defend us from the savages."

"And you're bothering me with this why?" He crossed his arms over his broad chest, listening to her at last. Naomi hurried to tell her story.

"Whoever they were, the outlaws carried away my students. The deputy said you're the best tracker in the country. I need you to find them."

Mr. Wolf's stoic expression didn't invite more but she added, "The morning started as usual with the academy boarders seated at the table eating porridge. The real cook and the kitchen supplies were to arrive later this week with the rest of the girls." It occurred to her that the rest of the students wouldn't arrive now and her teaching position might be at an end. "I don't know what will happen now."

"How did you escape?" Charlie asked.

"I had opened a window hoping for a breeze. When we heard shots, the girls ran toward the front of the room to see what was what."

That was such a mild way of explaining it. When the first shot resonated from the area of the barn, interrupting the stolid silence of breakfast, the girls had sent benches flying as they hurried to the front window.

Gently, girls, she'd admonished them, demonstrating restraint and proper deportment. *Remember, a lady always maintains poise and calm, even in dire circumstance. Nor does one show extreme curiosity, as it is an emotion of the lower classes.*

"I told the girls to stay seated. There had been problems with a skunk. I assumed the noise had been made by Mr. Wilson shooting the varmint."

"Was Wilson the hired man?" Mr. Wolf asked.

"Yes." Patrick had greeted her at the Flat Rock stage depot three weeks before when she'd arrived in Texas. Naomi had been prepared to meet a board member or at least the headmistress. Instead, the caretaker had been assigned the task of transporting her and later her students as they arrived. Naomi swallowed bile, picturing the old man the last time she'd seen him—dying from gunshot wounds.

"The girls claimed that watching the hired man shoot a polecat was probably the most exciting thing they'd see for a while." Admitting that she'd been unable to control the girls embarrassed Naomi. The young ladies had ignored her, pushing and shoving to be the first at the front view.

Though Naomi had silently agreed that boredom lay ahead of them, she'd continued walking slowly toward the door to illustrate gracious dignity. Even though she was secretly as interested in the outdoor disruption as her students, she was careful to model restraint. As she passed the open side window, she looked out, prepared to enjoy the meadow below, the one spot of green in a world of brown dirt, red dust, and gray sky.

"From the side window, I saw the riders attacking." Reliving the moment of horror, she told Charlie Wolf, "Wild savages raced across the meadow, whooping and screaming as if they were banshees. I shouted a warning to the girls but it was too late. Men rode their horses up on the porch and burst through the door."

"You going to tell me how you got away?" he asked, showing remarkably little sympathy, reminding her he was also part wild savage.

"I jumped out the window, landed on the ground, rolled under the school, and hid in the crawlspace under the building, listening as my charges were attacked." Naomi bit her lip to stop its trembling. She knew from the rough sounds, thumps and cries she'd overheard that terrible things had happened above. "We need to go after them. The outlaws didn't linger at the school."

"You plannin' on huntin' 'em down?" Charlie Wolf asked.

Naomi nodded. "I was unable to think of any way to save my students at the time, but I listened to what the gang leader said." It had gotten quieter and she'd watched the savages push and drag the girls to the extra horses the bandits led. "A man named Jericho was in charge."

"You sure you heard the name right?" Charlie demanded, his expression changing from grim indifference to fierce attention.

"Of course I'm sure about it." Naomi snapped. "He bragged about how they were going to trade the girls to a man named Harvey Collins. While they were celebrating their success, the gang leader said, 'Collins didn't lie. White girls like these'll bring us plenty across the river. We ain't out a thing if he don't come up with his part of the trade'."

She blinked back tears before appealing to the bounty hunter's better nature, hoping that he had one. "Another outlaw said, 'Hell, Jericho, I'm for takin' 'em to Mexico even if he does come up with his end of the deal'. Mr. Wolf, I can't abandon my charges. They only have me right now to rescue them. I need you to help me find them."

"And then what?" he growled.

"I haven't come up with my plan yet, but it's imperative that we catch up to the kidnappers. My students are resourceful and if they are able, they will participate in their own escape."

Naomi stood outside the barn trying to find some way to persuade a man who looked every bit as savage as their attackers to help her. She'd thought all day about it. She could reach the girls sooner than the proposed posse if she had a good tracker. She gazed at Charlie Wolf and knew he was her best hope.

"How many riders hit the place?" His indifferent attitude had changed to interest.

"I think there were at least twenty." Naomi hurried to answer. "When I saw them coming toward the school, I didn't count, but…" Her words faltered and she shuddered, hugging her arms around her body, suddenly cold.

"Take a drink, you'll feel better." He didn't wait for her to agree but handed her the bottle again.

"No, thank you." Naomi returned the bottle, the contents untasted, watching the sinews in Charlie's neck tauten as he tilted his head, swallowing the whiskey in deep gulps before he stopped drinking and gave his attention back to her.

"You were smart to hide." Praising her cowardice, he covered her hand still lying on his arm and led her into the barn.

"Get your ass out here, Wallace," he yelled loud enough to reach into the shadowy dark corners of the building.

"You heat that water for me?" he asked when the old man shuffled into the open pointing a pitchfork at them as if for defense.

Naomi might as well have been invisible as the men transacted business, but Charlie Wolf didn't release her so she couldn't disappear. She drew herself upright and waited while he gave the old man orders. She had no intention of leaving until Mr. Wolf agreed to help her with her rescue.

"Did just what you said, Charlie Wolf." The old man's head bobbed ingratiatingly. "Filled the trough half full of hot water and set the buckets of cold beside."

"Get lost for the rest of the night." Instead of the thank you that Naomi thought such a task should receive, the bounty hunter rudely ordered Wallace to get out.

The old man's unintelligible mutterings accompanied a speculative look at Naomi. She stared back at him, offering no explanation. Charlie threw him some money and the old man's curious expression changed to a grin. He left, smiling and pocketing bills, evidently unconcerned with what happened in his barn the rest of the night.

As soon as Wallace disappeared through the door, Charlie Wolf released her hand and walked away without word or glance. Standing where he'd left her, Naomi watched him strip his vest and drop it on the floor.

Following that, he tossed his hat on a bale of straw and the handkerchief from around his neck fluttered to the floor. Testimony to her years of picking up after others, Naomi automatically stooped and retrieved it. When she was again upright, she saw that he'd stopped by the horse trough at the end of the aisle.

"As I mentioned outside," she said, trying to continue their conversation, "I want to hire you."

Mr. Wolf unfastened his gun belt and laid it on the bale of straw. Then he untied the leather thong securing a second weapon to his thigh and placed a long-bladed knife next to his gun. He turned then, scratching his bare chest and meeting her gaze as if just remembering her presence.

She licked dry lips, focusing on Charlie's hand gliding up and down his bronze skin. She had felt his strength only moments before and her arm still tingled where he'd touched her.

Muscles in his chest rippled as he rubbed his nipple. She couldn't help herself. Her gaze skated lower, examining the colorful loincloth that covered his groin. Naomi's throat tightened, making it difficult to speak even if she could find words to say.

Naomi, most people don't want to think about what to do. Tell them. Give them directions and take charge of the situation. She tried, as her sister had always advised, to assume a position of success.

Although it was impossible to picture the bounty hunter doing anything for her, she had to convince him to pursue the kidnappers. She realized belatedly that she had neglected introducing herself.

Before she could remedy that oversight, Mr. Wolf pointed at the trough as though it held some significance of which she should be aware.

CHAPTER FOUR

"MY NAME IS Miss Naomi Parker."

Charlie didn't know why she held out her hand until she said her name. He grabbed the extended limb and pulled hard, rolling her down his arm and into his embrace before she realized she'd been captured.

He wrapped her in a bear hug and she tilted her head, looking at him with astonishment, not fear. He did a quick assessment. If it weren't for the unusual shade of her eyes, Miss Naomi Parker would be written off as old-maid material. She was a tall, narrow-flanked female past the first flush of womanhood.

Not being a prize himself, nor considered civilized, he rarely came in contact with women of society. He wasn't quite certain how to get rid of the lady with whom he now found himself standing thigh to thigh. Plain speaking seemed the best course.

"I'm planning on being in that tub of water naked as the day I was born whether you get out of here or not." Remembering how she'd witnessed his antics with

Molly, he didn't waste time pretending to be anything but a red-skinned savage.

He released her abruptly, expecting her to hurry from the barn. Instead, she allowed an inch of space between them, still close enough so the heat from her body caressed him.

"I need your help." Her lips trembled as she repeated her request.

"You've been following me all over town." Charlie studied her thin face, brown hair confined in a tight knot, straight teeth, and freckled nose. Above sun-reddened cheeks, cornflower-blue eyes met his gaze.

"Yes." The woman didn't even deny it, leaning against him.

He tightened his hold on her, pulling her so close her chin brushed his bare chest. The contact sent a frisson of heat coursing through him, which made no sense since her body was encased in what felt like iron.

"What the hell kind of contraption do you have on, Miss Parker?"

"I don't understand," she whispered, her expression confused.

He rapped his knuckles against the sturdy corset encasing her, making a loud thump before he dropped one hand to her hip. The other, he stroked down her back to her rump, pressing her against the swell of his erection, stealing a moment's pleasure before she ran screaming from the barn.

Dammit, I need a woman. On closer inspection, her steel-bound breasts appeared to be about the size of robin's eggs, and fury, not terror, made her eyes sparkle. *I wonder what color they are when she comes.* Charlie flinched at the thought. Spinster schoolmarm or not, his cock was erect and urging him to make friends.

He eased slightly away, ready to turn her loose, and hope his actions hadn't guaranteed a rope at the end of his bath. Flat Rock wasn't a town for an Indian to get frisky with a white woman. He noted all of this pragmatically, surprised at the desire still coursing through him.

Gripping his handkerchief in one hand, she braced her other palm against his chest, tilted her head, and glared up at him. Charlie liked the way she fit in his arms. Her hips moved against the swell of his cock and her expression changed to stunned surprise. She froze.

"Stupid to offer your hand to someone you don't know." He figured it was only fair he give her some sound advice since his erection rubbed against the juncture of her thighs and the thought of another man using her so rudely didn't set well with him.

"If you would focus on what's important, here, Mr. Wolf, we could have an intelligent conversation. My students were kidnapped due to my negligence and I must see to their rescue. I need your help."

"You're lucky you survived the raid. Think about that instead of wallowing in guilt and let the law take care of the kids," Charlie said in disgust. He had a cigar, the rest of a bottle of good whiskey waiting for him, and moments before he'd thought that enough. She'd made him want more, which aggravated him.

"That trough half-full of hot water still has some steam coming from it. That's the only thing on my mind right now," he lied.

Awkwardly, the teacher fit her body to his—hip to hip, thigh to thigh, bosom to chest. He'd thought her too thin but discovered her to be a willowy armful, her gentle curves hidden under the iron corset she'd encased herself in.

Charlie stifled his groan, thinking about long, white legs riding his hips as he sank into her heat. It had been a while since he'd lain with a woman and his groin ached with need.

"You trying to have your way with me?" he asked in disbelief.

"If that's what it takes to get you to listen," she answered primly.

He let his thoughts play over the impossible possibilities for a moment before stepping away from her. Considering the likelihood Miss Parker was touched in the head from her outlaw encounter, it wouldn't be fair to take advantage of her almost offer. He studied her for more signs of crazy.

Nope. She knows what she's doing. Her cheeks glowed a shade pinker than the burn beneath as she turned away to set his clothes on the straw. When she turned back he released his loincloth and started unlacing his pants.

"Do you have soap and linens for your bath?" She parsed her question carefully, her husky tone the only indication of anxiety.

"In here." Intrigued, he dropped the saddlebags next to her, watching to make sure she didn't steal anything. Besides spare buckskins and a pair of long johns, he carried a wad of money and his extra Colt six-shooter.

Since catching Jericho and his ragtag band of renegades was a lucrative prospect dear to his heart, Charlie at least owed her a listen-to. He figured she'd already pretty well told him all she knew and that little bit would help when Sam, Deak and he started out in the morning. He could have explained that now that he knew Jericho was involved, his help was secured and she could leave. But—he didn't.

Charlie had a hard time concentrating on her words. He needed a woman and she looked better to him every moment she stood there. She fumbled through the contents of his pouch before withdrawing the soap and drying cloth and laying them next to the tub.

So she wants to seduce me, huh? The thought tickled his fancy. "Naomi." After he said her name, enjoying the way his mouth formed the word in a motion almost like making a kiss, Charlie sat on the bale of straw and stuck out his foot. "Grab my boot and pull," he ordered her, deciding to test her desire to please him.

He could remove his own boots. He'd spent a lifetime taking care of himself. But she jumped to do his bidding, worrying her bottom lip with her teeth as she avoided his gaze, concentrating instead on his foot. He deliberately clenched his toes inside the leather moccasin to keep the boot from coming off.

"You'll have to turn around and stand astride my leg," he drawled when she tugged without success.

She looked askance at him, a blush creeping from beneath the once-white scarf she had wrapped around her neck. Embarrassed or not, she climbed over his extended leg and tugged his boot off. When he stretched out the other foot, she straddled that leg, expecting to do the same, but he pulled her down so that her female parts rubbed against the soft suede of his deerskin pants.

She squeaked in surprised shock but her voice was back under control when she looked over her shoulder and repeated yet again, "I need to hire your help in rescuing my students."

Her thighs caressed him through his pants and he felt the heat of her woman's place teasing his leg. He had to give credit where it was due. She was determined.

"What part did you plan to play in this rescue?" He wasn't really listening to her answer, mesmerized instead by the feel of her sex separated from his flesh by no more than thin cloth. Her angles had curves and the spinster was looking better by the moment as he gazed at the

GEM SIVAD

round rump presented to his sight when she bent over him.

He'd already re-estimated the size of her breasts, raising the expectation from robin eggs to apples. She wiggled higher, her rump cheeks easing apart, her heated center brushing his thigh while she looked over her shoulder at him. Pink lips shaped her answer and lust distracted him for a moment.

"I intend to ride with you." *I intend to ride you?* His cock jumped inside his pants. But she looked at him so trustingly he parsed her words again and figured out what he'd missed.

Ride with me like hell. "No." He started shaking his head, doubly rankled at both his mishearing, and his heated response.

"The girls will need me," she muttered stubbornly, ignoring his loud denial. Her grim tone made it clear that she understood what fate awaited her kidnapped students.

"I don't work for free, teacher. How do you plan to pay me?" He flexed his thigh muscles, brushing hotly against her, feeling her heat through the material that separated his flesh from her core. Given the state of his arousal, it was a dangerous move.

"I get paid once a month at the school." She looked worried staring over her shoulder, making her female parts slide along his thigh. "I'm not sure now who will tender my pay. It's not clear to me what's going to happen."

Well, it's clear to me what's going to happen here in about two moments if you don't get the hell out of this barn. But Charlie didn't say it aloud. Instead he looked at the fullness of her bottom lip and her face scrunched in worry.

He had the almost uncontrollable urge to lift her up and bury his face between her breasts. They were definitely looking more like apples to him now. His cock stretched as if reaching to fill her and he wondered if she noticed the elongated club on the inside of his pants.

First, I need to get her out of that god-awful wire contraption she's wearin'. All sense had left his mind. He was concentrated on one thing—her body and how to get into it. With real reluctance, Charlie struggled for control and offered her one last chance to get out.

"How you get paid is none of my concern. I don't take IOUs in poker or for chasing danger, so if you don't have something to offer me in payment, you best be leaving and you best do it now."

"I need to hire you," she repeated before her chin tilted up and she turned back to her task. As she slid down his outstretched leg, grasped his boot and tugged, wiggling her hips teasingly, he wondered if she knew her effect on him.

An unusual grin softened his expression as he looked at her backside. *Well, maybe we can work a deal.* His cock drooled in need, creating a wet spot on pants pulled taut across his shaft.

"Scared or cold?" he asked her when she shivered.

"I lived through an outlaw raid because I hid." She looked over her shoulder and answered firmly. "You are not frightening. The only thing that scares me is the thought that I won't be able to help my students escape those men—so I guess I'm cold."

"Not for long, teacher," he growled, his inner beast excited and stretching to get out.

"We should proceed with your bath, sir, before your water cools." It was the barest murmured suggestion but his erection throbbed painfully at her sweet drawl.

It would be the right thing to do, telling her the truth. Whether she hired him or not, come morning, Charlie and his cousins would be on the trail of his old enemy Jericho. Since word had come of Jericho's emergence from his lair in Mexico, Charlie had been following elusive rumors. The half-breed renegade led a gang of cutthroats, some former Comancheros.

Traveling under cover of night, the outlaws had progressed across Indian Territory. But according to Miss Parker's information, Jericho was in Texas now. The abduction of the students gave Charlie a trail to follow.

Right now though, he had other things on his mind. He no longer tried to resist the temptation of bedding the schoolteacher. Reaching for her, he brought her up into his lap, nestling her rump against his cock, making certain she understood the bargain.

"So you have need of a tracker and I have need of you."

"Exactly," she answered quickly. Casting aside doubts, Charlie fumbled with the buttons on the back of her dress.

"Why don't I wash your back while we talk?"

Her question made him pause. He'd never been bathed by a woman. He'd heard of it, sometimes dreamed about it, but in thirty-two years of living, it had never happened.

The combination of the bartender's antics and the rejection of the saloon whore had launched an evening Charlie intended to spend in a drunken stupor, smoking a cigar in a tub of hot water. An hour before his plan had sounded like a good time to him. Now he had a woman offering to bathe him so he would listen to her story of woe.

If she doesn't get off my lap and hike on out of here, I'm going to jump her and get myself hung. "I don't want to talk. Don't have a thing to say." Giving her one last chance to leave was the hardest thing he'd ever done.

"I am sure that my monthly stipend will be forwarded here. I asked the sheriff to contact the school officers for assistance." She continued to squirm, pressing her rump into his cock as she looked over her shoulder and talked to him.

She's really not as skinny as I thought earlier. He drew in her scent, rolling it over his senses. Beneath the road dust and everyday sweat, she smelled sweet and womanly. He turned her on his lap and held her face in his hands, squinting at her skin as he ran his thumb down her smooth cheek.

I'll be damned. She's not as old as I figured either. He felt oddly aggrieved, as though she'd been laid out as bait and he'd taken it without looking close enough.

"I will do whatever it takes to hire you, Mr. Wolf." She calmly clasped her hands. Turned the way she was, her breasts brushed against his chest. *The woman is asking for it and doesn't even know it.*

"Anything?" He shifted her in his arms again, facing her away from him so he could finish slipping the buttons free before she changed her mind. "My name's Charlie Wolf, not Mister Wolf," he murmured into the shell of her ear as he nibbled there and then sucked on her earlobe.

"Yes, anything," she answered softly. Miss Parker wasn't as composed as she'd have him believe. She trembled in his arms and her fingers laced together in a white-knuckled grip.

Deliberately he rolled his hips under her. She didn't run away screaming or have a fit of vapors so he forged forward, murmuring his question against her neck. "So these girls at the fancy school..." He paused in his nuzzling long enough to finish his question. "They're your friends?"

"No, they are my responsibility. I hid, saving myself

instead of protecting my charges." She glanced over her shoulder, frowning as though he was a dimwit and not looking the least bit afraid of him.

"You think you should have taken on the renegades single-handedly?" From her expression, Charlie understood that's exactly what she thought.

"I did nothing but hide. Now it's my job to rescue them. The sheriff here refuses to get a posse together and by the time the U.S. Marshal finds a tracker and deputizes men..." Her voice piddled off and she shook her head, denying that inevitability before continuing. "So yes, I'll do anything, including trade you servicing for service," she answered grimly.

Well there it was. She knew what she offered and at the moment, it seemed a fair deal to Charlie.

She straightened on his lap, her back pressed to his chest, buttocks against his engorged shaft. He wasn't playing with her anymore. He murmured his last warning, "If you don't leave this barn right now, Naomi, we're going to get naked together and you'll be the lowest of the low—a white woman who fucks redskins. Because make no mistake, if you stay, I'm going to be inside of you."

He nuzzled the delicate shell of her ear until she shivered and moaned, tickling the lobe with his tongue before taking it between his lips and sucking. Biting on the soft flesh between his teeth just a little bit harder than a lover should, he muttered, "Best get out of here now, or you'll meet the same fate as your students."

He stood, dumping her from his lap as he had Molly, rejecting temptation before he gave in to stupidity.

She rose from the floor, brushing off her skirts before meeting his gaze with her own determined stare.

"It's not the same at all. My students have no choice, I do." Her voice and expression contained no simpering or sham seduction.

"So you'll trade your life for theirs?" He watched shock blanch the last of her color.

"Yes," she answered quietly.

Charlie folded his arms considering the school teacher's bargain instead of reaching out and shaking sense into her. Miss Parker's girls had been kidnapped by Jericho—the outlaw Charlie most wanted to catch. Beings how his future and Naomi's were already entwined, Charlie saw no reason to deny fate.

"So be it." Reaching behind her, he drew his knife from its leather sheath. "Hold out your hand."

CHAPTER FIVE

C HARLIE FOUND IT UNSETTLING how Naomi stood with eyes closed and extended both palms, trusting him. He could have just as easily cut her throat as her hand. Using the tip of the sharp blade, he cut a thin line on his palm. Before he changed his mind, he made a matching incision on hers.

"What?" Her eyes popped open and she looked at him, puzzled.

Pressing the bleeding wounds against each other, Charlie said the necessary words in Kiowa before fumbling a strip of cloth, binding their hands together.

"What are you doing?"

"Making sure our blood is well-mingled." He gazed up from their bound hands to her face.

"Is this some kind of Indian ritual denoting a contract?" she asked, her tone polite.

"Yep," he said gruffly. "Have to do." He took the bindings from their hands, releasing her to step back while he dropped his buckskins without further warning.

"Surely scaring me to death with a knife wasn't necessary." Her outraged glance traveled from her palm to his face. She didn't try to disguise the irritation in her voice. "I thought you were going to kill me." Her complaint piddled into quiet when she realized he was naked.

"My clothes need washed." Before she could change her mind, he directed her the way a buck would his squaw. He laid his knife back down and handed her the dirty buckskins he'd just dropped to the floor.

"Of course," she said, reaching for them.

Charlie suppressed a grin when she stared intently at his dirty clothes and not his bare flesh. Standing around naked wasn't something he usually did. But he enjoyed the way the air played over his cock as he watched her bend over the trough, wet his pants, then lean on a bale of straw, frowning at the soiled buckskins as she scrubbed them.

When she was finished, she harrumphed in satisfaction and laid his laundry out to dry. Charlie felt he'd waited long enough. He reached out to pull her close, deliberately pushing his cock between her thighs.

"Still sure you won't mind layin' under a dirty Injun?" He mimicked the saloon owner's words and tone. Holding her gaze, first he ground his groin against her mound and then, lifting her slightly, pushed his hard length against her dress material until it rode up into the juncture of her legs. He held her still with one hand on her hip, while he languorously rubbed his naked cock against her cloth-covered nether lips.

He didn't dare linger there or he'd spill his seed without ever getting inside. He wanted to pull up her skirt and take her.

"If you will use the water Mr. Wallace provided for your bath, you won't be dirty." Her tart answer accompanied an annoyed look as she studiously ignored his body moving against hers. But the cloth that rode between them was damp and he could feel the heat of her flesh through the thick fabric of her dress.

"Yes ma'am," he agreed and started to turn away. And then his original desire to test her limits revived and he turned back. "Touch me," he ordered.

"Whhhat?" He could have lit a cigar from the blaze in her cheeks. He took her hand and put it on his engorged flesh.

"I mean—touch me, like this." He clasped her slender hand around him, even though her long, tapered fingers didn't meet.

She looked down in astonishment before jerking her gaze away from his flesh and he knew she'd never seen a man's naked dick before.

"You a virgin?" he asked.

"Are you?" Her brow wrinkled and she frowned at him.

Good answer. He wrapped his big paw around her fingers, stroking her hand up and down his shaft.

"Think you can manage a big man like me?" he asked gruffly when her odd-colored eyes rounded in astonishment. She was trembling so much he was afraid she might fall down, but she didn't cavil or whine. She didn't answer his question, staring instead at his bare chest as though she'd never seen one of those before either.

"You need to bathe now," she repeated her earlier suggestion in a conversational tone that made him almost laugh. Miss Parker was set on pretending her hand wasn't pleasuring him below.

"Trough's plenty big enough for a little bit more. Take your clothes off and get in with me."

"Don't be silly." Her face primmed up and she removed her hand from his shaft, stepping back. This time he'd shocked her beyond docile cooperation. He didn't bother arguing. He picked up his knife, ready to cut away the iron trappings that compressed her flesh.

"What are you going to do, cut my hand again to punish me?" Her words were derisive, not the respectful tone of a squaw nor the fearful response of a white female. It occurred to Charlie right then that Miss Naomi Parker wasn't like any woman he'd ever met before—except maybe his mother.

"You don't need one of these damned things. You're slender as a girl." Truth was, she was so long-legged and narrow-hipped he'd almost compared her to a boy. In one motion, he cut through the fabric of her clothes—the dress, the chemise underneath and the lacings of the corset constricting her. He stroked his finger down the pinch mark that marred her flesh, pleased to see pink rounded breasts spring free.

Apparently struck dumb, she said nothing when he shoved the cut material wide, pushing it off her shoulders to the floor where the corset landed with a loud *thunk*. She stood before him in nothing but cotton drawers.

"That was my only dress." All the spunk seemed to drain out of her, leaving her looking tired and vulnerable.

"It had blood all over it." But he would have cut if off of her had it been clean. The dress was a mockery of her surprising delicacy. Done talking, he took hold of her drawers and pulled them down.

The bleached cotton skimmed right off narrow hips but caught for a moment on a surprisingly rounded bottom. He followed the cotton, bending to unlace the half boots she wore.

"Step out of your shoes," he ordered. On his way down, when his head was even with her feminine curls, he noticed their light color and nuzzled her there for encouragement.

"Stop that," she gasped, regaining some of her spirit. He grabbed one shoe and started work on the second. She clutched a wad of his hair and pulled.

"Quit that," he smacked her bottom, feeling the silken skin under the rough calluses on his palm. When she twisted to kick him, he caught her foot and pulled off the second shoe, and then her bloomers.

"Long legs." He admired her alabaster flesh stretching from toes to the delicious V at the apex of her thighs. Regretfully he noted the boyish hips, not wide enough for easy childbearing.

Bent over like a man shoeing a horse, he began working his way back up her leg, nuzzling her dimpled knee, kissing the inside of her thigh, brushing his lips across her lower curls. His movements were accompanied by her squeaks of shocked distress.

Charlie inhaled her scent, savoring it. Molly, earlier in the night, had reeked of old sex and sweat. Naomi smelled sweet even though perspiration dampened her limbs. Tentatively he licked her thigh, sampling her light, salty essence. She shuddered under the stroke. Goose bumps chased across her skin and he rubbed his face against her belly, holding her hips as he learned every inch of her.

He didn't have it in him to be mad about the hair-pulling when he stood upright. She looked like a wild woman, ready to go toe-to-toe, bare-knuckle brawling with him.

"I am not ready for you to begin," she said desperately, her face flushed, and her hair falling loose from the sedate bun she'd worn earlier. Dark-brown strands now appeared to be covered with an oily mixture hiding the color that matched her lower curls.

"Too late, we already started," he growled, cupping the delicate breasts that were flushed with a rosy hue. A brown areola surrounded each nipple and her budded peaks thrust jauntily at him in response to his touch. His mouth watered looking at them. "Get in the trough," he told her gruffly.

"I'm hiring you. You cannot tell me what to do." And then, ludicrously, she crossed her arms and glared defiantly up at him, challenging his right to give her orders. He mimicked her stance and stared back.

"I can and I just did. You told me you'd do anything to get your students back. Well, this is what it's costing you."

He lusted for her creamy white flesh and the softness of her woman's body, which now he could fully appreciate. His cock bobbed, pointing at her strongly. *I want that, I want that, I want that.*

"You've taken up my time and already owe me. You can either take a bath with me or bend over the nearest bale of straw right now while I settle our account." His voice emerged as a guttural growl. She glared but he ignored her hostility, focusing instead on the flush that warmed her skin. "Until I say otherwise, you'll follow my directions. Now get in the tub."

"Don't be silly. I can't bathe you and be in the water too." She stated her opinion as fact. He smiled.

"Yes you can," he assured her. He concluded that he might have to coax her into the water and stepped closer, brushing her arms aside to thumb her nipple. It stood at attention as he palmed her breast, squeezing the small ripe fruit. "Looks to me like you're ready for me, Naomi."

"What are you doing?" She gasped, displaying real horror as her nipples reached for him. He waited expectantly as her glance dropped lower and she remembered that her full glory was exposed to him.

"Ohhh…" she moaned, backing up and covering the pale silken curls with one hand while wrapping her other arm across her breasts.

"Better be care—" His warning came too late. The edge of the trough caught Naomi mid-thigh and she lost her balance, falling backwards into the water. Not one to miss an opportunity, Charlie climbed in behind her as she sat up, sputtering in shock.

"Like I said, the trough's plenty big enough for both of us. Now settle back down and enjoy yourself." He surrounded her slim hips with his thighs, his cock standing at attention against her back while he slid his arms around and cupped her breasts in his hands.

"Beautiful," he murmured, caressing her surprisingly plump breasts.

"Really?" she asked, twisting around so that she could peer up at him.

"Really," he assured her, brushing a kiss over the sensitive spot where her neck joined her shoulder.

She moaned. Her breath came in shallow gasps, moving her tender flesh against the edge of his palm. He pulled her head back against his chest, savoring the feel of her in his arms.

CHAPTER SIX

THINGS WEREN'T GOING according to Naomi's underdeveloped plan. Her directions were delivered as moaned suggestions suborned to Charlie's will. While she marshaled her arguments, he explored her body, top to bottom.

She'd already been with him through the dusk into darkness. It was time they needed for traveling. But the bounty hunter seemed intent on coupling with her before they set out on the trail of the outlaws. There was no diverting his attention. He acted like a terrier after a rat— only she was the rat and he appeared ready to devour her.

"Charlie Wolf, we need to get on the trail of the men who kidnapped my students. Surely we could conduct this part of our transaction after we have completed the rescue." She tried to reason with him.

It was a difficult proposition to sell since as she spoke, he ignored her suggestions and explored the valleys and hills of her body. His fingers ran willy-nilly up her ribs, seeming to count them, possibly to make certain she was real.

For a man who had needs, he was certainly taking his time. And now she was held captive between his thighs and unless she turned around and risked bumping that waving protrusion of his, she couldn't see his eyes.

She needed to be able to see his eyes to do her reasoning. But it wasn't to be. He held her back to his chest, controlling her body as her will to resist evaporated rapidly.

When he slid his hand between her thighs, she stiffened her legs and made her back rigid. He gave her a reprieve from his lower exploration when he cupped her breasts again, this time pressing his thumbs against her nipples. She exhaled in a loud, thankful breath, only to gasp in shock. Not finished with her nipples, he rotated them before pinching each bud between finger and thumb.

She had never felt anything like that in her life. Even in moments of her own self-explorations her breasts had remained—well—breasts. Cradled in his hands, they had become something else entirely. They ached, itched, tingled—demanding that she turn and rub them against his skin.

Unable to stop, she arched her back, shoving her flesh against his roughly calloused palms. "Ahhh." The groan of pleasure escaped her lips before she could suppress it.

"Pretty." Heat flared in her belly. He cupped her

flesh in his large hands and whispered in her ear, "I'm going to taste these." He lifted each one and squeezed the plump mounds intimately.

Taste? Struggling to control her responses didn't help because he was everywhere. She backed away from the merciless hands cupping her breasts but her thighs and rump bumped and ground against his male length. The tactile assault confused her.

He nibbled and nuzzled her ear, her neck, her shoulder, under her jaw. All the time he murmured, sometimes in words she understood, sometimes in a language foreign to her. She had no time to protest or refuse, swept along on the tide of his passion.

He roused sensations in Naomi never stirred before. She didn't know how to act. Her woman's book of etiquette and decorous behavior had never discussed this. Cooking plentiful meals, sewing ruffled curtains, pouring afternoon tea—but not the feel of Charlie's hands on her breasts as he nibbled on the crease between her neck and shoulder.

She was certain that no mention had ever been made of the frustration felt from such attention. It made her feel a totally new way—fierce, almost angry. She wrenched free and turned violently on his lap.

"You will listen to me now," she declared militantly. Straddling him, her knees bent on either side of his narrow hips, she leaned forward, her breasts heaving in passionate indignation.

She stared into molten heat, his gray eyes and the jagged scar on his brow accentuating the exotic masculinity of his face. He smiled, stealing her breath away and she couldn't remember her message of outrage.

"Thank you," he growled, closing his lips around her sensitive nipple, his teeth scoring the swollen button before sucking it into his mouth, milking it erotically.

"You can't—" She gasped, trying to understand as he lit the internal fires of hell and they burned in her body. "Charlie Wolf—what are you doing to me?" Her words spilled out as a moan instead of a protest.

He didn't stop though. Instead, he doubled his attentions, teasing her other nipple in time to the pull of his lips. Naomi clutched his shoulders, holding on to him, her back arching to capture more of the pleasure beyond anything she'd ever imagined possible.

She'd touched his erection before. But now Charlie held her, prodding her with his male member until her nether lips parted and he rubbed it inside her tender folds. It was an invasion of the most egregious nature. Startled out of her sexual haze, she froze.

"Let's see what happens when we do this," he murmured. She followed the trail as his hand stroked down her ribs and paused, resting on her stomach.

"Want me inside of you?" he asked, tracing lightly across her skin, inflaming the unnamed desires pulsing in her core.

With his other hand, he slid his shaft against the

slick flesh inside her folds, rubbing it against the sensitive nub at her apex. She jerked, feeling as though a flash of fire had jolted through her.

"Like that, do you?" He grinned, obviously pleased at her uncontrolled response.

She was fascinated by the smile on his face. He looked nothing like the stern bounty hunter who had ridden into town leading a string of dead men. He continued brushing back and forth across the spot that tingled until she pushed back, needing more.

"That's it," he directed her. "Give yourself to me. Let me in."

Let him in? Deliberately, holding her gaze, he centered his shaft against the entrance to her body, moving his other hand to her hip.

"Nowww," he growled. Pressing her downward, he nudged his shaft higher, penetrating her channel in tiny increments, making her want more. The tip of his engorged flesh breached the opening to her body. She waited breathlessly for her fate.

Using his chin, he scraped aside the wet hair to better reach the sensitive spot on her shoulder. The motion momentarily distracted her from the lower invasion, embarrassing her at the way her chignon— pomade-covered and once tidy—now lay in limp clumps. Thank God, he didn't seem to notice as he nibbled on the bend in her neck.

"What the hell do you have on your hair?"

Of course, he noticed. "Does it really matter right now?" Even in this moment, poised above his shaft, ready to change her destiny, Naomi couldn't quell her exasperation.

He snorted and her already sunburned cheeks burned hotter. She crouched helplessly, aware of his flesh intimately touching hers, her body's heated response telegraphing her desire. It probably wasn't the best time to tell him she found his tone insulting.

She shivered and forgot her combative words as the whiskers along his jaw brushed the tender flesh on her neck. She was focusing on that when he moved the hand on her hip lower, petting her nether curls before sliding his fingers between her legs, brushing the bit of flesh at her apex that had proved to be so sensitive.

They needed to talk. She had his attention, now she needed to remember what they were talking about. Oh yes, her hair. "My hair is curly-wild unless I pomade it."

"Wild is good," he said, barely looking up from the nipple he suckled.

Maybe so. She wasn't in a position to argue when he scraped his teeth across the tip of her bud and she melted inside, squirming to get more of his shaft inside her. It hurt. She stopped.

The enormity of what she was about to do wiped away the sensual haze he'd created. Naomi stiffened, looking at him with panic-stricken eyes. Breathing in short gasps and holding on to his broad shoulders, she tried to gather her wits and steady herself lest she descend farther onto his shaft. She knew what she'd bartered but… Instinctively, she tried to close her legs against him.

"No ma'am," he said sternly, removing his lips and teeth from her breast where he'd been giving her so much pleasure. Charlie squeezed her rump and inched his shaft higher inside her. "You'll not keep me out of this sweet honey. This belongs to me now, Naomi. Open for me."

Sweet honey? His very words made her sex clench. Her arms dropped to her sides as she leaned back and looked at him in astonishment.

"Hang on to me, teacher. I won't hurt you." Charlie lifted her arms, draping them over his shoulders.

How will I ever be able to take it inside of me when just the tip has stretched me so unreasonably? His promise was a complete falsehood. It burned like hellfire when he forced the broad head of his member farther through her entrance. Even as her body stiffened at the intimate act, her channel clenched tight around the invader. Breathlessly, Naomi analyzed each sensation.

"It is truly a remarkable act, isn't it?" She didn't really expect an answer. It just seemed fitting to acknowledge the moment in her life she thought would never happen. She looked with approval at the man who would divest her of her innocence.

Pain… She shuddered, widening her stance to allow

his intimate invasion as he learned the shape and size of her parts. He rotated the nub of sensitive flesh at her apex, making her hips sway following the sensation. *Pleasure…*

Naomi leaned closer, rubbing her nipples against Charlie's chest as ripples of heat pulsed through her. Her hips swayed, chasing the enthralling spell his magic fingers cast until his member forged higher, burning a path inside her.

"Shoot, teacher, you're not even broke to ride." His words came out in a husky growl. He probed gently, at the same time pressing her body downward.

"I would prefer not being compared to a horse if you don't mind." She struggled to reply, staring at the barn wall instead of him. Her words, meant to be caustic, emerged as a weak whimper.

His chest vibrated tickling her nipples and she knew without looking that she'd made him laugh. Charlie stroked her belly, his hand gliding lower, teasing her sensitive pearl. He toyed with it, caressing the nubbin and making her pelvis tilt toward him seeking more. She winced.

He did it again. As soon as it feels good he pushes farther inside me. "You're too big." Disappointment flooded her. She'd not get to experience the act because any fool could tell they didn't fit. Trying to expel the foreign intruder, her body strained away from his touch.

Her protest didn't matter. Mr. Wolf's rigid shaft

connected their bodies and he seemed resolved to do the impossible. Abruptly he handed her the soap.

"My back needs scrubbed. Reach across my shoulders and get at it." His rough order turned her disappointment to disgust, giving her reason to climb out.

"I've changed my mind," Naomi muttered, trying to disconnect their bodies in order to scramble out of the tub of water.

Gravity and the slippery trough conspired to aid in her deflowering. Sharp pain accompanied her fall as his manhood filled her, impaling her fully. His groan of pleasure accompanied her shocked gasp. Charlie drew her toward him, his turgid member scraping the walls of her sex like rough sandpaper.

"Why is this purported to be such a grand thing?" she complained, hiding her face against his chest and mumbling petulant words before she could stifle the sound. As so many other experiences she'd anticipated, the truth of this great mystery had proven disappointing.

His chest muscles moved under her cheek as if he silently laughed at her. But he also stroked her back and petted her body as if she were a child. Embarrassing as the situation was, she risked a glance up at him.

His eyes crinkled at the corners and he gave her such a look of approval it warmed her insides. Even better, he lathered the soap on his hands and rubbed white suds across her shoulders and down her back, easing her closer, fitting himself deeper.

Perhaps it's not so bad. Certainly no one has ever bathed me before. She groaned, arching into his touch, her muscles relaxing as her womb tentatively clenched, exploring the invader. Naomi closed her eyes, inhaling his spicy male scent. Experimentally, she rotated her pelvis against his groin. Pain—but also a new pulsating pleasure.

Heat radiated from her core. Tentatively squeezing the walls of her sex around his shaft, she made Charlie growl. It delighted her that she could call forth a groan from this powerful man.

Eager for new sensations, Naomi reached for the elusive ecstasy tantalizing her. Instead of helping her find her quarry, Charlie wet her scalp, letting water trickle down her face and neck and attacking the pomade she'd used to flatten her curls.

Lathering his hands again, he washed the oily mixture from her hair, untangling the wet strands, using his fingers to comb them back from her high forehead.

"I don't have anything with me to make it lay down now." Reality set in. *I must look like a skinned rat.* She rebuked him to cover her dismay.

It seemed a silly complaint but it was easier to focus on than the hard body connected to hers. Now that he was inside her, he seemed perfectly willing to sit in the trough under her all night long. It made her want to snap at him.

Their intimate experience left her feeling inadequate

and incomplete. Disappointment again simmered in her veins. She didn't understand the importance he'd placed on the activity but she'd kept her promise and the deed was done.

Naomi drew in a frustrated breath and pushed upward. Leaving him was easier in mind than body. Her channel tightened around his swollen flesh as if trying to prevent her withdrawal.

"Whoa there, teacher. We're not finished yet." Charlie grabbed her hips, his soapy hands sliding across her skin as he brought her back down, filling her with himself again.

CHAPTER SEVEN

"**J**ESUSMARYANDJOSEPH," Charlie groaned as her gyrations sent her plunging back down on his ecstatic cock. One more up and down and it would be all over for him. His release was so close. He had to clench every muscle in his body fighting it off—not now—not yet. *Breathe in... Breathe out...*

He concentrated on getting the lacquer out of her hair to keep from losing control while she purred under his hands like a kitten. He hooked the wet strands behind her ears, relieved that once he'd removed the gunk, it matched the light brown of her lower curls.

"Don't we need to be moving on, Mr. Wolf?" she asked. She peered at him from cornflower-blue eyes, as if assessing the worth of their continued connection. Seeming all set to climb out of the tub, her words startled him from his enthralled contentment.

"Yep." He sure as hell did need to move. "You do it," he told her. "Ride me." He wanted to thrust into her wet heat all night long. But mindful of her virgin flesh he resolved to let her set the pace.

"Like this." Lifting her by her hips, he noted her surprised dismay as his cock almost pulled free. She smiled, glowing with pleasure when he penetrated her again. She blinked, her expression thoughtful before tentatively trying it.

Charlie closed his eyes in bliss as she settled on him, tilting her pelvis and taking him deeper. Her channel clenched around his cock, squeezing it so tight he felt as if a fist gripped him.

Charlie leaned against the back of the tub, experiencing heaven as Naomi lost her irritated expression. In fact, she looked mesmerized. Aside from giving him the pleasure of her body, she also explored him, touching his chest, rubbing his shoulders and then nuzzling his jaw. The last was so unexpected his cock swelled bigger and jerked inside her.

"Oh," escaped her as she resumed hold of his shoulders, levering herself up and down briskly on his cock.

"Ahhh," she sighed, leaning backward, holding the sides of the trough, her eyes closed as she found another position.

Charlie held her by the waist, helping her find her rhythm as she pumped up and down, squeezing him with her internal muscles, grinding her pearl against his groin and rising only to slap down again in an erotic mating dance.

Inclining forward, she cupped his face in her hands,

tracing the scar that ran from brow to chin before kissing the spot marking his jaw. Miss Parker learned fast how to please him. While Charlie was still recovering from her lips against his scar, she tilted her pelvis, grinding her pearl harder against him.

He forgot about her burned cheeks, lumpy hair and narrow hips knowing only that she caressed his face and made a place for him inside her body.

Groin to mound, joined as they were, her sweet breath feathered across his chin and he watched her bite her bottom lip. He shifted, settling her tighter against him, reaching for a spot deeper inside her as if he were a spoiled child.

Beads of perspiration dotted her forehead and liquid flooded her eyes. He leaned forward and kissed the end of a lash, capturing a drop of moisture with his tongue.

"Even your tears are mine now," he told her gruffly before catching her full lower lip between his, biting it gently and then taking her mouth with a kiss. Charlie jerked in surprise when he felt her brush across *his* bottom lip. He teased her tongue, luring it into his mouth, following her retreat back to the warmth of hers.

It was a first for him too—part of him held on to her as though she were a sacred moment—he was almost scared to proceed. He'd never bedded a virgin. She moaned, tasting him as though she liked his flavor. His hand came up, cupping the back of her head, steadying their connection. Before he ever finished this first claiming, he wanted to be the only man who ever gave Naomi this pleasure.

She ended the kiss, lifting up again as though leaving him.

"Huh-uh," he disagreed, his hips following her rise.

"You told me to scrub your back." She had the wash cloth and soap in her hand and presented her breasts to his lips as she reached over his shoulder. He didn't know if it was accidental or intended. Either way didn't matter.

Charlie butted against her soft flesh, seeking comfort as if he were a baby. He suckled her like a man long denied. She tasted sweet, her skin tender and her nipples responsive. He flicked the budded peak with his tongue and then bit it lightly. Her hips jerked and her cunny squeezed him.

She liked that. Kneading the muscles in his shoulders, she pressed her flesh against his lips. Her sheath milked his cock in time to the slow pulls of his mouth on her breast.

He nipped the sensitive tip and she shuddered, thrusting her breasts higher against the pain. He felt the pulsing rush of her release as her internal muscles clamped down on his rod, spasming in a long, drawn-out orgasm that pulled and milked him, demanding that he shoot straight into her womb. He had to fight to prolong the pleasure. Staggering to his feet, he lifted her with him.

"Wrap your legs around me," he told her. He carried

Naomi across the barn to an empty stall. She clung to him as he cradled her close, cupping her rump as her thighs circled his waist. Her fingernails scored marks on his shoulder and she made soft noises of satisfaction. So did he as she moaned her delight when his cock pressed against a point of pleasure inside her.

He needed to ram, to pound, he needed... *Damn* As he held her gaze, her blue eyes darkened into midnight skies and another release swept over her.

"Sweet Jesus in the morning," he muttered, backing her against the wall of a stall and draping her legs over his arms. He pressed his thumb on her pearl, rotating, squeezing and teasing at the same time he pumped into her hot wetness.

Virgin tenderness forgotten, he slammed his cock deep and hard, riding her through one orgasm and into the next. At some point, he covered her mouth with his, claiming that part of her too.

Charlie breathed for her, held her like a sacrifice before his need and rutted on her until the walls of her channel clenched in aftershocks, muscles tightening and relaxing, fading into gentle twitches. He growled, pouring his seed into her core, his hips maintaining their pounding tempo until the last drop.

They both collapsed from exhaustion in the straw. He curled possessively around her, surrounding her slender length without crushing her, aware of her every sniffle, sob and sigh as she lay vulnerable next to him.

When she shivered, he reached up to drag a horse blanket across them, trapping his heat for her. He knew when she was awake—she held herself stiffly, her breathing controlled and shallow. He knew when she fell asleep because her body relaxed, letting her natural contours fill the planes and angles of his form.

She's not a Kiowa woman to barter for. What the hell was I thinking? He looked wryly at the palm of his hand marked by his cut. Her palm wore the same mark.

He'd been like a bull on her the moment he'd gotten her into the building. And then to claim her in such a brutal manner—but he wasn't sorry as he held her in his arms and breathed her scent into his lungs. He hoped she wasn't.

Charlie forgot about the Kiowa squaw he'd planned to trade for someday. Looking possessively at Naomi, his teeth flashed in a wolf's grin. She'd never had a chance. If she'd tried to leave any of the six times he'd offered her reprieve, he doubted he'd have blocked the door even though he'd wanted her to stay.

But she hadn't tried to leave. She'd stood up to him and made a bargain to save her charges. Charlie closed his eyes and relaxed. Satisfied with the night's events, he lay awake stroking her hair as it dried in light brown curls. Their *agreement* might get him hung but he had no regrets. He'd found his mate.

Now he had to figure out what to do with her. He lived a nomadic existence, riding with his cousins on the hunt, visiting his Kiowa relatives when he wanted and drifting in between jobs. At the McCallister house, he felt the taint of his long-dead grandfather so when he visited his mother, he camped out on the range.

On the day Jonas McCallister died, Charlie's cousins Deacon and Sam McCallister had renamed the place the MC3, claiming the ranch for him too. He hadn't taken the McCallister name and hadn't considered moving to the spread. Looking down at the woman in his arms, Charlie reconsidered his living arrangements. The schoolmarm couldn't travel with him on his hunts the way a squaw would have. He figured bedding Naomi had changed the course of his life.

At dawn, Charlie covered her better with the blanket and went in search of clothes for her. He'd mangled the dress she'd worn the night before, but he excused that with the knowledge it had already been damaged.

He passed the livery owner, Wallace. The old man had crawled under a wagon outside. Snoring loudly, he sprawled on his back, a bottle of whiskey lying next to him attesting to his drunken stupor.

Quietly, Charlie edged past the sleeping drunk, heading down the street for the back of the general store. He planned to roust the store owner and buy Naomi a new dress. No doubt he'd have to pay double for it, but he didn't care. He wanted something that would put a smile in her pretty blue eyes—something that would make her like him.

CHAPTER EIGHT

A LOOSE STRAW POKING her hip prodded Naomi from contented sleep. She groaned as she realized she was unclothed, stiff and sore, lying in a stall of the stable and curled under a blanket smelling of horse. Thankfully though, she was alone. She took a moment to explore the cut on her right hand. She wanted to believe that she'd had a bizarre dream but her itching palm proved that her memory was sound.

She sat looking down at her nakedness as though she'd never really seen her body before. Red marks covered her breasts. The light whiskers on his jaw had scraped, his teeth had nipped and his lips had sucked. She flushed, remembering.

She clambered out of the stall, hastily looking for the remnants of her clothing. Parts of them were in the stable owner's scrap heap. Thinking she'd tie it on somehow, she searched through the rags for her dress, but it was missing altogether. The rest of the damaged goods she bundled to take along.

Her eyes drifted to Charlie's change of clothes

drying on the bale of straw. *So he's coming back.* He'd be wearing the spare clothes she'd seen in the saddlebag when she'd pulled out the bathing supplies.

"You owe me, Mr. Wolf." She pulled the nearly dry set of buckskins from the straw and shimmied into them, enjoying the subtle brush of the leather against her skin, savoring the freedom of male clothing. Naomi had been taped, tucked and tortured by corsets ever since Ma Lancaster, her childhood neighbor and adopted grandmother, discovered her bosom coming in. The absence of the rigid confinement left her feeling liberated.

Charlie's clothes were too big, of course. His buckskin trousers were twice the breadth she needed. Although as Naomi remembered his body, she conceded that not an ounce of fat marred his muscular frame. He was taller than her by at least a half a foot, something else that set him apart from most men.

Our behavior was absolutely wicked. Her womb clenched, intensifying the unfamiliar ache in her sex. Naomi smiled at the sensation as she climbed into the too long pants. Thoughts of Charlie Wolf both pleased and irritated her.

"He should have roused me before he left." On the other hand, she was rather glad not to have to face him this morning. Her limited experience with males had proven them to be unreliable so his disappearance didn't surprise her.

She frowned at the mark on her palm confirming their agreement. If he proved untrustworthy, at least he'd furthered her education, giving her an unforgettable experience she'd felt doomed to miss.

"Yes." She shivered and grinned. *We were in a trough when I gave him my virginity* Shaking her head in wonder, she remembered his barbaric seduction culminating in the loss of her maidenhead.

My sacrifice was for a good cause. He'd delivered a sharp, rending pain when he'd first tunneled into her body. It had hurt, inexplicably in a good way. That thought made her womb flex again as heat pooled in her loins.

As she assured herself she'd done the correct thing in making her bargain, she hitched up the loose pants, tying a corset string around her middle to keep the buckskins in place. Evidently Charlie Wolf only wore vests because she couldn't find a shirt.

She pulled the sleeveless leather garment over the top of the shift she'd salvaged from Wallace's trash barrel and belted it all with a strap she found hanging on the barn wall. Pleased with her own ingenuity, she stomped her feet into her boots and rolled up the extra length of Charlie's pants until they rode ankle high.

"*Godey's Lady's Book* says we must deal with challenge in a calm and creative manner." She spoke aloud, remaining composed until she smoothed her hands over her hair and realized that unredeemable disaster had struck. Her once slicked-down and tamed mane billowed around her in a halo of snarls.

What the hell's on your hair? His words came back to her. Her neck tingled where he'd pushed aside the limp mess to nuzzle her sensitive flesh. Lifting a knotted strand, she glared at it, focusing on her hair rather than the carnal experience she'd had the night before.

Just look at this mess. She couldn't cry over her coiffure when there were so many more important reasons to have hysterics, but she wanted to. Trying to get a grip on the reality of her situation, she walked from stall to stall until she found Patrick's mule.

The stable owner had grudgingly stabled it the morning before, telling her he'd keep the animal for payment if she didn't come up with cash. He could have the old mule. She needed a horse. She frowned, continuing down the aisle to the string of horses the bounty hunters had brought to town. Charlie's stallion stood in line with the rest.

She studied the buckskin. The three bounty hunters had said it was a good horse, certainly in better shape than Patrick's mule. When she heard the creak of the door, Naomi stepped into the mare's stall.

Wallace came into the barn grunting and complaining. She didn't risk a look to see what he was muttering about this morning. When he walked down the aisle on the far side of the barn to the trough where she and Charlie Wolf had bathed, his presence jarred her from her dithering. She grabbed a bunch of hair and tied it back with a broken corset string, peering through the slats to keep track of the old man.

Good Lord, I should have found that. Naomi cringed. Wallace had her dress slung over his shoulder. He remained oblivious to her presence, continuing to grumble as he left the building and closed the door behind him.

She really did expect Mr. Wolf's imminent return. However, lingering in the barn and being at the mercy of the stable owner held no appeal. She considered the possibility that she was borrowing an already sold animal and decided to let Charlie sort that matter out. Rather than face Wallace on his next trip inside, she saddled the buckskin mare and prepared to leave.

When she rode the mare from the barn, early morning dew covered the ground. The Flat Rock streets were empty when Naomi headed toward the Sparrow Creek Young Ladies Academy.

Except for the ache between her legs, Naomi felt physically none the worse. She clasped the sides of her mount and thought about coupling with Charlie Wolf. Her cheeks flushed and she squirmed in the saddle, pressing down and gripping the leather with her thighs, the apex of her thighs grinding against the hard seat and reminding her of her previous night's activities.

I had a lover. The fact both stunned and delighted her. She'd actually experienced the often heard whispered about mysterious coupling. She feared she'd pay dearly for that memory. She knew from the smirk on the stable owner's face as she'd ridden past he wouldn't remain silent.

At the very least, my reputation in Flat Rock is gone. "I secured Mr. Wolf's services to save my students, which makes it a splendid sacrifice," Naomi murmured defensively.

She wavered in between naming him Mr. Wolf in her thoughts, or the more familiar Charlie. Incongruously, she fumbled in her mind, trying to recall the proper address.

Godey's Lady's Book *didn't cover this. I certainly know him. But he is a male close to my age and an employee.* She decided it would be most appropriate to retain formality when dealing with him.

Since it was unseemly to think about physical gratification when her students' lives were at risk, she reminded herself that her actions had gained Mr. Wolf's help.

It is I who seduced Charlie Wolf. No doubt he was a libertine who accepted her attentions with alacrity, nevertheless... *Plain Naomi Parker seduced a beautiful man into helping her.*

She was quite proud of herself. Mr. Wolf was the best tracker in the country and he'd agreed to find her students. In her estimation he had an honorable character—after all he'd paid the saloon girl for the small gratification he'd enjoyed in the bar and Naomi had certainly tendered a greater pleasure.

He might not come after me, but I'm betting he won't let me steal his horse. Naomi's practical honesty asserted itself.

She was quite relieved at midmorning when Charlie Wolf rode up on her right side and grabbed her reins, halting her progress. She was completely flustered by his teasing manner.

"My vest will never fit me the same since you've tented it that way." He nodded at her clothes. Naomi's skin flamed as she stared down at her chest where her breasts were rounded mounds under the rough fabric. His usual stoic expression replaced his grin when the other two bounty hunters moved in on her left.

"You need a hat. Your face is burned red by the sun." Almost sternly he tipped her head up, studying her. Then he had the nerve to add, "Your hair's wild today."

"If you recall, Mr. Wolf, my hair got wet." She brushed ineffectually at the tendrils of curling fluff escaping the corset string. Naomi knew how bizarre she must look and resented that he pointed it out. Her words were a tart reminder he'd caused her hair disaster.

"Call me Charlie." He nudged his horse closer, looming nearer as he reached to pull the vest tighter across her bosom. She looked down and caught her breath as his bronze hand glided beneath the leather and brushed against the soft chemise covering her chest.

"Mr. Wolf, really, you are being…"

His caress changed to a gentle squeeze as she repeated her formal address. Naomi's indecision about what to call him was resolved.

"I can dress myself, *Charlie*," she sputtered.

Apparently satisfied that he'd gotten her attention and also arranged his clothes on her to his liking, he caught a strand of her hair between his fingers and pulled on the corkscrew curl. Releasing it, he smiled when it bounced back into a tight coil.

"Stop it," Naomi ordered him. She kept her face turned forward, blushing at his familiar attentions as Charlie handled her in front of his relatives.

He grunted, dropped the curl and moved his horse farther from hers for the rest of the ride to the school. Once through the gates, she dismounted, staring at the rocks and rough ground instead of toward the caretaker's body.

"I need to give this man a burial." The horror of the earlier event seeped through her bones, leaving Naomi shuddering under a wave of panic—she couldn't look at poor, dead Patrick.

His body was a gruesome reminder that the girls had been captives of the outlaws for over a day. Every other consideration was outweighed by the need to hurry after them. She wasn't stupid. She knew she couldn't rescue her students without Charlie Wolf. If his bounty hunter relatives helped, that was even better.

By this time, someone would have notified the school trustees that the school had been attacked. The headmistress, Eleanor Beecham, scheduled to arrive in a fortnight with the remainder of the girls, wouldn't come. Naomi didn't know what would happen to her own position.

Charlie Wolf came to her side and put his hands on her shoulders, scrutinizing the way his buckskin pants drooped and his vest reached her thighs.

"Go back to the horses and get your clothes out of my saddlebag." He turned her around, pointing her away from Patrick's violent death. "I'll take care of the burial."

"Thank you for tending Patrick," Naomi said. Then, perplexed at his words, she frowned. "I don't have any clothes in your saddlebags."

"I bought you a dress," he said gruffly. Confused, she stared at him, then down at his buckskins.

"I like what I have on better. On the trail it will be easier to get around." She ignored his proffered offer of clothes and went into the empty school dormitory where green-eyed flies crawled insolently over the uneaten porridge.

Overcome by all that had happened since the morning before, she pushed the bowls aside and, resting her head on her arms, looked outside. The three men were dubious heroes at best. She could see them through the door as they dug Patrick's grave. Her gaze slid rapidly over Charlie moving on to his cousins. It was telling that Charlie Wolf was the most civilized-looking of the three.

Deacon McCallister's size would have intimidated most, even without his harsh expression and low-slung gun.

Samuel McCallister was startling in his handsomeness. His light hair and well-chiseled features made her think of angelic perfection. But his gaze chilled her, especially when he accompanied it with a smile.

All three men looked competent. Capable of fighting outlaws and... As she remembered the gang of renegades, she looked at the three men doubtfully. Including her, the rescuers numbered four against at least twenty. When she counted in her eight students, bringing their numbers to twelve, she decided winning the lopsided fight might be possible.

She reminded herself she'd paid for his assistance and tactical problems were Charlie Wolf's job now—with her insights, of course. The bounty hunters would find the criminals and defeat them in battle, saving the young ladies of Sparrow Creek Academy.

She was startled from her reverie when a body blocked the light streaming through the open door. With the three men digging, it hadn't taken long to bury Patrick. She sat upright, waiting.

"Better get dressed." Charlie threw her his saddlebag and stood watching.

She was too weary to argue that the buckskin

worked better for her where they were going but his next words surprised her.

"Put the long johns on under the pants. It'll take up some of the slack and give you some extra padding between your rump and the saddle. You'll thank me tonight." He left her dressing, returning to his cousins.

She climbed the stairs to the small room she'd been given. The kidnappers had been up there, scattering the bedding as well as her personal items. Grimly, she removed her shoes and Charlie's clothes, hopping on one leg and then the other, pulling the long underwear up and then the deerskin pants back over those.

After she traded her thin slippers for boots, she tentatively moved toward the door then looked around at the rest of her things.

Hastily she picked up the books, shoving them into her carpetbag. She heard Charlie Wolf climbing the steps and her body tensed, anticipating his arrival.

"You can't take much with you. We're riding light and fast if you want to catch up to your students." He bent his head to avoid the low ceiling in the room and pointed at her bulging valise.

Embarrassed that she had to be reminded of their mission, Naomi tipped most of the books into the trunk and packed underclothing, lightweight blouses and a brush, comb and soap. She carried it back where he stood waiting but Charlie shook his head at the bulging satchel.

"Take only what you need."

As he watched, she replaced her mutilated chemise with one from her trunk and added a shirtwaist. Taking up his vest, he put it on her, patting her rump before he stepped back and headed for the steps.

At the last moment, Naomi tucked *Godey's Lady's Book* in the waist of her pants.

Charlie's eyebrows went up but she ignored him. When she left, her valise was considerably lighter, holding only the brush, comb, soap, two drying cloths and underclothes.

Just as he supervised her packing, he commandeered the mission. Naomi told herself she allowed his authority because they'd made a bargain to save the girls. For that she would listen to his advice. She knew he was right about the excess baggage, but leaving her worldly possessions behind was hard.

She cast one last look at the interior of the school, girding her loins for battle as she followed him to the horses. As she reached for her horse's leathers, his hand closed over hers and she was uncomfortably aware of his larger size pressing her against the animal. She tilted her head to look up and he set a hat on her head. She recognized it as the handyman's wide-brimmed straw.

"I can't take Patrick's hat."

"Don't figure he'll be needing it and the sun'll burn you to a crisp without it." He ran his thumb across one already painfully reddened cheek. "Wear it," he ordered, walking away, clearly not doubting she'd obey. Then, as if he had an afterthought, Charlie turned back and spoke mildly.

"We'll be stopping in Buffalo Creek and leaving you there to wait."

"I told you I'm going with you to rescue my students, Mr. Wolf." Naomi glowered at Charlie. She'd just known he would try to leave her behind. She bit her tongue to keep from reminding him she'd paid for the right to ride with him.

Sam McCallister openly listened while he tied a shovel on his saddle.

"Introduce us to your woman, cousin. It appears she has a mind of her own." Deacon McCallister stood behind her though she hadn't heard his arrival.

She flinched, uneasy around these men who moved so stealthily. He spoke across her shoulder to Charlie Wolf. Then he shifted something inside his mouth and carefully spat, creating a brown stain on a tuft of parched grass.

"I am not Mr. Wolf's woman," she corrected him firmly.

"Deacon and Sam McCallister," Charlie nodded at each and back to her. Then he boosted her into the saddle, adjusting her stirrups when she was seated.

"Please tell me you do not engage in that filthy habit," she whispered, taking the opportunity to lean close to the most civilized of the three men. Charlie turned sharply in time to see Sam hit the same spot

Deacon had stained a moment before.

"No ma'am," he said, swinging lithely onto his mount. His gray eyes crinkled at the corners and glinted with humor when he added, "But I have other proclivities."

Then he squeezed his thighs and his horse, incongruously named Old Mossy, broke into a dancing sidestep, arching his neck and snorting in response to his rider. Charlie swayed in the saddle, his muscles rippling and his bronze skin shining in the sunlight. Naomi's first impression remained—*Charlie Wolf is a beast riding a beast.*

Coming in beside her on the right, Charlie nudged her mare into motion. As they started down the trail, his cousins brought up the left and he finished the introduction, moving his horse closer to Naomi's buckskin and speaking across her.

"Cousins, this is Naomi Parker, former teacher at the Sparrow Creek Young Ladies Academy." He paused, reaching over to straighten the straw hat on her head before adding, "Meet my woman."

Sam and Deacon tipped their hats respectfully, having no comment other than a nodded, "Ma'am."

CHAPTER NINE

I T WAS LATE AFTERNOON going onto evening when they rode into Buffalo Creek and dismounted at the town livery. Sam and Deacon went on to the sheriff's office to report on the kidnapped girls they were about to rescue. Aside from the bounty on Jericho, the McCallisters anticipated that the grateful relatives of the hostages would offer their thanks in cash or more probably, future goodwill.

Deacon had already researched the students on the list Naomi had given them. Among the eight, he'd discovered the niece of a state senator, the granddaughter of a federal judge, the sister of a U.S. Marshal and the daughter of the President of the Texas Banker's Association. The Quince girl and three others had big ranchers for their daddies.

Charlie had a feeling every bounty hunter in the state as well as the army and dozens of lawmen were already on the trail. But because of Naomi, the McCallisters had a head start.

Except for the Quince girl, he didn't know any of the hostages and didn't give a damn about their welfare. Charlie thought about the job pragmatically. He pursued Jericho and intended to get him. Though profitable, freeing the girls represented no more than a side issue. But the rescue, though incidental to him, might please his woman into liking him. So, it became important.

It would be a spell before Sam and Deacon returned and Charlie hung back in the barn with Naomi. It was time to speak to the teacher about what had transpired between them. He'd made up his mind about her from the moment she bartered her life for her students.

An opportunity to have a woman such as Naomi for a mate comes only once. That she'd been ignorant of a man's touch before him only heightened his determination to keep her.

He intended to settle her with enough money to make do in Buffalo Creek under the sheriff's watchful eye. Charlie figured Potter would keep her safe until the McCallisters returned with her students. Then—when he got that far in his thoughts he stalled.

For one thing, she didn't seem to realize she belonged to him now. He suspected that if he left Naomi with much money, she'd be long gone before he hauled Jericho to justice. She didn't pay much attention to his orders either, not in a manner a squaw should. Charlie assured himself she'd eventually know her place. He'd train her.

It didn't matter how she primmed up trying to be a straitlaced schoolteacher. Her hair betrayed the wild woman within. Coiling in improbably tight curls and bouncing around in the string she'd tied it back with, her hair softened her flinty-eyed glare.

"I'm making arrangements for you to stay here." He brushed a stray curl from her cheek and then pulled it to its full length before releasing it and watching it corkscrew again. Against his callused palm, her skin felt as smooth as silk.

Naomi studiously avoided his gaze, stepping sideways indicating by her stiff posture he'd gotten too close.

"Don't you want to ask me anything?" Charlie searched for something to say. He didn't want to leave her behind thinking hostile thoughts about him. But, try as he might, he couldn't come up with a smart comment.

Naomi didn't say anything but rebellion warred with outrage in her expression.

"You're staying here." Charlie felt the need to declare his order again as he pulled her into his embrace, tilting her chin and forcing her to meet his gaze.

Her clenched jaw signaled her effort to hold back argument but he could tell she was madder than a wet hen when he handed her a roll of bills. Her glare was a threat.

Probably a look she gives her students. She stood stiffly in the circle of his arms, staring up at him accusingly. Charlie sighed, pulling her against his length, wishing they had the time for another joining.

"We made a bargain. You were going to help me rescue my students." Her voice held stubborn anger and her arms had become rigid barriers between them.

"Woman," he scolded her, rubbing her fanny possessively, "you can hardly stand up. I can tell by the way you're walkin' that your rump hurts and from the sounds your belly's makin', you're more than a little hungry. Besides, you'll be in the way." He was happy to end that conversation. "When did you eat last?"

She grabbed his vest, fisting the leather in both hands, jerking him closer. "I'll keep up and I'm not hungry. You can't leave me behind." When he said nothing, her fierce expression softened into a smile and she slid her hands under leather, caressing flesh.

Awkwardly delivered though it was, her touch made Charlie shudder, his spirit reaching from within him as though finding its true home. He groaned, enfolding her in his arms, urging her against the swell in his pants. Naomi's effect on his body fascinated him. He wanted nothing more than to follow her around all day on the off chance he might get to slip his cock inside again.

"Mr. Wolf, we need to talk," she whispered before planting a kiss on his left nipple.

She's doing it again, trying to seduce me. The idea both amazed and delighted him but he wasn't falling for it. Though his cock threatened to split his pants his brain grabbed hold of his lust.

"Be glad you get to stay behind." His tongue felt thick in his mouth and his body rebelled as he rasped out the words. "You've got the services of three bounty hunters who will rescue your students. While I sleep on hard ground and eat trail grub, you'll be comfortable waiting here." He swatted her butt, laughed gruffly and peeled his body from hers.

"I hired you to lead me to my students. I didn't hire you to think for me."

Charlie watched with interest as Naomi transformed from siren back to school marm. During her attempt to sway his judgment, her full lower lip had curved invitingly in a smile, creamy skin had warmed to pink and her blue eyes had become points of midnight desire. Now she wore a militant expression, pressing her lips to a thin line and glaring at him from eyes of blue steel.

"You're worn out."

"I don't need to rest," she muttered, fisting her hands this time on her hips.

"I'll get you a room and some supper. Hiram Potter's a good man, at least as much as any lawman can be. You'll be fine until we get back." Charlie ignored her fury and turned toward the barn door. He hesitated. She looked forlorn standing there with his clothes drooping on her slender frame. "Put your new dress on. You can't go into the hotel wearing my buckskins."

"Mr. Wolf, you're the most arrogant, dictatorial

male I've ever encountered." Not being one to hold back her observations Naomi stated her opinion. Her intended insult made him smile inside.

She doesn't see white man, Indian or half-breed when she looks at me. She sees a mule-headed jackass. For the first time in his life his two worlds fit themselves together and he became one entity, Naomi Parker's man. To celebrate the fact, he pulled her into his arms and hefted her up so the ridge of his hard-on notched in the juncture of her legs.

"See what you do to me, woman?" He kissed her opinions silent, holding the back of her head still and exploring her mouth with his tongue. She pressed her mound against his cock and pulled his head back down, taking over the kiss. Wrapping her arms around his neck, she held him tight and used what she'd learned the night before.

When she touched him this time, carnal hunger rumbled deep in his chest spreading to his throbbing cock. Charlie scooted them back into a vacant stall and slid his hands down inside her waistband, stroking his fingers through the lips of her sex. She was hot and needy, wet for him, making it easy to slide a finger inside.

"Hold your shirt up," he growled, forgetting the hunt, the bounty, his partners and his two worlds, focusing every part of him on the woman in his arms.

Her breasts were small, plump treats. He captured a

stiff nipple between his teeth, biting it gently as he penetrated her tight channel. She flinched and, knowing he'd made her sore, he should have stopped. But her cunny clenched around his finger and she thrust her breast against his mouth, asking for more.

He pressed against her, tweaking with his fingers the nipple he couldn't attend with his mouth, laving the peak before him with his tongue and matching the pull of his suckling with the rhythm of his lower thrusts.

She held his head to her breast as he pleasured her. Liquid heat coated his finger and he added a second, curling enough to find her sweet spot and make her sway and moan. Touching her inside, feeling her sheath tighten as he stroked in and out, Charlie lost the will to deny his cock the same joy.

"Kick a leg free from your pants." He fumbled his loincloth aside and his buckskins open as she obeyed. Taking his shaft in hand, he hoisted Naomi high enough for groin to meet mound, fitting his hard flesh to her entrance.

"Yes," she moaned, wrapping her legs around him, meeting the full force of his thrust with her own.

He feared he'd go off as soon as he entered her. As it was, he held her rump and hunched over her, pumping his hips slowly trying to draw the experience out as long as possible.

"Mr. Wolf, I need—"

"Charlie," he muttered, covering her mouth and

penetrating her lips with his tongue.

"Charlie," she panted. "I need—" her words broke off in a gasp when he stroked her pearl, pressing his thumb on the sensitive bundle of nerves.

Her release rippled through her and Naomi whimpered, "Oh, oh, oh Charlie…"

The feel of her flesh spasming around his flesh broke his control. He grunted, heat pulsing from toes to heels, chasing up his legs and centering in his cock. His back bowed with the force of his orgasm and he stroked in and out of her in short hard jerks, his sex deliberately spurting cum into her womb.

Slumped over her and drained, Charlie continued holding her in place, sealing the connection between them and hoping his seed found a home.

Naomi rested, stroking his hair absently with one hand, her forehead on his shoulder. Charlie could feel the strength of her heart thumping and realized the cadence matched his own. He stood, savoring their moment of oneness. *That's the difference with this woman. She makes me more than I am.*

"When I come back for you, we'll have more time," he promised, nuzzling her neck as the ripples of her orgasm quieted. She released her legs from around his waist and self-consciously stood, making a moue of alarm when his seed spilled out of her and slid down her thigh.

"I'm wet. I, uh, I…"

Glad he carried a clean one, Charlie pulled his handkerchief from his pocket and folded it. Dropping to his knees in front of her, he kissed her belly, before wiping her thighs and sliding the soft material between her legs.

"Thank you, Mr. Wolf," she murmured, her cheeks bright red when he stood and kissed her forehead.

"Charlie," he corrected her again. He hid his amusement when, recovered, she patted her clothes in place, trying to regain her dignity. He could have told her that it was hopeless where he was concerned. He could see now how to master her—using her susceptibility to his sexual prowess. Primal satisfaction curled in his chest that he'd established his dominion over his mate during their mating.

"I'm renting a place for you at the hotel. I'll be back for you when I get your room fixed up." He left her satiated and drowsy in the barn and kept his eyes on the dirt street while he walked toward the two-room hotel situated next to the sheriff's office. There was no sense in advertising his movements this evening. Only a fool would expect no problems with Charlie's choice of a woman. Irritating female though she remained, she made him smile inside, an infrequent emotion in his life.

"You be careful, Charlie," she whispered as he left. Her cautionary words warmed him, making him certain she cared at least a little bit about him.

He'd expected more of her caustic arguments but she

remained uncharacteristically quiet as he walked away. Maybe she was in shock. He didn't think many people had ever managed to make Naomi Parker mind their orders and it filled him with smug satisfaction that she obeyed him.

He'd have preferred taking her along, but aside from the fact that she'd be in danger and a liability on the trail, she moved like a woman pure worn-out and their recent coupling hadn't improved matters a bit. Mad at him or not, she needed a hot soak and a good meal followed by sleep in a soft bed. Much as he'd like to climb in behind her, he'd told her the truth. He'd be sleeping in the saddle or on the hard ground, as usual.

Before he stopped at the hotel to rent a room for Naomi, he visited Sheriff Potter's office where he found Sam and Deacon. Because the sheriff had always been indifferent to Charlie's half-breed status and had given him the same respect he gave the other McCallisters, he'd earned Charlie's trust.

"I'm leaving my woman at the hotel while we're outlaw hunting. I'd take it as a personal favor if you'd watch over her while I'm gone."

After the Buffalo Creek Sheriff agreed to keep an eye on Naomi, Charlie went across the street to get her fixed up in a place to stay. He banged on the counter until the clerk, frowning and wiping his mouth on a napkin and irritated at having his supper interrupted, came out from the back.

"I need a room." Charlie opened his saddlebags and found his money still nestled in a roll where he'd left it. But she'd taken his gun. He should have seen that coming.

She seduced me senseless. "Never mind." He turned, heading back to Naomi on a run. By the time he got to the barn, she was gone. His irritation with the school marm ever increasing, Charlie saddled Old Mossy and rode into the dusk, following her trail through the quickly fading light. He hadn't ridden far when Deacon swung in on his left and Sam took the right.

"Following the schoolmarm, cousin?" Sam gave him a cocky grin. "You two set the town of Flat Rock on its ear."

Charlie remained focused on the trail and refrained from punching his cousin. On his other flank, Deacon began.

"First you told Hiram Potter you were leaving *your* woman in his care. Second, you attempted to rent a room for Miss Parker." Deacon numbered Charlie's recent sins in a calm voice. Then he turned to less recent events. "After Wallace trash-talked the two of you this morning, I doubt there's a soul in Flat Rock who remains ignorant to your tryst with the Sparrow Creek schoolteacher. Are you planning to ruin this good woman's name in Buffalo Creek as well?" Deacon McCallister didn't have much to say on most occasions. Like most other people, Charlie tended to listen when the former minister roared as he did now.

Charlie gritted his teeth, sick at the idea of Naomi's name being sullied. All of the warnings he'd mocked her with the night before were real and looming in front of him. She'd treated him so normally he'd forgotten he was half-breed, she was white and they were never going to have a real life together.

"I must have hit the dry goods store before the owner heard," Charlie snarled. "He didn't have any trouble taking my money this morning."

"Yes, the town was duly informed you bought her a dress." Deak eyed him expectantly but when Charlie volunteered no further explanation, he started talking again. "Last night, Wallace came into the bar with a wad of cash, claiming you'd paid him to get lost from the barn after you'd dragged the schoolteacher inside."

"It didn't happen like that," Charlie muttered.

"It better not have," Deacon continued, "because he said he sneaked back and she was struggling to get away from you and you had your knife out."

"Funny, no one came to rescue the school marm." Charlie didn't bother hiding his disgust, nudging Old Mossy into a faster gait aimed at leaving his cousins behind. They matched his pace and traveled three abreast.

"Not saying they would've tried, but with Deak watching the front of the bar and me eyeing the side door, no one even considered it." Sam trotted next to

Charlie openly savoring the memory of danger as though it were a tasty dish. "There's gonna be hell to pay over this one, Charlie."

Making one of his quicksilver shifts in mood, he grinned and clarified his warning. "I'm just saying, because I was protecting your chance with a woman, I didn't get my monthly fuck. I'll be damned if even the sway of Old Mossy's rump isn't looking good to me."

"Nothing's funny about this." Charlie glowered at. his cousin. "You'll laugh skidding into the fires of hell."

"Hope so," Sam drawled. "But you've got more to worry about than dousing my hellfire."

Charlie agreed. Naomi was blundering around unprotected. As soon as word circulated, a lynch mob would be uncoiling a rope for him and she'd be fair game for any man's attentions. Her teaching days were over whether she realized it or not.

White folks having nothing better to do than spew hate about Indians, news of the incident would spread like wildfire. Flat Rock citizens might have turned a blind eye on a half-breed bedding a whore, though from Molly's actions in the saloon, it seemed doubtful. But in the eyes of most, Charlie had committed a hanging offense by bedding a white woman, let alone, a schoolteacher. He figured if they could find a way, they'd hang him twice.

I'm not giving her up. "Naomi Parker and I have an agreement and she's under my protection," he told his cousins belligerently. "That's all any bastard needs to know."

"You will do right by the woman?" Deacon asked, settling back in his saddle.

"She wears my mark." Irritated, Charlie slowed to a walk and waited until his cousins did too. When their horses walked in tandem, Charlie loosed his grip on the reins and showed his cousins the red slash on his palm.

"Well, damn me if you didn't go and take a squaw." Sam clapped him on the back hard enough to knock Charlie from the saddle if he hadn't been expecting it. "So why's she riding off without you? And where's she going?"

"Does she know she's your bride?" Deacon asked, cutting right to the heart of the situation.

"She knows we're partners," Charlie hedged, not really ready to discuss the odd way he'd found and claimed his woman. "She'll make a fine wife."

"Congratulations, Charlie." Deacon's words declared the union a done deal. His smile proclaimed his approval. In spite of all the obstacles in front of him and Naomi, not to mention their current state of separation, Deacon's words bolstered Charlie's determination to keep his mate.

His cousin was a curious fellow. Until a few years back, Deak had visited a widow once a month. But when she'd married another man, he'd shrugged it off indifferently. Since then, he'd lost interest in females in general and made it a point to ignore Sam's carousing. His indifferent attentions to females obviously didn't extend to Naomi. He worried out loud over Charlie's good sense when it came to his mate.

"She'll take some gentle handling, not being used to your rough ways."

"Yep," he agreed, though remembering her determination to make him listen to her and her ability to fuck him senseless, Charlie had a feeling Naomi was a lot tougher than she looked.

Damned if I didn't find a prize. "Chasing after my woman's students will get Jericho for us too." Unwilling to let his cousins see his enthrallment, he refocused the conversation. If the situation hadn't been so tangled with danger for Naomi, he might have laughed at the McCallisters' abrupt departure from the business of his claiming a squaw to the business of bounty hunting. Sam wasted no time embracing the new subject.

"Hiram Potter said he's already asked for authorization from the U.S. Marshal to hire a tracker. Figure we'll get it since we're after a bunch of outlaws who've kidnapped daughters of important Texas citizens."

"As opposed to unimportant citizens," Deacon murmured grimly.

Charlie understood Deacon's rage simmering beneath his calm demeanor. Seven years before, Robert McCallister had been a young minister and an *unimportant citizen* when his wife had been savaged in their Abilene home. The sheriff had refused to go after her killers, so Robert had set aside his Bible and gone hunting for the murderers. Sam joined him. Charlie was already on the trail.

After they'd executed the men, the three drifted on together, picking up handbills and catching outlaws for pay. Robert McCallister quit preaching and became known simply as *Deacon*, one of the most feared gunfighters in the territory.

"The band of renegades will be travelling fast, heading due south toward Mexico. With luck, maybe if we get right after 'em, the gang'll be too busy riding to stop and abuse Naomi's students." Charlie guided the conversation back to the current problem.

"We'll get the girls and Jericho too," Deacon said, stroking his beard thoughtfully before he gave Charlie a hard look. "But be that as it may, your woman is running loose and from those tracks it appears she doesn't have any idea where she's going. While she's out there stumbling around she could run into a lot of trouble besides rattlesnakes. On top of Jericho being in the area, a band of Apaches slipped off the San Carlos reservation and are heading through Texas toward Mexico."

"I'm going on to Eclipse and have the sheriff there contact these families." Sam pulled out the list of names Deacon had written for him. He stuffed them back in his shirt and added, "I'll double back and join you on the trail. Maybe by the time the families get word, we'll have the girls safely home."

Charlie agreed. "Deacon, you follow them and I'll join you as soon as I can." When his cousin frowned, Charlie assured him, "Hell, they didn't even try to hide. You don't have to be a tracker to find their trail. Looks like they didn't care who knew where they were going. Stay alert because that's not a good sign."

"I'll catch up to you later," Charlie told them before Sam rode east and Deacon south. "It appears I've got some work to do corralling Naomi Parker and seeing to it that she gets to Buffalo Creek in one piece." The trio split up and Charlie went west, following where the buckskin's prints led.

CHAPTER TEN

NAOMI HAD TIME TO WONDER more than once why folks always thought they knew best for her. Her sister Comfort had started the trend, sending her to the neighbors to stay when Comfort left Alabama for Texas.

Her older sister had put food on the table however she could. But when an offer of marriage had been made, she'd grabbed it, leaving Naomi alone with a brush, a comb, a copy of *Godey's Lady's Book* and orders to leave the ramshackle cabin falling down around her and go live with the neighbors.

Back then, she'd climbed under the porch and refused to say goodbye to her sister, sure that Comfort would come back. She hadn't. Naomi spent a full week telling herself she didn't need anyone while she fished and stayed alone waiting.

When Harvey Collins had kicked open the door to her shack and tried to rape her, she'd hit him with her only pitcher, breaking it across his head and running all the way to the Lancaster Farm. In the end, fleeing a monster in the night, she'd been happy to be taken in by the neighbors.

Glowering at her satchel, which contained much the same paucity of valuables, Naomi felt the same sweep of rebellious rage she'd felt then. She also felt guilt. If she'd just...

Last week an old man had come calling at the school. He'd been driving a wagon with a sign painted on the side that read, *Harvey's Travelling Wagon of Interesting Items*. Naomi had recognized the peddler immediately, refusing to allow him to stop and show his wares to her students.

Collins was a remembered bogeyman she'd thought she left behind with her childhood in Alabama. But there he'd been, leering at the young girls hanging off the porch, even as she'd chased him away with threats.

"We have no use for your items. You'll need to drive on." Naomi had walked to the wagon and ordered him gone.

"I 'member you. Yer *Nomi* Parker." He'd grinned, displaying a mouth full of broken teeth. "Turned into a dried-up old maid, didn't ya?" He'd smacked his lips and cackled his question louder for any listeners. "How's that sister of yers? Knew her pretty well, but then again, so did half the men in the county."

She'd been horrified seeing him and had tried to find a way to shut him up. He knew she came from a played-out dab of dirt, sharecropped by her father and brother until they'd both been killed in the war.

"Get out of here, you wicked old man. I'll send Patrick after the sheriff if you don't go now," she'd dropped her refined pretense and threatened him.

"Everything all right over there, Miss Naomi?" Patrick had called to her, lending the knowledge of his presence to the tableau. For all her bravado, she'd been glad to see the hired man limping toward her.

"I've explained that we have no use for his potions or fribbles. He's leaving now." Naomi had felt so safe with Patrick Wilson there to protect her. But both Becky Johnson and Missy Cotter had defied her instruction to stay on the porch and swooped down on the wagon.

"I have money to buy what I want, Miss Parker." Missy Cotter was the product of intense spoiling and never missed an opportunity to brag about the money she came from.

"Go back to the dormitory porch, ladies. The peddler has nothing you would want." Naomi had been firm and Becky Johnson's snobbery had helped.

"Really, Missy, would you want anything that dirty old man is selling? My mama would swoon at the thought of buying such as that." The silly child had raised her voice, intentionally insulting the merchant and impressing him with her superior social status.

"Your day's coming, Miz Parker." He'd sneered at her. "You and all yer prissy females will get your comeuppance." Harvey Collins had driven on down the road, but Naomi felt certain he'd engineered the kidnapping days later.

My fault—Patrick dead and the others stolen—it's my entire fault. She should have realized it had been too easy getting rid of him. She should have told someone about Harvey Collins. Her stomach churned with shame.

Her hand clenched, brushing her fingers across the cut on her palm. It was tender, still fresh evidence of her bargain with the bounty hunter. As far as she was concerned, Charlie Wolf had reneged on his part so she was going out on her own looking for the girls.

"I haven't had a lot of luck in my life with people doing what they say they'll do. I don't know why I thought he'd be any different," she muttered. Regardless of their agreement, in her heart, she didn't trust Charlie to keep his word, regardless of the way he'd marked her hand and body.

"You'll trade your life for theirs?" Her palm tingled and the cut itched as Naomi uneasily remembered his question. Of course he hadn't actually meant her life—as in the rest of it—had he? Resignedly she shrugged.

I'll either have his help or I won't. But I have no time to argue. Fulfilling her duty to her students was what she had to do. When the starless sky turned dark, closing down around her like a blanket thrown over her head, she forgot about any misunderstanding that might exist between her and the bounty hunter and hoped that Charlie would catch up to her soon.

The buckskin mare put one foot in front of another

as though she had a destination in mind, so Naomi left the reins slack and gave her the lead. The animal traveled swiftly as Naomi rode her, tensely straining to see through the darkness.

Her legs were trembling with fatigue and she wasn't sure she would be able to stand if she slid from the buckskin when Charlie's dark stallion edged beside her. He pulled her mount to a stop, dismounted and caught her as she toppled over.

"I told you to stay put in Buffalo Creek." The whole time he was scolding her, he led her away from the open flat land and toward a shaded gulley. She could see better now as dark turned to shades of purple in the early morning sky.

"Best stop for a time. The animals need rest and so do I." He loosened the girth on the buckskin mare, slid the bit from her mouth and hobbled her, all while Naomi stood, weaving on her feet, watching from exhausted eyes.

When both animals were cared for, he strode to a spot under a tree, brushed away the dead limbs and debris and unfurled his ground cloth. Then he laid his blanket on top of that and pointed at it.

"Rest here before you fall down."

Naomi obeyed without question, too tired even to ask where he would be.

The sound of horses greeted her when she woke. She kept her eyes closed, sorting through her most recent memories. Charlie Wolf had ordered her to bed and his attitude had seemed quite high-handed.

Hesitant to deal with his wrath, she kept her eyes shuttered, peeking stealthily from under her lashes. Charlie was near. His horse stood next to the buckskin mare. Both ate leaves from the tree Naomi rested under. She sat up, wincing at the ache in her body, stiff from both the hard ground and all the unusual activities in which she'd recently engaged.

In the time it took for her to rise from the blanket and look around the camp, Charlie took his place beside her.

"There's a catch basin of water down below. Bathe." He handed her linen and a bar of soap.

Grateful for the chance to soak, she left comment about his dictatorial behavior for another time and hurried to the water.

"Watch out for snakes," he advised.

Naomi didn't like snakes or other slithering critters but she did like being clean, so she watched her step, shed Charlie's clothes and plunged in the water, wallowing like a kid in the semi-warm pool. Her hair hung in rough strands that would become snarled balls when dry. She worked ineffectually at one tangle until she felt his gaze on her.

"I wish my hair was straight like yours," she muttered.

He held out his hand, indicating it was time for her

to quit the water.

"Just gawk at something else besides me," she told him, exasperated at his boldness when he didn't look away. She covered her breasts with one arm, her triangle of lower curls with the other and grimaced at him as she emerged.

He snorted at her attempt at modesty and wrapped the blanket around her, rubbing the drying cloth across her hair. Then he handed her a tin.

"Work that into the snarls, then rinse it out of your hair."

"What's in it?" she asked suspiciously, sniffing the mixture. It smelled like him, or at least the spicy wood scent she associated with him.

"Bear grease." He grunted impatiently. "Now rub it on your hair."

It was odd how right away her hair felt different. It hung in soft wet strands that felt like silk when she rinsed his concoction from her head.

"It feels like when I was a child and rinsed my hair in rain water." She let her hands play down the silken length and looked at him doubtfully. "Bear grease?"

"No. My mother makes it for me to use on my hair," he growled.

She'd noticed how shiny his hair was. "It's indecent for a man to have hair that hangs down his back and is prettier than a woman's." The tart words escaped her before she could stop them. Then she fastened on the important part of his sentence, excusing her own rude comment.

"You have a mother?" She was surprised. He didn't look like a man with a mother, let alone one who made him beauty products for his hair.

"Did you think I was born in a cave with wolves?" He capped the tin and stuck it in his pocket.

"Does your mother live with the Kiowa tribe?" she asked politely, ignoring his sarcasm because frankly, she could picture him in a cave with wolves.

"My mother is Rachel McCallister of the MC3 Ranch. She's a white woman, like you." While she digested that information, he did one of his silent maneuvers, moving much closer, leaving Naomi very conscious of his nearness.

"Sun ointment—should make your face quit burning." She could feel the heat from his body as he rubbed a different salve on her cheeks.

His nearness and gentle application of the medicine flustered her. No one had taken care of her since her sister had left. Naomi had grown up taking care of others. Now this man leaned over her and squinted as he dabbed another kind of cream on her cheeks.

"It does soothe the burn." She couldn't resist touching his hand as he carefully applied the balm to her burned cheeks. "Why are you being nice to me?"

She suspected that Charlie Wolf never made a move that didn't benefit him, but at this moment she didn't care. It was wonderful that he was showing her kindness during the day.

"Your skin's too chapped. I want it soft under my lips when I taste you," he drawled.

"It's daylight. We need to travel now that I've rested." Naomi blinked at him, confused.

"We're hidden here and it's a good place to hole up until dusk. My horse will let me know if anyone or anything gets close."

"It was dark last night. How did you find me?" Naomi asked.

"Old Mossy took a fancy to the buckskin mare you pilfered." Charlie's eyes crinkled at the corners just the slightest when he answered. "She's in heat. He followed her scent." The almost smile changed to a frown and he asked, "Where the hell did you think you were going?"

"The buckskin mare belonged to one of the criminals you captured and I felt certain she was returning to familiar horses," Naomi answered smugly.

"And even if that blockheaded idea was sound, you thought you'd just ride into an outlaw camp and do what?"

Naomi blushed and squirmed under his gaze. Her plan had been more an impulse.

"Woman, you have no sense." He shook his head. Shrugging, he leaned close to her, his nostrils flaring as if testing the air.

"What are you doing?" she asked nervously.

"Fixin' your scent in my mind for if I have to go chasing after you again," Charlie growled.

His words brought a flush of arousal flooding her body. She could smell him too and she liked his spicy male scent. She was reminded that only a blanket separated her nakedness from Charlie and her skin pebbled with awareness as her womb clenched. Thankfully he didn't notice her unseemly response and continued explaining his plan.

"The stars'll be out tonight and it'll be clear enough to see." He turned her toward the camp and her bed under the tree. "Meanwhile, you can tender the next installment of your payment to me."

"What?" Her voice sharpened, her disappointment a twist of pain. He didn't need to remind her that she'd traded him liberties for his care. The hair and face creams seemed less special and her momentary pleasure at being tended disappeared.

"How many such installments will it take to close this account?" she snapped.

"Depends on the amount of danger I incur in the course of the rescue," he murmured, leaning over her to claim her lips. And then his shoulders blotted out the sun and he laid her to the ground, coming down on top of her.

CHAPTER ELEVEN

A S NAOMI PEERED UP at him, Charlie supported his weight, blanketing her with his body. A few pulls and he removed his vest and then his pants, baring his flesh to press against hers. She gasped, her husky sound of desire turning his gray eyes to dark smoke.

Holding her gaze, he hovered above her as if waiting for her to protest. When instead, she traced the scar on his face before running her fingers through his hair, his stern expression softened and he fit his knee between her thighs, pressing her open.

Naomi closed her eyes, savoring the feel of his muscled leg. He nudged and she willingly spread her thighs wider until his hot flesh rubbed against her folds. Arousal made her spine arch and her breasts thrust upward, the heat in her core becoming an inferno demanding satisfaction.

He trailed the long silk of his hair across her flesh, tickling her already sensitized nipples and she moaned, begging without words for his mouth to follow the same carnal path. His lips closed around one bud and when he suckled it, heat radiated downward, pooling in her womb.

She squirmed rubbing the tender and swollen outer shell of her sex against his thigh, reaching for some relief from his torment though she was sore from their previous coupling.

Naomi winced when he touched her pearl as he played in her slick folds, flinching when his finger circled her entrance. She wanted him inside her but…

Charlie grunted and stopped petting her, cupping both breasts and pushing them together to tease first one nipple and then the other. When she tried to wrap her legs around his hips, seeking relief, he laughed and abandoned her breasts.

"You will stop teasing me, Charlie Wolf," she panted, her hands fisted and her eyes tightly shut. Naomi lay gasping for breath, her body on fire with need.

"Yes ma'am," he murmured, trailing his lips down her midriff to her navel.

Her eyes popped open and she leaned forward, balancing on her elbows, watching him. He held her gaze, rimming the sensitive area before his tongue flicked inside and she felt the spear of that small penetration in her loins.

"Charlie, that's indecent." He sipped and kissed around her belly, making Naomi shiver and gasp.

"But good," he growled, tracing a lazy path of licks and nips down to the soft curls covering her feminine secrets.

She knew he wouldn't do such a thing but... Charlie's fingers parted the lips of her sex and his tongue swiped over her intimate folds, tasting her.

Fevered want fought waves of embarrassment. Want won. Like a wanton, she raised her hips, reveling in the pleasure of his mouth. Charlie stroked and petted her to a such fevered pitch she was too aroused to feel sore. Her flesh pulsed under his searching lips as he arranged her body to his liking, holding her rump high and feasting on her.

Naomi couldn't control her movements, undulating against his mouth, shuddering when he used his tongue on the sensitive nub at her apex, laving her pearl before taking it between his lips and sucking. He eased one finger than two into her passage and she arched her back, bucking her hips and clenching internal muscles around his digits as he stroked deeper.

His chuckle sent her flying into bliss as the vibration from his rumbled laughter cascaded through the bundle of nerves he sucked. She couldn't stifle her moans as one orgasm chased another, thrumming through her even as the first still pulsed in her veins.

Finally, when she slumped boneless without will or strength to move, Charlie looked up, flashing a smug grin before he lowered her rump to the ground. His fingers continued pumping in and out, following the sway of her body as it clenched and released in aftershocks, sucking him back when he pulled almost free.

"Please," she whispered. She didn't feel satisfied although her body shimmered with Charlie's sweat and ripples of release continued to pulse through her.

"Please what?" he teased, rubbing his face against her belly, licking her navel, then swooping lower to flick her pearl before gently sucking on it again. Abruptly, he sat back on his heels, taking his fingers from her body. She sighed, replete but not.

"Want something else?" He no longer teased, his voice husky, aroused.

"Yes." She wanted what he'd given her before.

He urged her thighs farther apart and took his place between them. Naomi leaned on her elbows, watching him part her nether lips with his shaft, penetrating her slowly, filling her with *him*.

Thoroughly prepared, her honey coating his cock with her emissions when he nudged slowly through her passage, she wanted more. Impatiently, she pushed up with her hips, taking him on a quicker journey to her core, groaning at the delicious feel of his flesh stretching hers.

"You're greedy," he accused, but laughed gruffly when he said it.

Yes. This part of you I want. This part of your company I'll miss. Naomi wrapped her legs around his waist and rode his passion, matching it with her own until his muscles tightened and his back arched, flattening her swollen breasts under his chest as his seed pulsed in hot jets inside her.

Charlie eased from Naomi, tucking the blanket around her. He would have liked to run his hands over her again as she slept. But he didn't want to wake her, figuring she needed her rest, having survived both an outlaw attack and him.

He pulled his clothes on, checked the horses and prowled around the camp, coming back to the blanket from time to time to watch her sleep. Finally he couldn't resist the mop of light-brown curls and crouched next to her, lifting a strand of hair. When he released the coil and it bounced back in place, her eyes opened.

"Obviously, it'll take more than your mama's bear grease to quell this mess," Naomi said wryly, looking sideways at him.

"Better get dressed," he told her. Not because it was time to leave but because if she didn't cover her white skin and long limbs he'd be on her again and she was already sore. He replaced her corset string with a leather thong, gathering her hair in his big hands and tying it low at her nape.

"Groom your mare. It will be a long ride tonight and the horses need pampered a little." He retrieved the brush and curry comb from his saddlebags and handed one to her. As soon as she had clothes on, Naomi primmed up.

"Tell me about your students." Charlie oversaw her

work and questioned her as she started brushing the mare.

She put her head down on the mare's side, hiding her face for a moment before she took a big breath and began. As usual, it took her awhile to get to the point.

"The twelve-year-olds—Justine Garner, Mary-Beth Calloway, Marnie Mullins and Ambrosia Quince were delivered to my care two weeks ago."

Charlie was sorry to hear the Quince girl was one of the captives. Her folks lived over Eclipse way where the McCallister ranch was located.

"This week, when Rebecca Johnson, Emily Erdman, Daisy Meadows and Millicent Cotter arrived, the first four having been there longer, felt proprietary toward the school." She frowned, struggling with her story. According to Naomi, she'd quickly lost control of her charges as the girls went to war in a pitched battle for control. Clothing had been hidden, bedding short-sheeted—even Naomi wasn't exempt—and Justine's specialty was fainting.

"Justine's tiny but willful. Whenever she can't get her way, she swoons. Or at least that's what she calls it. I call it falling down to get attention.

"I was supposed to teach them deportment. I couldn't even get them to deal politely with each other," she admitted.

"Anybody get hurt?" he asked.

"They are creative," Naomi conceded and then

shuddered. "When I heard the first shots fired, I was studying Marnie Mullins' hair hoping that when the headmistress arrived, she'd understand. Even after repeated washings black streaks still stained it from the ink Daisy put in her rinse water."

Charlie shrugged. It sounded like a bunch of female silliness to him but it didn't offer much to work with as far as the girls helping in their own rescue.

"Brody Quince got even," Naomi said flatly. "Patrick had been fussing about a skunk and the day before yesterday, she trapped it in the shed, then lured Daisy Meadows and the other fourteen-year-olds out there."

"You discipline 'em?" he asked, hiding his grin, picturing four of the state's finest locked in with a skunk.

"That's why the window was open. The odor was quite punishment enough since we all lived closely together. I'm sure you'll agree when we rescue them."

"I'm taking you back to Buffalo Creek," Charlie broke the news to Naomi.

"No you're not, Mr. Wolf." She turned on him fiercely.

"I told you, I'm not Mr. Wolf. I'm just Charlie Wolf. My father was Gray Wolf my mother is Rachel McCallister," he growled, irritated at her formal address.

"You act like a wolf," she told him snidely. "Whatever you call yourself, I hired you and I'm going along."

"If I *was* a wolf," he warned her, "I'd bite your neck and hump you into submission."

"You already tried that and it didn't work." She sniffed, turning her nose up, dismissing his threat.

"If you were a squaw, I'd beat you," Charlie growled, stepping close and cupping her face, staring down at her and trying to scare her into minding.

"I don't believe you." She turned her head and lightly bit down on his thumb. When her tongue touched his skin, she blushed, maybe remembering the way he'd used his tongue on her. "I'll follow you if you leave me behind," she whispered.

At dusk, Naomi rode beside him when they traveled toward the mountains and away from Buffalo Creek. Charlie didn't argue too long or too hard because he figured the schoolteacher was safer with him than running loose on her own.

Chapter Twelve

"**Y**OU WERE RIGHT. It's almost as bright as day out," Naomi complimented Charlie. The stars and moon lighted the arid landscape and even from horseback she could see the tracks.

She'd prevailed. Regrettably, their afternoon interlude of mutual satisfaction had been replaced with discord. Nevertheless, she rode beside him when they followed the outlaws' trail.

Charlie dismounted, crouching by the hoofprints, studying them. "See these deeper tracks, Naomi?" He pointed and she slid off her horse, peering down too. "The girls were transferred from horseback to the wagon here."

She walked beside Charlie Wolf, following the trail as it veered off in one direction while most of the horse tracks went in the other. They followed the wagon the rest of the night. Gradually the terrain changed as they entered foothills dotted with scrub pines. More often than not, they traveled by foot.

"Look up, Naomi. I'll teach *you* something." He pointed out the Big Dipper, a group of stars that formed a flat frying skillet.

"Pa Lancaster showed me that," Naomi said. But Charlie taught her how to use the knowledge.

"Imagine a straight line from those two stars to that bright star standing alone. That's the North Star. When you know that, you've got the top of your map. The rest is easy."

It wasn't easy, but he was patient and persistent, first showing her the ground each time they stopped, then directing her attention to the stars to mark their journey. Naomi found it quite exhilarating.

When he stood behind her, pointing out the constellations, he laid his palm on her belly, leaning over her shoulder. Before Charlie Wolf, she'd never experienced lust. Now, she recognized the pulsing need in her core for what it was.

She tried to concentrate on the outlaw trail, the stars in the sky and the wisdom he imparted, struggling to not let his overwhelming maleness distract her. But thoughts of what they'd done during their afternoon tryst pulled her mind from attending his instructions.

"Naomi, once we rescue your students, you might need to find your way without me." He scolded her inattention, reminding her of their goal, making her set aside the miasma of pleasure in which she'd wrapped herself.

Naomi staggered with tiredness by the time Charlie finally stopped. Since he'd found a rest spot, she wanted to drop to the dust and sleep. He made her help him tend the horses, chiding her on her lack of stamina.

"If you were a squaw, you'd pitch the tent, build the fire, fix the meal, and then and only then, lay in sleep with me."

"Those poor women," she said, staring at him in horror.

When Charlie finally prepared the ground cloth, she dropped like a stone, closed her eyes and barely felt his arm curling around her as she fell asleep. It was much later when he nudged her awake. She ignored him, too tired to care what order he now gave.

"Quit," she snarled when he pinched her rump. She looked at him blearily, wondering why the man wouldn't leave her alone.

"It's time for more education. You need to be able to protect yourself." Without further discussion, he pulled her up and ushered her to a clearing he'd already prepared.

It didn't take more than a few moments in combat to understand that Charlie used the instruction as an excuse to interrogate her.

"What happened to your family?" He'd started immediately.

"War." Naomi declared the word flatly, not sure if she spoke of what had been or the strenuous exercise that

Charlie forced on her now. The men in her family had marched off to defend the South's honor and left daughters and sisters to defend themselves.

"Your daddy keep slaves?" he asked.

"Daddy and Johnny didn't care about holding slaves or letting them go. They just didn't want to stay at home on a played-out farm another moment." A tide of long-suppressed anger accompanied her answer.

"He and my brother both joined the Confederate army the day we heard the South had seceded from the Union." Her hands clenched and her words were delivered in enraged gasps.

"Did he give you the deed before he left so you could sell when he died?" he asked to distract her from his move. She stalled in her dance and dodge and he caught her around the waist. She had to drop to the ground to escape, laughing to herself at his mistake.

Charlie's question assumed she'd been valued. It was a novel idea, a myth she'd fostered all of her life. Rage and pain filled her as she cast aside her façade and revealed truth. It felt rather as if she ripped a scab off a tender wound.

"My father was a sharecropper who could barely scrape together the rent for the land he finally abandoned." Her usual reticence in things personal forgotten, she dodged the savage tormenting her, ducked under his hands when she could and, for the first time ever, declared her grievances against the males in the world.

"So you're not a rich girl?"

"Of course not." She had to stop and stare at that question. Rich? Charlie would never understand the degree of poverty she'd escaped unless he saw the shack she'd lived in.

"If you think that, then my sister Comfort—wherever she is—is vindicated. When she left to get married, she gave me her copy of *Godey's Lady's Book* and told me to memorize it. I did."

"Why?" he sounded puzzled.

"It's how we learned what to wear, how to walk properly, what we should speak about if we were invited to a social gathering." She glared at him proudly. "It was how we decided who we'd be."

There was no way to make him comprehend how she and Comfort had based their futures on a magazine's instructions. She was amazed herself. But if he thought she'd been rich, it was a compliment of the highest order.

"How old were you when she left you alone?"

"Eleven and I wasn't alone long. I went to live with the Lancaster family next door. That lasted for two years until they both died six months apart."

She stood, hands balled into fists, waiting for him to come at her from the left. He feinted right and swooped in on her, taking her by surprise and tossing her to the ground once again. This time, he followed, coming down on top of her.

"Then what?" He was so close his breath ruffled her eyebrow.

"Then," she said tartly, squirming under the very personal way he pressed his length against her, "I went to work taking care of myself as I have done ever since."

"Don't think much of men, do you, Miss Parker?" Charlie rubbed his groin against her mound, taunting her.

"I never think of them at all if I don't have to." She tried to push him off as she made a statement that of course wasn't true. Recently, she couldn't seem to think of anything other than the man sprawled on top of her.

"Is that why you picked a school for females?" He held her face between his hands and stared down into her eyes as if he could see truth there.

Naomi stared right back, ignoring the way he pressed his hips against hers. She had worked her way up from a one-room schoolhouse teaching twelve ruffians to a position of importance teaching deportment to young ladies. Of course she'd chosen to work with girls. She prided herself on being able to choose since most women couldn't.

"I accepted employment that would get me to Texas. I'm here to find my sister. That's all." Her purpose for being in Texas didn't include the man pinning her beneath him but her senses disagreed, stealing her will.

"I haven't seen my sister since she left seventeen years ago. I plan to return to Alabama once I've assured myself that she has a good home."

"Why would you want to find someone who went off and left you?" He kept her from rolling away when his words made her angry. She tried to punch him when he stood, pulling her to her feet.

"She's family," Naomi snapped. "She's all I have."

"You need a man. You're a weak, silly woman who can't even defend herself." He whirled her around, forcefully demonstrating that she was at his mercy.

"I've managed alone." She didn't like to think about the day that Comfort had left, or the years in between, when few letters had changed to no letters. "I don't have to answer your questions." Her tone was harsh, brooking no dispute. It was the one that she used with students who didn't respond to soft persuasion.

"I say you do." Charlie Wolf prodded her secret fears from her. "What's got your back up—questions about your sister?"

"The man she left home with was a bad man if I ever saw one." Naomi admitted this to Charlie, wishing she was wrong, but knowing she wasn't. "Comfort married him because he was the only one who ever asked." There had been plenty who took without asking though. Naomi held that back, not wanting to reveal the sisters' shared shame.

When Comfort had brought home her first meal paid for with her body—she'd prostituted herself for a chicken and two ears of corn—the girls had cried together. But the memory of what they'd endured and the knowledge of what they'd survived had given Naomi strength to keep striving for better.

"And you, Naomi—how come you remained unwed?"

She blinked at the question, trying to discern his reason for asking before she told him the truth. "I guess I was just fortunate. No one ever wanted me."

A rough growl escaped his throat and his gray eyes darkened to the color of pitch.

"What?" she asked, backing away from him.

He stalked after her, his manner predatory. Never dropping her gaze, she retreated as if facing a true wolf. Ready to spin and run, her foot grazed the blanket and she realized he'd herded her there. He pounced, sweeping her off her feet, removing her clothing with furious haste.

Perhaps she was as needy. She pushed his buckskins low and grasped his shaft, testing its stance. It pleased her mightily that he was ready for her.

"You will not tease me today," she ordered him, emboldened by the sparring they'd just done. Also, it was the first time she'd spoken of her sister to anyone in too many years to count. In listening, somehow, Charlie had stepped into her life more securely.

He rolled her under him and mounted her with no caresses or tender foreplay. She didn't care. Her body had prepared for him and liquid heat eased the way as his shaft filled her with one thrust.

"What if I say you're my woman?" he asked, bracing on his arms. He held himself above her but remained linked below as he studied her face, waiting for her answer.

"I would say until we free my students you can claim whatever you please." Her snippy statement ended on a gasp as he stretched the walls of her channel, finding that spot high inside her that made her melt and shiver and fly.

She didn't know what she'd done to anger him, but their coupling during the afternoon was rough, forceful and prolonged and she was tender and aching inside by the time he took his satisfaction. He held her to him, her face pressed against his bare chest and she could smell her scent mingling with his.

"You're with me now," he growled, playing with her hair, which he'd tumbled into erratic curls.

"Obviously," she said wryly, repeating his earlier threat, "you've humped me into submission." Leaning her head back to look up at him, Naomi asked with false sweetness, "Are you going to give me more self-defense lessons?"

"You'll have to use your brain to get out of trouble, I can't teach you violence unless I can figure how to harness your tongue."

She didn't know why she'd ever thought his expression unreadable. She didn't need to hear the disdain dripping from his words. She could see it in the jut of his chin and arrogant tilt of his head.

CHAPTER THIRTEEN

T HAT NIGHT, before they set out again, Deacon McCallister rode into their camp. A short time later, Sam McCallister joined them. The men didn't comment on her presence and spoke as if she wasn't there.

"Jericho and his wild bunch are camped up ahead in a box canyon," Deacon said. "I didn't get close enough to hear the gist of the argument, but he and an old man named Collins have been going at it all day. Jericho sent more than half his men out scouring the countryside, but I have no idea for what."

"I wired the families, notifying them of the abductions and then lit out before I had to deal with a bunch of bawling mamas." When Sam McCallister shared his lack of sympathy with a grin, Naomi prepared to reprimand him for his crass disregard for the magnitude of the event. But before she could speak, he added more interesting news.

"The U.S. Marshal telegraphed his approval for

payment. The reward money is waiting in Eclipse. All we have to do is bring in Jericho, just like we planned."

"When did you start chasing Jericho?" Naomi asked, after playing his statement over in her mind once and then again.

"We've been dogging his heels all summer," Sam admitted. "And I'll be for damn sure glad when he's dead and we can quit."

"He has a large reward?"

"The biggest ever," Sam stopped, aware of the silence behind him. "What?" He turned, asking the question of Charlie, who glared in his direction.

"You talk too much."

"What is the plan?" she asked the brothers, since she knew she would get no answer from Charlie Wolf.

"The plan is for you to wait here. We'll go in, rescue your students, bring them back to you, after which, we'll take the bad men to jail." Charlie gave her a gun to protect herself while he was gone and explained her role as just stay put.

She would have preferred to shriek and demand he let her join the hunt. Had they been alone, she would have, but somehow the presence of his relatives made her hold her tongue. She remained rooted to the spot where he left her when the men rode into the night.

After he was gone, it occurred to Naomi that her bounty hunter rode toward danger. He could be killed. She assured herself that Charlie could take care of himself. But still, she was too far away from the outlaws' camp to know if something went wrong.

She waited as she'd been instructed—for a while. In the half-light of predawn, overcome with anxiety for both her students and Charlie, she climbed on the already saddled buckskin mare and rode toward the outlaw camp.

The mare's head came up and she broke into a trot, alerting Naomi that they were near. Had early morning sounds not carried so clearly, she might have blundered into the camp and become a captive too.

A horse ahead of them nickered a greeting. Naomi pulled up fast and slid to the ground, covering the buckskin's nostrils. At first she was pleased. Then she looked around, recognizing her vulnerability this close to the camp. She didn't actually know it was outlaws. She dithered, the morning light increasing as she indecisively filtered through ideas for ascertaining the identity of those in the camp.

The fact Charlie would be angry with her was a given. She felt certain she'd be able to sense his presence if he were near. She couldn't. Somehow, the McCallisters had gotten lost in the night. More importantly though, Naomi felt certain she'd found her students. Bringing her chaotic thoughts to order, she tried to assemble a plan. Unfortunately, the weaknesses outweighed the strengths of her position.

She was somewhere unknown with a gun she didn't know how to use. Pa Lancaster had spent plenty of time teaching her how to snare, clean and cook a rabbit, but shooting hadn't been among her lessons.

Naomi considered riding back the direction from which she'd come, but the laws of probability told her that all of her blundering on horseback would get her in trouble.

If her speculation proved correct, those were the men she'd hidden from when they attacked the school. They'd killed Patrick. The reality of her danger frightened her, telegraphing her panic to the nervously sidestepping horse. Naomi kept her hand over the mare's muzzle, stroking the velvet nose and imparting calm as Charlie had instructed. The mantle of his knowledge blanketed her and she steadied.

Looming to the right of where she stood were shadowed boulders that had tumbled down from the cliffs above. Naomi led the mare to the first dark area. The boulder was tall and bigger across than her one-room shack in Alabama.

In the sheltered niche, there was just room for the horse to turn around. It was almost a perfect hiding place. The buckskin fidgeted, reminding Naomi she needed to secure her. If she turned the mare loose, the animal seemed destined to walk straight toward the unsuspecting outlaws.

Naomi scanned the area and found a rock to anchor the reins to the granite floor, hoping the animal had been taught to ground tie.

As she left the mare and walked into the morning light, facing toward the sounds now coming clearly from the camp, she recognized the voices.

Multiple outlaws were camped not too far inside the canyon and Harvey Collins was with them—she could hear his agitated tones sporadically, even though she couldn't understand individual words. A deeper-voiced male cursed at Harvey in several languages.

Good, the miscreants are arguing among themselves. I need to get inside that camp while they are looking at each other. She had no idea how to rescue her students. She'd hoped Charlie Wolf would tell her his plan, but wasn't surprised when he hadn't.

It appeared the payment of her body she'd tendered in advance for Charlie Wolf's bounty hunter expertise was a sham. He'd let her seduce him knowing that he was going to capture Jericho anyway.

She wasn't sure how that knowledge affected her. She felt like a fool and admitted that self-esteem blossoming under Charlie Wolf's attentions now wilted under the knowledge he'd tricked her.

"Stop sniveling," she admonished herself. "Pa Lancaster taught you how to sneak up on quarry and Charlie Wolf showed you how to fight. You are not without resources."

She shrugged off Charlie's less than honest behavior, at least temporarily, and assembled her own plan. The time of day was on her side. The hazy predawn had given way to soft light, showing her the way.

She needed to know how many men were inside, where the girls were located, what armaments were on display and how to sneak the girls past the guards without being seen. Naomi crept around the boulder and dropped to the ground.

She was reminded of early morning trips through the woods with Pa Lancaster. He'd fixed her up in baggy trousers, treating her as though she was a son. He'd taught her to walk lightly, crawl carefully and slither smoothly. She could almost hear his voice as she obeyed old teachings.

Crawling on her knees, Naomi was thankful for Charlie's thick pants. As she approached the clearing where ground cover became sparser, she carefully lowered herself flat to the ground. She was unfamiliar with the Texas night life, but in Alabama, the snakes would have been delighted to eat her alive. Hoping her path was free of creatures, she belly-crawled toward the sound of the quarreling voices until she lay behind a scrub bush not ten feet from the two men arguing.

Excluding the leader and Harvey Collins, Naomi counted six men—three squatted by the fire, a fourth stretched flat, leaning his head on his saddle, while two still remained asleep, although Naomi had no idea how that could be with all the shouting going on.

"Old man, I brought these girls to you for a price. Deliver the guns or get out. I can find a different use for the women."

"I figured you'd not have need of an old man once you got your shipment. I told you, I stashed the guns close to where I picked up the girls." Harvey talked fast but not fast enough. The leader slapped him across the face and brandished his knife, threatening to cut Harvey's throat.

"The sweet young girls will remain ours—right, my friends?" The outlaw leader directed his question to the three men squatting by the fire. They looked with interest at the wagon, showing Naomi where she'd find her students.

"Not so young as all that, boss. Couple of those girls look ripe for the pickin' to me." The man lying on his saddle, hands behind his head, leered suggestively at the wagon.

Naomi listened to the leader harangue Harvey in a mix of languages, shifting angry words back and forth from English to utterances Naomi didn't recognize. Harvey Collins seemed desperate to soothe the outlaws but determined to keep the girls for his own scheme.

"Don't be greedy, Jericho." Harvey was adamantly protecting the kidnapped students. "I can't ransom those girls back to their families if you've ruined 'em. Hell, there's thousands of dollars riding in that wagon. We made a deal. You get me the girls, I bring you a shipment."

"Until I receive payment, the girls belong to me."

The outlaw leader lowered the knife and put it back in its sheath. "If that's later than sooner..." He shrugged and nodded toward the other men. "They'll find a use for the girls."

Naomi held her breath, willing herself to concentrate, studying the camp layout as Charlie would have. Thrilled terror pulsed through her veins. Half the quest had been accomplished. She'd located her students.

Harvey's *Wagon of Interesting Items* stood next to the only scrub pine in the small clearing but no students were in sight. She inched sideways, flat against the ground, her gaze steadily scanning the terrain, careful not to linger on those she surveyed.

Suddenly the smell of coffee hit her and her stomach growled loudly. Had the volume of the argument not increased, the quarreling men might have heard it.

"I'm telling you, boys, use that one I ruined but leave the rest of the healthy ones alone. I can't get nothin' out of 'em if'n you've poked 'em to death first."

Naomi froze as he spat in her direction.

"Sheeet." He drew the expletive out for emphasis. "You boys have any idea how much these females are worth? I've got the children of Texas's wealthiest in that wagon. The mighty will pay through the nose to get their flesh and blood back. I'll be rich as a king." He cackled at the thought of his illicit treasure.

CHAPTER FOURTEEN

*U*SE THE ONE *I'VE RUINED.* Dear Heaven, what had Harvey done? Naomi slithered on her belly, crawling toward the wagon, desperate to reach the girls before the camp fully awakened. A mound by the side of the back wheel was enough to send her in that direction.

Naomi shimmied under the wagon and slipped as close to the child as she could. Dried blood streaked Justine's hair and fresh red trickled across her face. Naomi hugged the shadows, studying the shallow rise and fall of the girl's chest.

"Justine," she whispered with little hope of a response. Naomi's shock changed to relief when the nearest eye popped open, closing again in a distinct wink.

Well, that surely makes a difference. Suddenly Naomi didn't feel so hopeless. Then Justine's finger twitched the slightest bit, pointing above Naomi.

Naomi wanted to warn her to save her strength. She knew the girls were in the wagon above. She nodded fiercely, beginning her crawl to the other side, planning to climb inside the wagon and free the other students.

She heard nothing but as she eased backward through the wet morning dew, a hand came over her mouth. At the same time a hard body sprawled on top of her, pinning her to the ground. Silently Naomi bucked upward, trying to free herself.

"Naomi," Charlie whispered before he took his hand away. As soon as he freed her, she rolled over and stared into the face of Charlie Wolf. He motioned her to follow, shimmying backward quicker than she could keep up. When they were on the outside of the camp, he pulled her to her feet.

They remained silent until they reached her earlier hiding spot. Now two horses stood waiting. Charlie's stallion's reins trailed the ground. The mare's leathers were looped over Charlie's pommel. When she would have spoken, Charlie shook his head, boosting her into her saddle and leading her mare instead of giving Naomi the reins.

Having no choice in the matter, Naomi followed where Charlie led, wondering if she would have to return his gun before she had her showdown with Harvey Collins, because sin or not, she intended to kill the old man.

"Teacher, did I not tell you to stay put?" He was furious.

As soon as they were far enough from the camp to talk, he slid from his horse and lifted her from hers.

Shocking both of them, she wrapped her arms around his waist and hugged.

"Mr. Wolf, I am so glad I found you." Her words tumbled out as he held her, squeezing her to him until she thought her ribs might crack.

She didn't care. He could hug her as tightly to him as he wanted. She squeezed him right back, liking the feel of his power in her arms.

The girls were alive, Justine wasn't as badly hurt as Naomi had feared and Charlie Wolf had found her in time to help her with the rescue. She leaned her head against his chest for just a moment, drawing upon his strength and then she stepped away, dropping her arms.

"I have a plan," she said briskly. His eyebrows beetled into a frown and impulsively she touched his arm again. "I came to help. Justine's playing possum. She's not nearly as hurt as they think."

Charlie grunted, his feral expression most disconcerting.

"I heard the outlaw leader arguing with Harvey Collins." She drew a deep breath before continuing. "For once in his no-good life the old man did something right, even if for the wrong reasons. At least 'til now, he's kept the other girls unharmed."

"How do you know this man, Harvey Collins?" Charlie's gaze looked more wolf than man as he listened.

Her fingers clenched nervously around her reins. "The law in the county I'm from in Alabama ran the peddler out of the district for misdeeds. He claimed he sold household necessaries, but it was more commonly thought that he was a merchant of sin and evil. Young girls had a way of turning up missing when Harvey was in the area."

Charlie didn't exact details, just nodded at her assessment as if he understood. She wasn't so naïve that she didn't realize there were flesh peddlers who roamed the territory ready to do business with the outcasts from society, who always found them.

"Now that you're here, it will be easier. I'm going back into that camp and crawl up on the wagon seat and drive the wagon out. They've left the mule hitched up and they won't be expecting trouble. You can climb onto that shelf above the canyon and use your rifle." She paused for breath and then asked, "You can shoot, can't you?"

Charlie Wolf stood listening to her with arms folded across his chest. She had no trouble reading the expression on his face—rage.

~~~

There were seven outlaws in the camp wanted for varying deeds of lawbreaking. Eight, if he counted Harvey Collins and nine with the man guarding the horses. After listening to the fat windbag, Charlie had no trouble adding him to the potential body count at the end of the forthcoming shoot-out.

Deacon had circled around to the other side of the ravine, so he had a clear shot at the clearing from above. Sam was busy cutting loose the remuda of horses the gang used for travel.

Waiting for the call of a mourning dove, Sam's signal, Charlie gave Naomi her directions. He wanted nothing more than to turn her over his knee and whale the daylights out of her.

She'd belly-crawled like an Indian right up to the camp. Part of him swelled with pride—he'd chosen well—another part of him long dormant trembled from aftershocks at seeing her so close to death. For thirty-two years he'd waited for a woman to claim his interest. Miss Naomi Parker had his full attention and he didn't plan on losing her to her own stupidity.

"Stay here." When she started to shake her head, he asked, "You still have my gun?" When she fumbled it out of her pocket, he frowned. It had a hair-trigger and it was loaded. "You know how to use this?" Without waiting for a reply, he took it out of her hand, checked the chamber for a round and handed it back.

"Anyone besides Sam, Deak or me comes running this way, shoot 'em." Then he left her standing behind a boulder, holding the reins of the horses in one hand and his Colt .45. in the other.

Timing was important. Charlie acknowledged the weakness of his plan to himself as he walked into the boxed canyon. If the girls were unable to help themselves, it would be hard getting them out alive. But if they died in the shootout, it was better than leaving them in the hands of the kidnappers.

While Naomi crawled around risking her life, he'd had time to watch the seven gang members in camp. Jericho wouldn't be able to hold them back much longer. If the old man didn't deliver what cargo he'd promised, the girls would soon be forfeit.

Maybe they would be anyway. Charlie hoped to get them all out alive and walk away with his own skin intact. But if any of Naomi's students died in the rescue, he figured they'd be going to a better place than the renegade leader had planned for them.

———

"Hola!" Charlie called as he walked into the camp, his six-shooter drawn and ready. It was enough to stop the tirade being delivered upon Harvey Collins.

"Jericho, your guard's asleep at his post. A child could steal your remuda and gut you at the same time." In fact, the guard, a Mescalero killer with a hefty bounty on his head, wouldn't be waking up—ever.

Jericho whirled, going for his gun as he turned to face the voice he knew well. As soon as he saw the aim of Charlie's gun, he stopped in mid-draw and finished his turn, a smile on his face.

"My old friend, Charlie Wolf! What brings you to my camp this morning?" The hand that had been resting on his holster carefully lifted, matching the one he raised above his head. The smile on the outlaw's face broadened as he took in Charlie's horseless state. "Dropping in for coffee?"

"You have something that belongs to me." Charlie nodded at the wagon as he spoke.

"What the hell? You sold the merchandise more than once?" Apparently outraged, still holding his hands high, the outlaw turned on Harvey Collins.

"No," Charlie answered for the old man. "He was stupid enough to steal from me. I came to get my own back." He nodded toward the wagon. "The flesh peddler's cart and what it carries belongs to me."

"Old man, I will kill your useless hide right now." Jericho pulled a knife from a neck sheath.

"Another move and you die." Charlie shot the knife from Jericho's hand before he could throw it as Harvey Collins gurgled in fear.

"You can't walk into my camp and kill me." The outlaw turned slowly and looked at Charlie in amazement.

"I'm not planning on killing you." Charlie aimed his gun at Jericho's crotch. "I'll just leave you with something to remember me by." The two men stared at each other, hatred so deep it was a tangible force between them. "You wanna tell your friends I'm not bluffing?"

"Don't shoot," Jericho gritted through clenched teeth, as much to his outlaw friends as to Charlie. He glared at the bounty hunter. "What do you want?"

"I told you. The wagon and its contents belong to me."

"That's my wagon and it sure as hell don't carry nothin' that belongs to you." Harvey Collins chose that moment to join the discussion.

Charlie ignored him and spoke again to Jericho. "Have one of your men put that bundle laying over there into the wagon with the rest of what you stole." The gun never wavered from its aim.

"Pete, do it!" the gang leader yelled and one of the men lifted the girl from the ground.

Charlie held his breath, hoping. The child on the blanket remained limp as the man settled her inside the wagon and out of sight. Charlie lifted his gun so that it was again aimed at Jericho's heart and then stepped close, whirling him around.

"We're going to walk over there now and we're going to drive the wagon out of this camp and if you're fortunate, I might let you live." Jamming the gun against the outlaw's back as he pushed him, Charlie ordered, "Move it."

"You're surrounded." Jericho turned his head, smirking. "How you going to get me into the wagon and out of this camp while my friends are here to stop you? You're a dead man."

"Not today, I'm not," Charlie disagreed. "But keep running your mouth and you won't be so lucky."

"Justine," he called out. A young girl, blood matting the side of her face, poked her head through the canvas opening. Charlie had reason to appreciate Naomi's earlier visit, although it stuck in his craw to admit it.

"Untie the ropes on the other girls and one of you get up top and drive this rig." Charlie raked the outlaws with his gaze. "Draw leather and I shoot Jericho."

The daughters of Texas didn't falter or faint, as Justine, the little girl who'd been playing possum came alive to free her classmates.

Charlie walked behind Jericho, keeping the gun against his back, heart high. A different girl crawled to the wagon seat and picked up the reins.

"I'm Ambrosia Quince," she introduced herself grimly and, as if remembering her manners, added, "I'm very glad to meet you."

Charlie eased the gun out of Jericho's holster and handed it to the Quince girl. Then he called to Justine, "You got a length of that rope they used on your friends?"

"Drop that right here," he told her when she waved a loop at him. He shoved Jericho forward, forcing his head into the noose until it circled his arms.

"Now give me another one, Justine." This time she dropped the rope around Jericho's neck.

"We're gonna walk out of here, Miss Quince."

Charlie nodded reassuringly at the driver who held the reins with confidence. "Your teacher hired me to get you to safety. Let's get started. If things go bad, run this old mule and don't stop 'til you get to Flat Rock."

Naomi's girls were better than he'd hoped for. One of them slid a noose around Jericho's neck from the back and tightened it while another wrapped another length of rope around the outlaw until he was trussed up and unable to move anything but his legs.

As Ambrosia Quince slapped the leathers against the old mule, the wagon rolled out of the camp. Jericho stumbled along beside it, his choice to keep up or be dragged behind, choking to death.

Charlie kept his back to the wagon and shifted his gun, training it on the remaining outlaws. On schedule, Sam hazed the remuda of horses into a frenzy, chasing them from the box canyon where they'd been corralled. They stampeded through the camp.

The old mule broke into a run to get out of their way. Charlie used the chaos for cover and leapt on a passing bay, leaving the other seven outlaws behind for his cousins to deal with.

Jericho ran beside the *Wagon of Interesting Items*, trying to keep from being trampled or strangled. Charlie hauled him up, slinging him facedown across the back of a passing animal. Jericho agilely rolled until he straddled the mount, wrapping his legs around the horse's sides. He was smiling until Justine tugged on the noose around his neck.

"Keep moving," Charlie called to the Quince girl driving but it was unnecessary. She was running that old mule hell-bent for leather. Charlie didn't worry about her grit when an outlaw jumped in front of them. At the last moment when she didn't waver, the man leapt aside. Charlie shot him on the way past.

Behind them, a hail of bullets sprayed over the outlaws, keeping them pinned as the mule sped down the trail. The wagon bounced over hardscrabble rock and dirt and Charlie feared it might shake itself apart at the pace the driver set. But it hung together and when the Quince girl reached the boulder where he'd left Naomi standing, Charlie didn't stop, but shouted instructions at his woman, "Bring the horses and get a move on." She was already mounted and leading Old Mossy at a run as she urged her horse close to the wagon, craning her neck to see inside and count her students.

"We're all here," the Quince girl yelled.

"Keep them rounded up for me in that wagon. I'll have 'em back in my hands by the end of the day." Jericho laughed, seeing the cart loaded with his hostages.

Charlie brought his gun butt down on Jericho's skull, shutting him up effectively. Then he pulled the mule to a halt and slid from the saddle.

"We need to go to Buffalo Creek," Naomi told him. He ignored her, talking to the girls in the wagon instead.

"Keep driving the wagon toward the sun." He tied

the limp body of the outlaw leader across his horse and roped the horse to the side of the wagon before mounting Old Mossy.

"I'll catch up to you but keep moving," he said to the Quince girl.

She shook the old mule into a trot that turned into a ground-shaking run, kicking up dust as the wagon moved away.

"Mr. Wolf, I can get help for the girls in Buffalo Creek." Naomi waited next to him with her plan.

"That's the wrong direction," he said grimly, finally looking at her. Naomi's frown irritated him so he said no more. She shrugged at his silence, nudging her horse into a lope, following close to the wagon's rear axle.

"Is everyone back there all right?" she called in an anxious voice.

As Charlie watched, three girls poked their heads out of the flap covering the back of the wagon from view.

"We knew you'd save us, Miss Parker," a young girl piped, looking out the opening at Naomi. "Justine was pretending to be out cold, but she really is hurt."

"I said keep moving and don't stop for anything," he thundered down on Naomi when she would have halted the wagon to examine her charge, slapping her horse's rump and sending it back into a lope. Then he rode even with the packhorse where Jericho was tied head down and ass up in the air. The outlaw was conscious and cursing.

"Head to Flat Rock—toward the sun," he repeated to

the driver.

"Keep that gun handy," he told Naomi. "If the prisoner gives you any trouble, shoot him." Then as an afterthought he added, "Don't kill the horse."

He turned Old Mossy and headed back toward the gunfire at a dead-run, aware that he'd left his cousins outnumbered three to one. He needn't have worried. Deacon was strapping bodies across an animal he'd caught. Four outlaws from the camp were wounded, three were dead including the Mescalero guard, and neither Sam nor his brother had caught lead.

"Where's the old man who set up the kidnapping?" Charlie looked around the camp. Harvey Collins was nowhere to be seen.

"He took off running when we were nabbing the others. I let him go. Figured if the snakes didn't get him, the sun would." Deak was right and Charlie had more pressing worries than a crooked old man.

"By my count, we've got another five or six thousand to divide up, not to mention the price on Jericho's head." Sam offered a sly grin. "Sure was fine of your schoolmarm to lead us to these outlaws."

"Better move fast and get this bunch back to Flat Rock," Charlie said gruffly. "There were only seven wanteds and an old man in camp with Jericho. More than half the men who ride with him were gone."

Sam and Deak mounted and strung the lead line behind them. Then they spurred their animals to a gallop, accompanied by the sound of Jericho's men groaning and protesting at the pace being set and the thud of hard leather against their wounds.

They soon caught up with Naomi, who had ignored his directions, heading away from the sun toward Buffalo Creek. She was pushing that old mule to go as fast as he would oblige. Three of the girls clung to the bench as it rocked and swayed across the range and five more were inside the wagon.

When Charlie rode up next to her buckskin, he expected her to pull up. Instead she dug in her heels and tried to get more speed out of the mare without leaving the raggedy merchant cart and her students behind.

His cousins waited for him to retrieve Jericho, still slung over a horse tethered to the wagon. Charlie kept his lips tight against harsh words, cutting the rope and hauling the last outlaw to join the string of others.

That done, he turned to ride back to the wagon of girls and his woman—his obstinate woman.

"That wagon is too rickety to take the speed she's travelling," he muttered out loud as Deacon came up on his left.

"Seems like she's in a hurry to see the last of you," his cousin observed wryly.

"Maybe I should ride along home with her," Sam offered. "It won't do for her to go back alone. That flesh peddler Collins is still loose."

"Get your own woman, McCallister runt." Charlie

slanted a warning glance in Sam's direction, making his cousin laugh out loud.

"You telling me that skinny schoolmarm caught The Wolf?"

"She'll come to Flat Rock with us and her brood." Charlie offered no answer to Sam, turning Old Mossy toward the departing clutch of females instead. "After that, we'll figure something," he muttered to himself.

"Charlie, you reckon you'll ever be able to make her mind?" Sam said, taunting him.

"Doesn't look promising," Deacon's answer followed him as he chased after Naomi again.

CHAPTER FIFTEEN

R EMEMBERING THE NOXIOUS SHERIFF in Flat Rock as well as the fact that most of her students lived on the other side of Buffalo Creek, Naomi made a decision counter to Charlie Wolf's. When the bounty hunter retrieved the last prisoner, his brooding expression left her fluttering nervously inside.

"I'm going to help all of you get home, girls," Naomi assured her students as soon as Charlie led the prisoner away. The young ladies trusted her judgment when she'd turned toward Buffalo Creek. She intended to keep that as their destination and see them home safely.

"Tell me how badly Justine is hurt," she called into the wagon bed, afraid to hear but concerned that the smallest hostage might need immediate attention.

"I'm all right," Justine herself answered. "I got knocked in the head when they first came through the door. Then I got hit again when I told that old man I wasn't going anywhere with him." Wound up like a top and ready to spin, Justine needed to tell her story. "I was out for a while, but mostly I've been playing possum ever since. I was bleeding at first and I moaned real loud, so they left me on the ground by the wagon to die."

"Justine, you could fall, sit back. Girls, make her be still, she has a head injury." Reminding Justine that she was an invalid prompted her to withdraw back inside the wagon. Naomi shuddered at the ordeal the little girl had survived.

"She'll live," Mary-Beth called snidely, gripping the wagon bench. It was a startling reminder of the girls' quarrel at the Academy and confirmed that things were getting back to normal.

"Brody, how bad is Justine's injury?"Naomi asked Ambrosia Quince, worried about Justine in spite of Mary-Beth's reassurances because there had been some fresh blood on her face.

"Drive." Brody handed Marnie the reins and said, "I'll look at the cut, Miss Parker." She climbed into the back.

"Whoa up there." Naomi was so focused on her students and travelling that she didn't see Charlie Wolf until he rode alongside the mule and reached down, grabbing harness to haul them to a stop. She wasn't sure whether he spoke to her or the mule. The mule, having been run quite hard, was more than ready to follow orders.

"We are on our way back to Buffalo Creek. We can manage there until the Board of Trustees makes a decision about procedure. Since the girls' parents have already been notified, they should be waiting there." Naomi couldn't stop her nervous flow of words any more than she could look at Charlie when he rode closer to her.

"We thank you for your help. I believe the charge for your services should be covered by the bounty you'll collect on the outlaws." She couldn't keep the sour note of displeasure from her voice. His duplicity still pained her but he'd rescued her students so her anger was unfounded.

She hid behind the word *we*—treating the episode in the stable and the days together on the trail as though they had never happened. Naomi risked a quick glance at his face and saw an implacable, surly scowl.

"We're ushering the outlaws and the girls back to Flat Rock," Charlie announced gruffly. "Before we get them there, you're parting from them and leaving with me."

In the distance, she could see his partners Deacon and Sam as they rode toward Flat Rock leading a string of horses carrying bodies. Naomi paused in her comments, inordinately pleased that Charlie wanted her with him. It was the first time in her life anyone had ever come after her.

"I need to be with my students while they wait." She shook her head regretfully and disagreed.

"They're waiting in Flat Rock," he said, lowering his voice so only she could hear the threatening growl.

"You're not safe there now. The girls are. We'll split off from the others before we hit town."

"No, we will not," she replied, treating it as the ridiculous suggestion it was. She would make her own decisions now.

"You have caught the outlaws and rescued my students. Our transaction is complete. I can arrange for the girls to return to their homes from Buffalo Creek. The sheriff in Flat Rock is an idiot." She clasped her reins in nervous fingers, explaining the end of their relationship to him in polite terms. When he made no comment, she tightened her knees, lifting the reins in preparation to move on, having said what needed to be said.

"You're wearing my clothes." His stoic gaze raked her form.

"I'll return them when I can," she answered stiffly, edging her horse farther from the wagon to prevent her students from hearing.

Before she could get the mare going, Charlie Wolf reached down and scooped her off the buckskin, transferring her to his lap, holding her in front of him on his saddle as he led her mount to the back of the wagon and threw the reins to one of the gawking girls.

"Miss Parker," Marnie called fearfully. They had just escaped one band of savages and Charlie's appearance wasn't reassuring.

"Name's Charlie Wolf," Charlie said easily, riding closer, holding tight to Naomi. He nodded at the two men going in the opposite direction and back to the frightened girls.

"We're the McCallisters from over your way. I need you to turn this rig around and go back to Flat Rock. It's closer than Buffalo Creek." He turned to Marnie Mullins and added, "Keep driving the wagon, you're doing a mighty fine job."

Naomi's student must have recognized the McCallister name because her fearful expression relaxed and she looked pleased when Charlie praised her. Naomi was surprised that the girls lost their fear of Charlie Wolf so quickly. They were looking him over with great interest.

"Flat Rock's closer than Buffalo Creek," he explained as he held Naomi in his arms, his horse prancing under them. "The old man who engineered your kidnapping got away and more than half the renegades in Jericho's band are still roaming the area."

Shame swept through Naomi as she realized she'd put her students in jeopardy again. Charlie held her in an iron grip, refusing to turn her loose as he gave the girls their orders. They accepted, nodding agreement. Naomi could see their relief and suspected that they'd lost confidence in her judgment and the presence of the bounty hunter soothed their fears.

"Follow me to Flat Rock," Charlie told Marnie.

She picked up the reins, clucking to the mule and turned him into the sun. The wagon bounced and the mule kicked in protest at the traces but Charlie leaned down and slapped his rump and the animal settled down and went to work, obeying authority.

Charlie said nothing to Naomi. Nevertheless she was conscious of her feelings of relief, wrapped in the safety of his arms. He turned his horse toward Flat Rock, the wagon of girls following.

Naomi sat ramrod straight until he roughly pulled her against his chest. He was angry. Waves of suppressed violence radiated from him. Her instincts warned her to remove herself from his arms.

"I would like you to put me back on my horse."

"You don't own a horse," he growled. "As far as I can see, you own one book, a comb and a hair brush."

"Oh." She'd forgotten that and realized how foolish she must seem to him. They'd just rescued her students and peril still surrounded them but every time the horse took a step, her rump moved against Charlie's groin, flooding her with impure thoughts and flashes of memory.

"You've got too much sun, Miss Parker. Your face is going to hurt soon," Marnie called out a warning.

Heat seared Naomi's skin but not from the sun. The temperature of his body had ignited totally inappropriate and wicked desire in her. Though her students were next to them in the wagon, in spite of the fact that the evil man who had perpetrated the kidnapping remained free, even as the outlaws belonging to the gang roamed the countryside, Charlie Wolf held her rump tightly to his groin, deliberately taunting her with his aroused member.

With every shift of her body Naomi rubbed against Charlie's manhood. At first she was resentful, then resigned to his outrageous behavior but finally aroused. Naomi was pulled from her fog of desire by Charlie's next words.

"You ever have an ass-beatin'?" he murmured in her ear, dropping his hand to rest on her belly.

Did he just ask me if I'd ever had... "I beg your pardon?" Scandalized, she turned to stare into his eyes.

"You heard me. And you'll feel my hand on your backside, soon as we get some privacy." His hand pressed harder against her midriff as if in silent warning. Seeming to feel better for saying his words, Charlie relaxed and pulled her tighter against him.

"The girls are looking at you, Mr. Wolf. You are holding me in an indecent fashion. I would like to borrow your spare mount until we get to Flat Rock."

"You're not going to Flat Rock," he repeated.

"You're making a spectacle of us. Behave." Naomi turned and reprimanded him, "Wherever I'm going, I'd prefer traveling alone, mounted on the buckskin mare and not riding on your lap."

"Can *you* behave?" he asked, waiting for her answer as if she were a child.

When she nodded, he dropped behind the wagon and set her in the buckskin's saddle once again. Eyes big but lips sealed, Rebecca leaned from the back of the wagon untying the mare.

Without another word to Naomi, Charlie rode to the front of the wagon, expecting her to follow, which she did.

CHAPTER SIXTEEN

B Y THE TIME THEY REACHED the outskirts of Flat Rock, the shock of their captivity and rescue had worn off and the girls were clamoring to tell Naomi the details of their abduction. As Charlie had pointed out when he'd tracked them, Harvey Collins had been waiting to load the captives in his wagon when the kidnappers delivered them.

Justine had a wicked cut that would probably scar her forehead. The girls called it her badge of honor and Justine grinned proudly at their praise. Nevertheless, she needed medical attention since the wound still trickled blood.

Naomi was all too aware of her own impoverished state. She had no means of paying a doctor for looking after Justine's injury. She also had no money to stay in a hotel with her students and no clothes to wear since Charlie had destroyed her dress.

Naomi's emotions ran amok, churning with relief, anger and dread. She knew the Sparrow Creek students were safe with the bounty hunters but she'd met the sheriff in town already and had no confidence they'd be safe with him.

She really didn't want to go back to Flat Rock. But her students were still under her care and would remain so until they were claimed by their parents. When they stopped outside town, Naomi braced herself for an argument with Charlie.

"I'm accompanying my students into Flat Rock," she told him.

"You have no sense," he growled, summing up his grievance in one sentence.

"I have enough sense to know I'm responsible for my students." Naomi shrugged away his opinion. "You're free to go, Mr. Wolf. I thank you for your services during our time spent together and certainly understand your desire to leave now."

"What's the hold-up?" Deacon asked when he rode to their side. "Charlie, you and your woman need to get clear of here. We'll see to the students."

Never mind that the girls were listening avidly and eyebrows went up when Deacon implied she had a relationship with the other bounty hunter.

"Doesn't matter," Marnie said bravely, looking at both men. "I'm for staying together." At that point, the other girls weighed in on the discussion, stating their desire to remain with Naomi.

"You see? That settles it. I'm accompanying the girls

until they join their families. The sheriff in town is a fool, but we'll be in civilized environs, safe from the marauding outlaws. I'll be fine."

Deacon's growled, "Females," sounded like an expletive.

"Let's go," Naomi directed Marnie, not seeing any reason to tarry. "We'll be safe here." She gathered up her reins and nudged her horse into motion, leading the girls into town. But when her horse brushed close to Charlie's on the ride in, she braved a quick look in his direction. His stern gaze promised a reckoning at journey's end.

Half the time Naomi was speechless with irritation at his arrogant assumption of authority, but half the time it was a breathless yearning for him that stole her words. She wished it were possible to feel his body on hers one more time and enjoy his manhood inside her again.

So much had happened since the day of the attack, and during that time she'd remained focused on rescuing the girls. But now that she had no such distractions, erotic memories flooded her mind. She was torn between embarrassment, disbelief at what she'd done and revisited desire coursing through her veins when she thought of Charlie's hands on her body.

I am a spinster of advanced years—twenty-eight and not one offer of marriage—an old maid, she scolded herself. *He was drinking spirits the first time and probably inebriated. Besides, he said men have needs. Obviously any woman would have been acceptable.*

Her stomach clenched and her womb flexed, reminding her of her own desires. Grimly, Naomi accepted reality.

He is a bounty hunter. I am a schoolteacher. It is best to pretend that it never happened. Nevertheless, the experience had satisfied a long-held curiosity about the coupling between men and women. She was still an unmarried spinster, but now she had a memory to cherish as she faded into middle age and it was a secret she refused to regret.

These girls were magnificent. I am so proud of them. Riding close to the wagon, she hovered over her students like a mother hen with chicks. *I'm proud of me too.* She'd done it. She'd rescued them and other than a severe fright and Justine's head injury, they were unscathed.

Naomi forgave Charlie Wolf his arrogant manner because he'd helped her. She couldn't have done it alone. She looked at the set of his fine shoulders and sighed.

Now that the girls were saved, it would be best not to see him again, as being around him was proving most awkward.

He seems determined to manage me up to the moment of parting. Naomi snorted softly at the thought but waited breathlessly for his next order.

It went to hell faster than they expected when Charlie and his McCallister cousins rode into town escorting Naomi and her wagon of students. They pulled up in front of Wallace's barn and the girls jumped from the wagon, jubilant at being safe at last. Deak went to find the sheriff and Sam headed for the telegraph office.

Naomi had on her snooty *I-don't-know-you* act as though she wanted nothing to do with Charlie but he stayed close, guarding her and the girls clustered around her as Naomi cleaned the wound on Justine's head and uttered soft sounds of distress.

"If there's a doctor in this town, I think Justine needs stitches. I don't think I can..." She gazed at Charlie helplessly, obviously worried.

"I'll get the doc for her if you think it's needed." He hesitated and then decided to risk it. He didn't like the idea of leaving Naomi unprotected for a moment, but the office of the town sawbones was just up the street.

"I'll be quick," he assured her. Naomi smiled at him as if he was her hero. It warmed a place inside Charlie. He figured, he'd ride a hundred miles to fetch a doctor for another such sweet look. "Stay close to the wagon and don't draw attention to yourself."

"We'll be fine. You worry too much," she advised him.

Charlie wasn't long fetching the doctor but by the time he returned, he had to clear a path to the wagon and its cargo. The ladies had retreated inside while Naomi stood facing the crowd. Jake, the saloon owner, sporting a white bandage tied around his head and carrying a rope, was ready to mete out his brand of social justice.

As soon as they caught sight of Charlie, two in the crowd grabbed hold of his arms, dragging him to stand in front of Naomi. The doctor was left pushing his way toward the wagon alone.

"Just tell us that the Indian jumped you," Jake said. "We'll make the dirty redskin pay for messing with a white woman."

"Don't be stupid, of course Mr. Wolf did not assault me." Naomi stood in the wagon, looking down at the saloon owner, denying his claim loudly.

"Hey, she called you stupid, Jake." The comment came from the back where the heckler remained far enough away to poke at Jake's anger without getting hurt.

"Why you Indian-loving slut, that makes you a whore, because we know you fucked Charlie Wolf." The bar owner looked even uglier than usual as he brandished his rope and yelled obscenities at Naomi.

"Your words are coarse and vulgar, the mark of an illiterate lout." She remained unruffled by the taunts and catcalls and treated the saloon owner as if he were a misbehaving student. Jake gaped at her astonished and for the moment Naomi seemed to have him under control.

"Best think about what you're gonna do when you

have to turn me loose," Charlie drawled, shifting his attention to the men holding him.

"Give me that saddlebag," Jake said, turning away from Naomi to reach for the leather pouch slung over Charlie's shoulder.

"You are a bully, sir. That we know. Do not ad thievery to your sins." Before the bartender could claim the leather pouch, Naomi leaned from her perch on the wagon and plucked it from Charlie's shoulder. "I'll guard your saddlebags, Mr. Wolf, until you've sorted out your disagreement with this merchant."

Charlie wanted to tell her to shush and lie low, but she continued chastising the crowd and Jake in particular.

"If your anger concerns the incident in the bar when Mr. Wolf hit you with a bottle of spirits, it doesn't appear to have done permanent damage." She paused and then added, "I'm sure Mr. Wolf will be happy to pay for the whiskey."

Since the teacher ignored and waved away the insults, refusing to entertain the first sentence concerning her night in the barn with Charlie, the men in the crowd began to shuffle and look for someone else to torment. She peered down at them from her make-shift stage, scolding the crowd of half-drunk men until the better part of them retreated as if they were schoolboys caught in a prank.

Jake's plans—hanging Charlie and tar-and-feathering Naomi—were momentarily derailed. Naomi turned a quelling look upon the two holding Charlie and even before the doctor interfered, most of the ruckus had stopped and they'd loosened their hold.

"Here now, I've got a sick young'n to look after. Clear the path to this wagon right now." Maybe because it finally looked safe, the doctor used his hard-sided bag to push and jab his way through the diminishing crowd.

The McCallister cousins, escorting a reluctant sheriff, joined them, stopping the worst of the physical abuse on Charlie, but the verbal assault on Naomi intensified when Wallace joined the mob.

"How was she, Injun? Did you ride her all night?" he pretended to ask Charlie, but directed the questions at Naomi. "Kinda long in the tooth, ain't she, half-breed?"

"That's enough. You'll not defile this woman's name again." Deacon shot his gun into the air, bringing order to the last of the chaos. Sam had both his guns out, adding more weight to Deacon's order.

"I'll bring the young ladies, you follow me with Miz Parker." The sheriff, unable to avoid his duty, sneered at her and motioned for one of Jake's men to lift her down.

"Your lady is in my care, cousin," Deacon assured Charlie, stepping to the wagon and gently lifting Naomi to the ground before any of the thugs could reach her. Then he turned, tucking her under his arm.

"If you have anything else to say about this young woman, you'll say it to me since we're relatives." His speech was that of an educated man and he spoke with the quiet authority of the powerful. Even the sheriff looked at the rough bounty hunter in surprise.

"What the hell? The teacher ain't no McCallister. She fucked the Indian and she's a whore." Jake wasn't turning loose his favorite theme.

"You're speaking of my cousin, Charles Wolf McCallister, the man who took Naomi Parker to wife three days ago and rescued eight daughters of Texas." Deacon's voice brooked no dissent. "So yes, I claim Naomi Parker Wolf McCallister as kin."

<hr>

Naomi listened appalled at the wild accusations and lurid descriptions the stable owner reported. He had remained silent through the verbal attack from Jake, but when it looked as though she'd stifled that bully, Wallace decided to stir things up again.

"Defiled her, that's what he did. Took his knife and cut her clothes off 'til she was buck naked." He held up Naomi's dress and shook it at the crowd. It had clearly been sliced from top to bottom.

"Do not prevaricate, Mr. Wallace. You are well aware my dress was covered in blood and destroyed during the outlaw attack. An attack, I might add, that no one in Flat Rock would respond to. Mr. Wolf loaned me serviceable clothing and I accepted. Together we rescued the young ladies from the school."

The crowd of mostly men looked at Naomi speculatively. She stared back, wearing the expression she used on recalcitrant students. She was startled when Charlie's cousin took charge of the situation.

"Give me your hand." Deacon McCallister grabbed her right hand and jerked it above her head, showing the crowd the cut mark on her palm. His voice dropped to a lower octave and he intoned as if giving a benediction.

"This man and this woman exchanged blood. Such an oath is common practice among citizens who wish to make a vowed pledge until the preacher can arrive. I say this woman is my cousin's wife. Any carnal knowledge they have allegedly shared was as husband and wife."

"I appreciate your assistance, Mr. McCallister, but telling that story isn't necessary," Naomi murmured softly, correcting him. Pressed as she was into the side of her newly claimed relative, she couldn't help but understand her danger.

"Hush," he murmured for ears alone. Cold blue eyes met hers briefly as he swept Naomi along, guarding his cousin too, as Charlie was dragged toward the sheriff's office. The doctor urged the rest of the girls to move quickly in that direction and Sam brought up the rear, carrying Justine.

It had seemed prudent to tell a better story when Wallace waved her torn dress around and maligned Charlie. She ached to defend their relationship but feared anything she said would add to his peril. Her stubborn insistence on coming into town had caused this danger. She was still trembling with shock when they arrived in the sheriff's office.

"Hell of a story you told out there, McCallister," the sheriff said sarcastically once the door closed them away from the mob.

"Of course there's been no time to satisfy Texas legalities." Deacon nodded at his cousin. "Charlie, I'd be proud to perform the ceremony."

CHAPTER SEVENTEEN

C HARLIE DIDN'T KNOW which was worse, listening to the bloodthirsty crowd outside or Naomi's obstinacy.

"Don't be ridiculous," the teacher refused Deacon's offer. "Neither Mr. Wolf nor I will be bullied by a lynch mob into marriage." Her voice trembled as she delivered her dissent.

"You don't have a choice," Sam explained slowly as though talking to a not-too-bright child.

"Of course we have a choice," Naomi replied firmly. "I choose to teach school and remain unmarried and I'm certain Mr. Wolf has his own future plans."

"You won't be going back to Sparrow Creek or any other school in the territory." Deacon broke the first of the bad news. "You signed a contract with a morals clause. Something they all have in them."

"I don't have a school to go back to?" Her expression became panicked. "But I have to go back. That's where I live." Charlie watched a look of horror spread over her face as Naomi processed Deacon's statement.

"No ma'am, not anymore. I wired the Sparrow Creek School Board and they sent word that you don't need to come back." Looking pleased, the sheriff read the message before handing it to her. "Miss Parker. *Stop.* Two weeks' salary tendered. *Stop.* No longer need your services. *Stop.*"

"You'll have to cash this at the bank." He smirked, handing her a draft for her salary authorized by the school board.

Charlie didn't enjoy watching bad news delivered, but it was better for Naomi to learn her circumstances now than have some old biddy in town gleefully impart the gossip, or the town's drunks pull her into an alley and have their way without reprisal. Charlie's blood boiled thinking about that possibility.

"But my personal items…" Naomi said, looking lost and fragile.

"I sent the deputy to the school and told him to gather up what he could. He brought back that trunk over there. Reckon you won't need your teaching supplies anymore." The sheriff was just a little too pleased with delivering his hurtful words.

Charlie stepped toward him, ready to wipe the sneer from the other man's face.

"I want my books," Naomi muttered, clutching her wages in her hand.

"Books are in here. Fill your satchel with 'em. We'll take 'em with us." Charlie threw back the lid of the trunk and looked inside. Her head came up and she nodded stiffly.

"Thank you for your helpfulness. I will go to the bank now." She headed for the door but was stopped by the sheriff's next words.

"Best not go out that way. Safer if you take the back door. I won't guarantee your well-being if you stay in this town." The lawman made it clear he thought she was more trouble than worth.

"What the sheriff means is—if you don't come out of this room hitched to a McCallister, you'll be entertainment for Jake's regulars." Charlie delivered the rest of the bad news. "If you're lucky, after they tar and feather you tonight they'll put you on a horse and run you out of town." When she remained silent, lips pressed tightly together, stubbornly avoiding his gaze, he grabbed her chin.

"Look at me." He forced her to meet the demand in his eyes. "Do you understand what I'm saying?" Hell, it was possible regardless of what they did in the sheriff's office Charlie might find himself strung up when they walked out. If that be the case, he didn't aim on leaving Naomi adrift and alone as he'd found her. He'd gotten a glimpse of the bank draft. It was a damn shame the piddly amount they'd sent. Her salary for teaching hellion daughters of Texas wasn't enough to keep a chicken alive more than a month.

He dropped his hold on her and crossed to the window, staring at the crowd milling outside in the street. Something had to be done and soon. It wouldn't surprise him at all if Jake had the tar heated and the feathers ready when Naomi left the safety of the sheriff's office.

⁓◦∽

Naomi studied the room's inhabitants, one at a time. The sheriff was even more obnoxious than he'd been on their first meeting. He sneered and hid behind his badge to say hurtful things. She suspected only the presence of Charlie and his cousins saved her from physical harm.

Sam McCallister lingered by the front door, a lazy smile playing around his lips, his blue-eyed gaze ice cold. Deacon McCallister though, assumed a different guise than he'd shown her in previous meetings.

Suddenly, he shed the manners of a rough bounty hunter and assumed a mantle of authority, speaking with learned words in a rich, resonating voice meant to reassure and persuade.

"Miss Parker, everything Charlie spoke is true. And it will happen just as he says. Charlie's my cousin and I can't let such a fate befall you because of him." He let the words hover in the air before clearing his throat and continuing. "If Charlie doesn't suit for a husband, then either I or my brother Sam will stand up with you. But you're not leaving this room today until you wear the protection of the McCallister name. After that we'll all leave together. What happens then is up to you."

Naomi began to understand the charade. Deacon would perform a mock ceremony and hopefully appease the Flat Rock citizens long enough for her to get out of town. It took so long for her to comprehend their strategy, she felt stupid.

She looked around the room, suddenly aware that everyone was waiting on her. The eight students who had been rescued draped themselves wherever seating could be had. Five sat on the side bench, two on one chair and Justine, her head neatly bandaged by the doctor, sat behind the sheriff's desk.

Everyone but Charlie seemed interested in who Naomi would choose as her groom. After his forceful warning, he'd leaned against the wall and stared out the dirty window, apparently indifferent to what went on.

She knew better. She could feel his rage across the room. The men outside had insulted him, attempted thievery against him and threatened his life. He had every right to be angry.

"Of course Charlie Wolf must be my husband," Naomi said crisply. She peeked at him quickly and felt a blush tint her cheeks when he turned his gaze from the window and held hers. Although his expression remained enigmatic, his gray eyes telegraphed approval and the hard line of his lips softened slightly. The knot in her stomach loosened.

"Charlie, you'll claim the McCallister name now to protect your wife," Deacon interjected another order, this time at his cousin.

Naomi didn't understand Charlie's frown or his grim nod. Since they'd wasted enough time, she crossed to stand by him and picked up his hand. He looked down at her in surprise then linked his fingers through hers, turning them to face Deacon.

Incongruous as the notion was, the red-haired bounty hunter she'd witnessed in spitting contests with his brother, now emanated dignity. The room quieted and Charlie's cousin did a convincing job of portraying a minister. Naomi was quite impressed by his performance.

When it came time for his vows, Charlie named himself a McCallister. Other than that, Naomi mostly remembered the ceremony later as consisting of, *Do you, will you and I do.* Heat from Charlie's body channeled itself through their joined hands and she was grateful for his strength but didn't feel married.

Afterward, what I do is up to me. She relied upon Deacon McCallister to make the mock ceremony appear real and counted on his promise for her future. If the sheriff's attitude was any indication, Flat Rock would not be a good place for her to stay, even if she now had funds since her stipend had arrived.

"Best get all this trash out of my town. You didn't get all the renegades and my jail ain't strong enough to hold the ones you've got. You'll have to take your prisoners to the U.S. Marshal." The sheriff ignored her and spoke to the McCallisters.

"Figure if you carry 'em over to Eclipse, you can wire the law and collect your blood money there." The sheriff shifted uncomfortably under the three bounty hunters' stares. "Go on then. I mean what I say."

"Girls can stay here until their folks fetch 'em." He nodded at the eight students. "They'll be safe enough without the taint of her around." He'd been waiting to slap an insult on Naomi and delivered it with relish.

"I'm not staying here with you. I'm going with Miss Parker," Justine Garner sat holding her bandaged head, arguing with the sheriff.

"It's Mrs. McCallister now, Justine. Pay attention. Miss Parker just married Charlie Wolf," Marnie corrected the other girl then added, "I'm also going where our teacher goes."

Naomi winced when the students wrongly believed her wedded status, but kept silent, allowing the sham to continue in order to win their freedom from the Flat Rock bullies. One by one the girls stood and began moving toward the door. Naomi followed.

"We'll pay a man to ride over to Eclipse and have the sheriff notify the parents that the girls can be picked up in Buffalo Creek," Deacon said.

"We were going there," Naomi mentioned the obvious. "You should have let us continue on our way."

Belatedly remembering the Indians and the rest of the outlaw gang still unaccounted for, she wanted to pull her words back as soon as they were spoken.

"So I could rescue you and your students all over again?" Charlie Wolf grunted his disgust at her opinion.

Since she knew he was right, she looked away and tried to quell the telltale blush staining her cheeks.

"Get yourselves ready to travel. If you need anything to make life easier for the next spell, we'll buy it at the town store." Charlie Wolf didn't give Naomi time to argue, speaking instead to the Sparrow Creek young ladies. The sheriff cleared his throat as if preparing to protest.

"About those prisoners, Sheriff, haul 'em out front with cuffs on and then get out of the way," Deacon ordered him. The rough-spoken bounty hunter was back, all signs of the sham minister erased.

Naomi watched with interest as the three bounty hunters coordinated their plan and herded everyone in the direction they wanted. Sam had melted from the room at the final, *I do* and already had the remuda of horses lined up and ready for cargo. The wagon stood waiting, minus the old mule but now hitched to a draft horse.

"Ever had an ass-beatin'?" Her sex clenched nervously as she met Charlie's gaze and recalled his question on the trail.

⌒⌒⌒

Each time Charlie thought he had a handle on what Naomi would do next, she proved him wrong. When offered the choice of marrying either one of the white McCallister men, she'd reached for him instead. Once outside though, Naomi tried to weasel out of it. Discreetly, aware of curious listeners, she stepped closer mentioning Deacon's promise.

"Mr. McCallister said my future is my own choice."

"Should've married Deacon then," Charlie said judiciously, admiring the way his buckskins pulled tight over her breasts when she folded her arms and glared at him.

"I understand the ceremony was a necessity—for show," she whispered conspiratorially.

"He's ordained." He laid the bad news on her, wondering what she'd do.

"Explain." Confusion wrinkled her brow and she stepped closer.

"Deak's a real minister," Charlie said gruffly. "His words are legal—binding." In point of fact, the marriage had to be registered at the county seat, but Deak had made two copies of the paper, leaving one with the Flat Rock Sheriff and keeping the other to drop off when he went to Abilene.

"So you really are my husband? I'm a married

woman?" Naomi wet her bottom lip, tilting her head sideways like a desert hen, her blue eyes assessing him.

He nodded and remained silent.

"All right." She dropped her arms, a slow smile shaping her lips before stepping toward her mare.

All right? What the hell does that mean? Not for the first time in his life, Charlie was thrown off stride by a female's words, which was why, except for bedding a woman when he got the chance, he'd stayed clear. The teacher was different though. She had his full attention and he planned on spending a lot of time learning her ways.

Charlie exercised control and didn't bawl out Naomi for the ten different things he had to yell about. Instead, he put her up on her horse without comment.

The three bounty hunters left town together, accompanying the daughters of Texas on their way to Buffalo Creek.

When the trail split, Deacon and Sam McCallister took their loaded caravan of strapped-down bodies, turning toward Abilene and the U.S. Marshal waiting there.

The prisoners were handcuffed and tied across their

saddles, riding facedown. Those who were capable groaned and cursed steadily. Their complaints were ignored as the string of horses headed east at a steady trot.

Charlie Wolf rode in the opposite direction, ramrodding the journey to Buffalo Creek where the families of the eight girls would meet them. Rebecca Johnson and Brody Quince took turns driving the wagon with the schoolteacher riding beside them on her horse.

For all his satisfaction at maneuvering Naomi into being his bride, Charlie's anger simmered inside. His fuse had already been lit when she'd run off from Flat Rock. It had sparked back into life again when she took out after the kidnappers by herself. His hand had itched to tan her behind when she'd crawled into the outlaw camp.

Now the distance between the end of the fuse and Charlie's control shortened considerably when Naomi chose to hover on the other side of the wagon instead of riding next to him. He wanted to talk to her. Hell, the truth was, he wanted to get so deep inside her she'd never be free of him.

Old Mossy had ideas about the buckskin mare as well. Charlie trotted close to Naomi's side and his stallion sidled close, nipping her horse's withers right above where Naomi's knee rested. The mare flicked her ears flirtatiously and resisted when Naomi tried to maneuver away from the big stud.

"Figure she'll throw a nice colt early summer next. You might too," Charlie said smugly. He leaned close to Naomi and straightened the reins in her suddenly slack fingers.

As he watched, her face turned bright enough red to scorch his fingers and his cock stirred. What was it about this woman that had him lusting after her as though he were a randy bull? Her mouth trembled and her teeth caught her plump bottom lip, chewing on it again. He couldn't resist, and reached across to touch her cheek.

God Almighty. As soon as he touched her skin, heat travel straight to his groin. Charlie kicked Old Mossy into a trot and moved to the front of their caravan, the motion of the horse giving him the painful pleasure of the slap of saddle leather against his rigid prick.

But aside from the log riding in his pants, he was settled and comfortable. He had his own woman. After refusing the family name for too many years to count, he'd claimed it without hesitation to wed Naomi.

He figured his bride would be a surprise for his mother. He also knew Rachel McCallister would welcome another female at the family stronghold. She held a third of the McCallister land in her name and through her, Charlie owned it too.

Naomi wouldn't be able to live like he did and damned if he hadn't decided he didn't want to live without her. It was almost funny how his need for her had trampled over his determination to live uncommitted to either part of his heritage.

Charlie hoped Jonas McCallister was writhing in hell at the thought of his Indian kin taking his name and residence on the McCallister ranch too. Charlie was feeling so pleased with himself he almost missed the faint sign of shod horses. Dismounting, he halted the wagon.

"Rest a bit," he told the girls. "But be ready to move when I say."

Naomi checked on Justine while Charlie studied the tracks mixed with the smaller prints of Indian ponies. They were heading toward Buffalo Creek.

Jericho's missing gang members were on the prowl. Charlie was betting the lives of Sparrow Creek Academy's young ladies that they'd just crossed tracks with the rest of the band of renegades.

CHAPTER EIGHTEEN

I F WHAT HE CLAIMED, was true—Deacon McCallister being an ordained minister—then she really was a married woman. A secret smile curled inside her belly as Naomi rode beside him and thought about that. So much had happened to her in the past days and the most exciting was the way Charlie Wolf had claimed her.

The part about me throwing a colt—child. Mentally Naomi rolled her eyes at his description at the same time the thought of having Charlie's baby spread molten desire through her.

Yes. I want that. I want him to give me children. Several. Images of beautiful bronze-skinned figures marched through her head—*daughters. I'd prefer girls.* She decided she needed to explain that to him before he planned a tribe of sons.

Her inner delight was interrupted when they stopped to rest and Charlie unhooked the string of horses and attached brush to the back of the wagon so it dragged the ground and erased the wheel marks. Tying the horses' lead line to his pommel, he motioned for the wagon to precede him across the open range until they hit desert land. He rode behind, erasing lingering wagon tracks under the hoofprints of the remuda.

"What's wrong? I thought we were going to Buffalo Creek?" Naomi asked when she reined to a stop next to him.

Change of plans," he answered gruffly. Charlie rode to the wagon and told Rebecca, "You need to move fast before you lose daylight. Head for those hills, find a secure spot and stay put."

Rebecca looked frightened but obeyed without question, slapping the horse into action. The old wagon rattled and shook, but held together as they once again bounced across the rough ground.

"What is it?" she asked, nudging her mare into a faster trot to ride beside Charlie.

"Outlaws," he answered grimly. "Get this wagon to those rocks ahead and into cover so that it can't be seen. I'll watch you to safety then go in the opposite direction, laying a false trail."

Before he turned away, he reached for her, pulling her half out of her saddle as he leaned close and took her mouth in a kiss. When he released her, he handed Naomi his saddlebag.

"Money inside is yours now. Use it to get yourself home." She clutched the leather pouch, unable to say anything, not even goodbye. Following the wagon slowly, she looked over her shoulder at Charlie. He had dismounted and was kneeling next to Old Mossy, covering each of his hoofs with some kind of boot.

Charlie looked up and caught her gawking at him and gestured for her to move on. Reluctantly, Naomi rode close to the wagon.

"Hurry," she told Rebecca, "Mr. Wolf thinks trouble's on its way. We need to drive to the foothills and hide the wagon."

The rocks ahead seemed near, but the sun had shifted westward in the sky before scrub pines announced they'd reached the foothills. As he'd promised, Charlie had waited, becoming an ever diminishing figure as he watched over them until they found cover.

As they climbed to safety, Naomi identified the speck in the distance as Charlie Wolf and the horses. He waved his hat as if he knew she still watched before whirling and loping away on Old Mossy, turning west after erasing the trail they'd just made. Naomi watched until the line of horses stretching out appeared no more than a distant haze of dust.

Charlie's using himself as a decoy. The saddlebags she'd slung across the mare's withers and his last words indicated that he might not return to her. Her throat ached, holding back terror, tears and emotions she couldn't name. She didn't want anything to happen to Charlie Wolf McCallister.

Daylight quickly faded into dusk as the ground underneath became rockier and the sheer face of the rock formation loomed in front of them. Rebecca drove the wagon up the incline and slapped the reins across the draft horse's back, urging it higher until they reached a stony plateau.

As soon as the wagon stopped, the girls climbed down and unhooked the traces before shoving the cart deeper into the shadows.

"Push the wagon back against the rock wall and cover it with sage brush," Naomi suggested, thinking of her childhood when Pa Lancaster had erected a camouflage screen for deer hunting.

"With all due respect, teacher..." It was Emily Erdman who wore glasses and now pushed them higher on her nose. "We're hidden by the rocks. We might need the wagon for shelter, Miss Parker."

"Of course, forgive my foolishness." Naomi was flustered and ill-prepared to establish a camp with the girls. She wasn't sure what to do first. As she stood trying to decide, her students took charge.

They chattered about the getaway, the ugly outlaws, a torn dress and Justine's head wound, but no one spoke of Charlie Wolf.

"The peddler didn't plan on going hungry. There's food here for a while." Justine crawled out of the wagon carrying tins of peaches and canned beans.

Naomi didn't know what to do. She tried to help set

up the camp, but the Texas born and raised ranch daughters knew more than she did about surviving in the wild. Worry for Charlie dominated her thoughts.

Most of the wares that Harvey Collins carried in his *Wagon of Interesting Items* were useless trinkets and beads. But the girls wrapped themselves in the thick wool blankets they found, passing them around until they each had one. They worked quietly by moonlight until Brody Quince took a length of rope from the side of the wagon and laid it in a circle.

"I've about had all the skunk I can handle," she said.

Naomi asked, "What's the rope for?"

"Pa says snakes won't crawl over a rope, so I should be fine except maybe for scorpions," Brody explained. She finished her circle, made a bed on the ground and lay down. "I'll take my chances with the critters. I'm sick of being cooped up in that wagon smelling of skunk."

The rest of the girls followed her lead, rolling into their blankets inside the rope as if it could ward off all danger. Soon the sound of sleep-breathing drifted to where Naomi kept watch. The girls depended on her to protect them. She swallowed back tears, feeling the inadequacy of her abilities.

Naomi shivered, pulling the blanket closer to ward off the cool night air as she waited for Charlie Wolf to arrive. She sat on a ledge atop the rock wall, situated so she could see anyone coming up the incline leading to the hidden plateau. Charlie had never failed to catch up with her and she was certain he would again.

As she waited, Naomi thought about Harvey Collins' part in the kidnapping. She remembered the shipment Jericho had spoken of and how determined the outlaw had been to get it.

Old man, I brought these girls to you for a price. Deliver the guns or get out. Evidently, Harvey had moved into another area of commerce, becoming a gunrunner as well as a kidnapper, extortionist and flesh peddler.

Harvey must have traded a shipment of weapons to the outlaw gang for their assistance in abducting the girls. He'd said he intended to ransom his captives back to their parents.

I figured you'd not have need of an old man once you got your shipment. I stashed the guns close to where you picked up the girls. Cagey and untrustworthy himself, Harvey had hidden the weapons.

Naomi shuddered, thinking about Charlie's mission. It seemed her husband was protecting everyone but himself. If Harvey met the remaining outlaws, he would tell them that Sam and Deacon were herding their fellow gang members to jail.

She suspected that Charlie had also used his string of horses to lay a false trail distracting the outlaws from his cousins and their prisoners.

Naomi pulled the scratchy wool material closer and sighed at the hard dirt and rough stone beneath her rump, assuring herself that Mr. Wolf was a fierce and wily warrior. He'd outwit the outlaws and return for her.

She frowned, remembering his parting words. He'd said to take the money and go home. He'd meant, of course, if he didn't return, which she assured herself wasn't going to happen. Still, she considered his instructions. Did he mean for her to go back to Alabama? She was tempted to dig in his leather pouch and pull out the wad of money he carried.

She wanted to count it, hold it for just a time. She had never seen so much money in one place as when he'd thrown bills at the stable owner. And in his saddlebag, there was a thick stack of greenbacks. It occurred to her that since her marriage to him was real, she had a husband who was a man of some material worth.

She kept herself awake thinking of sassy remarks she could say to him. She already knew how to ruffle his calm and get a response. She relived the first night, moved on to the school when he buried Patrick, analyzed his rescue of the girls and came to the end with him riding off to act as a decoy. *He's a magnificent hero.*

When the girls began to rise, Naomi curled up in a blanket next to the wagon, trying to sleep. But her rest was fitful, interrupted by the activity of her students and her anticipation of Charlie's return. She didn't want him to ride into camp and find her sleeping.

Finally she gave up napping and joined the girls.

During the day, pervasive unease gradually replaced her confidence in Charlie's safe return. The girls didn't speak about his absence and yet Naomi knew they all thought about his danger.

When darkness prevented any more movement, the girls again spread their blankets, circled them with a rope and slept. Naomi knew they were exhausted from fright as well as the ordeal they'd endured. She refused to let any of her students stand guard, deeming it her job to keep them safe. Also, she wanted to stay alert for when Mr. Wolf returned.

She sat alone all night, waiting. When the first light of dawn brightened the sky and she heard the rattle of stones falling she peeked over the ledge and saw Old Mossy's head bobbing as he climbed the rough path. She couldn't wait and hurried down the trail to meet Charlie. Dismay replaced relief. Charlie's horse trotted up to Naomi. He was riderless, wearing his saddle, his reins knotted under his muzzle.

CHAPTER NINETEEN

CHARLIE HAD RIDDEN far enough with the string of horses to feel safe in turning them loose. After stripping their halters, he hazed them into a run, watching as they left a cloud of dust behind.

Squinting against the sun, he stared at the sandstone peaks in the distance where Naomi waited. His heart beat faster at the thought of her being alone in the wilderness with a pack of girl children. He needed to get back to her quickly but he couldn't risk leading the outlaws to them if the renegades were close by.

He studied a pile of boulders, one of many unexpected outcroppings jutting up from the desert floor, like roots spreading from the mountains beyond. He poured water and scratched his horse behind the ear as the stallion drank from his hat.

"I'll be right back," he murmured. Capping the canteen, he carried it and his carbine to the lowest boulder and began climbing up the pile of rock. Once he'd arrived at a midlevel plateau, he scanned the area, noting the haze trailing behind his horses now far in the distance.

"Good," Charlie grunted, searching the vast empty wasteland for any other movement. The sun beat down mercilessly as he waited but nothing interrupted the day.

Satisfied that his way back to Naomi was clear, he started the climb down. One moment of inattention and things went all to hell. Charlie stepped on a loose patch of shale, skidding and dislodging rock and rubble as he tried to regain his footing.

Suddenly the stable mass he'd been climbing turned into a rockslide that carried him along with the avalanche of stone. Pummeled by earth and stones as big as his fist, he covered his head and dodged what he could. Finally, his downward plunge ended. During his fall, he'd knocked his head hard enough that it was a while before he regained his senses.

When he did, he discovered that he lay on a ledge, his leg pinned under a fallen slab of granite. He could flex his toes and hoped his bones weren't crushed. Though he struggled, he couldn't get leverage to push the heavy weight off him.

His canteen strap remained hooked around his neck and his rifle butt protruded from a pile of shale within reaching distance. Charlie pulled it to him, using it to snag his hat before checking his weapon's firing mechanism.

Too dizzy to continue, he rested, lying flat and

covering his face from the sun. When he opened his eyes, he forgot his circumstance for a moment and sent his mind wandering, trying to figure out why he hurt all over. When he remembered, he lunged, sitting up so quickly his hat fell in his lap.

"Shit." *Feels like I cracked a rib or two.* He grimaced, fighting back a groan as he stared at the night sky, realizing he'd been unconscious a long time. His body ached from the jolting fall. The side of his face felt scraped and raw. But agony shot through him when he flexed his knee and tried to move his leg.

He sat on a dirt shelf, not that high above the desert floor. Charlie spent the remaining hours of darkness using his knife to dig at the soil supporting the heavy stone, digging at an angle and shivering as the cool night air clung to his sweaty body.

Come morning, his leg remained lodged. He wedged the rifle butt under the slab of granite and strained, pressing his upper body weight down on the makeshift fulcrum. The rock moved incrementally without lifting the weight enough to free his limb but enough so that when it settled back down, it squeezed his leg torturously.

Making no progress in his efforts to free his leg, he called Old Mossy to him. Although he was higher than his animal's head, his horse thrust his muzzle toward Charlie, snorting and pawing the ground, announcing his disapproval of the situation.

Dangling upside down, Charlie twisted and stretched his arms toward the horse, reaching until he touched the animal's head, then working his way down the bridle to the bit and the attached leathers.

Fumbling to catch the reins, he soothed the stallion. By the time he finally claimed the dangling leathers, Charlie was lightheaded and his leg screamed in agony. Sick and dizzy, he knotted the reins high enough so they wouldn't foul up Old Mossy's progress, then hung in a half stupor, the weight of his body pulling against the rock pinning him.

The stallion nudged him into semi-awareness and Charlie realized he couldn't remain dangling upside down and expect to survive. He stayed conscious long enough to struggle back onto the earth shelf before collapsing. He woke to find his thigh swollen twice as big as it should have been and his horse gone. He felt like hell.

He had mixed feelings when he realized Old Mossy had disappeared. The stallion's disaffection surprised him, though he hoped the animal rolled the saddle off and managed to get shut of his bridle.

Get yourself a herd of mares, old friend. Charlie's throat clogged with emotion as he pictured the black stallion running free.

Situated as he was, his hat was his only shade. Sitting, he strained forward, focused on prying his leg from the rock. If he rolled one way, he went over the edge to dangle upside down. It wouldn't be long before predators discovered him. The coyotes were still intimidated by his man smell but no doubt that wouldn't last much longer. Soon they'd scale the rocks when they were sure he couldn't put up a fight.

Though he had no feeling now in his foot, his leg throbbed, radiating pain. As the day progressed, his body seesawed between bouts of sweating and shivers making his teeth chatter.

It wasn't the way Charlie had expected to die. He drew his knife, digging at the base of the rock again, trying to hollow out a deeper resting spot for his rifle butt. If he could get it in there just right, he might…

Perspiration dripped off him and too quickly he felt thick-headed, dehydrated by the sun. Finally, he sprawled on his back, pulling his hat over his head, waiting. He'd save bullets until the end.

His thoughts drifted to the event that had divided his life into white man and red man. His father Gray Wolf had become sickened by the war he waged on his wife's people and though he was Kiowa, he rode with the Cheyenne chief, Black Kettle to a place named Fort Lyons to speak of peace.

Charlie had been fourteen when he'd gone with his father to the fort. While they'd talked to the army representative, the cavalry had attacked the Cheyenne encampment on Sand Creek and shot, beaten to death or stabbed every woman and child they could catch. It had been a massacre calculated to bring the Indians to their knees.

Hearing the gunfire in the distance, Gray Wolf and Charlie had raced to rescue Charlie's mother. She'd been on the ground, firing her rifle at the cavalry, a white woman defending her adopted people. Gray Wolf had scooped Rachel McCallister from the ground, saving her from sure death.

It had been a younger Jericho, just as treacherous then, who'd circled behind the fleeing man and woman. Charlie hadn't realized the half-breed was fighting on the side of the whites. The renegade had thrown a saber, stabbing Gray Wolf before they'd reached safety.

Charlie had led them from battle and into hiding. But his father's wound proved to be a mortal blow.

"Take you mother home to her people," Gray Wolf had given his last orders before dying. Charlie's mother had held her Indian mate in her arms, refusing to let him go even after he'd taken his last breath. The son of two worlds had watched stoically, protecting her while she grieved.

Remembering, Charlie grimaced in pain and disgust. He'd returned his mother to the McCallister ranch as he'd been directed. Had Gray Wolf understood Rachel's family, Charlie doubted he'd have chosen that path for her.

Naomi kissed me here. He fingered the groove etched on his jaw, following it as it cut a line up his cheek, just missing his eye. The day he'd received the scar, he'd wanted to kill his grandsire, Jonas McCallister. The old man had always carried a whip, and the sound seemed to fill the desert air as Charlie battled delirium and faced the hate-filled man again in his mind.

Jonas had stood, his brawny height well over six feet, wielding a massive bullwhip with an even longer reach. He'd come after Charlie, flicking the tip over his skin and scoring a line of red before striking again in another spot.

"Nits make lice, boy. Get the hell off McCallister land. I'll flay more red skin off your hide every day you're here." The old devil had been in a rage every time he'd seen the half-grown evidence of what he called his daughter's defilement by savages.

Dripping blood, Charlie had rushed the old bastard, knocked him to the ground and wrestled the whip from him. Using Gray Wolf's knife, Charlie had mocked Jonas, slicing the bullwhip into leather strips and throwing them in his grandfather's face.

Sam and Robert McCallister, subject themselves to the old man's violent temper, had helped Charlie to a hiding place until his mother could get to him. She'd found him trying to tend the bleeding wounds on his body and face. Rachel had stitched the laid-open flesh, dabbing an Indian poultice on after.

"Charlie, he'll kill you if you stay here. Go back to your father's people. Ride with them and come back and see me when you can." His mother had cried as she'd sent him away. He'd left, but returned each full moon to check on her.

At those times, she'd ridden out to meet him or sent his cousins with word of her well-being. Charlie closed his eyes, a vivid picture forming in his mind of the time he'd slipped onto the McCallister ranch and his cousins had ridden with him into Indian country.

They'd been greener than new apples. Three haflings, too young in years to be men but too weathered by hard times to admit they were still boys. Charlie had been dressed like a Kiowa warrior which was probably the only thing that had saved their bacon. He'd led the other two as they'd belly-crawled to the edge of the rise and peered down at the Apache camp below.

He'd been determined to see Lozen, Victorio's sister—the Apache woman warrior who was said to be a witch, a healer and spiritual guide for her people. She'd been in the center of the encampment, surrounded by the men of three Indian nations.

Chief Nana had been there. It had surprised Charlie to see the venerable leader lean close to hear her words, paying her the respect he'd give a chief. The McCallister cousins had been so engrossed in listening, they didn't hear the Arapaho braves steal up from behind until they were prisoners. Instead of killing them, the braves had dragged the boys to the camp where the Apache priestess waited.

Charlie sipped a few drops of water and closed his eyes, reliving the experience.

The fire was just a fire and yet Lozen's image was unclear, sometimes almost transparent. She studied them and they stood silently under her appraisal. Sounds receded and left only them, the fire and the Indian woman—reading their souls.

"Why do you come here?" Her question was directed at Charlie Wolf, as it should be. He'd come and his cousins had followed.

"I've come to barter for a woman." It wasn't a lie. At seventeen, Charlie Wolf did want a woman. And that was more explainable than the need to see Lozen, the woman of magic who had sensed their presence when the Apache sentries hadn't.

She laughed and the rich, husky sound floated through the night, inviting the men of three tribes to laugh too. Filling three bowls, she carried one to each McCallister. When they all stood holding the noxious-smelling liquid, she spoke. "Drink and know your dreams."

Surrounded by warriors who'd rather kill him for entertainment, Charlie had swallowed the potion, emptying the cup as she'd watched. The power of the liquid had been immediate, taking him to his knees before visions claimed him. Lozen had sent him spirit walking in the otherworld to see his future.

When he and his cousins woke the next morning, the campfire was dead, the ground cold and all signs had been erased that over a hundred Indians from three different nations had been there the night before.

Seventeen years later, Charlie opened his eyes and wet his parched lips remembering the bitter taste of the brew. The dust whirls kicked up in the dry wind, reminding him of the red haze in his dream. His vision had been a jumbled replay of the past. He'd seen his mother stretching across a chasm trying to reach Gray Wolf.

Charlie had taken it as a sign that his life would be marked by both worlds, as it had been. He closed his eyes, but this time the image of his mother altered and became a tall, sharp-spoken schoolteacher reaching for *him*. He drifted through the escalating heat and pain, a smile of regret on his lips.

Naomi tried to be quiet, but the sounds of her readying for departure roused Marnie who woke the rest of the students. They all knew that Charlie Wolf would be on Old Mossy's back if he'd been able.

"I've got to go look for Mr. Wolf. He's obviously

been injured somehow and sent his horse to find us." She stared at Charlie's horse and not the girls ringing her. She did not want them to see her fear. Old Mossy stood looking expectant, nudging her with his head as though impatient for them to leave and none of the girls disputed her decision.

"He wiped our trail, how will you find him out there?" Marnie asked, frowning thoughtfully.

"I don't know, but I have to try." Naomi's uneasiness had given way to panic.

"He'll be mad. He said for us to stay put." Marnie teetered on her boot heels, thinking before she added, "But I agree you should go anyway. Keep the mountain straight behind you and you'll reach the place where he kept watch. From that point, follow the hoofprints he left. If you come across any unshod pony tracks..." She paused and looked at Naomi, frowning as she advised, "Ride like hell in the opposite direction."

Under normal circumstances, Naomi would have corrected Marnie's language. Instead she patted her arm and said, "I'll be fine."

They filled two canteens from the barrel of water strapped to the side of Harvey's wagon. Naomi had intended to ride the buckskin mare but switched to Old Mossy, mounting him instead.

"Maybe you should take the mare with you. You might need to bring back his body," Justine suggested. The other girls glared at the idea that Charlie was dead.

Naomi shook her head.

"After I find him, we'll ride double." Naomi pointed at the leather hoof covers on Charlie's horse. "I won't leave a trail leading back to you girls. Stay quiet and hidden while I'm gone."

She mounted Old Mossy and rode from their hiding place, frightened by her decision to leave the girls but determined to find Charlie. The stallion felt huge in comparison to the buckskin mare, but just as her previous mount had seemed to have a known destination, so did Charlie's horse.

As Marnie had directed, she kept the mountain at her back as her guide. By midmorning Naomi had begun doubting her plan, despairing that she might really be going nowhere, when Old Mossy turned and picked up his pace, trotting westward.

The sun was straight overhead when the big stallion broke into a lope, carrying them to a stand of rocks up ahead. Naomi tensed at the sight of buzzards circling in the sky, dreading what she would find when she arrived.

CHAPTER TWENTY

I T WAS NEAR NOON of the second day when Charlie
squinted at the sun overhead, watching the buzzards
lazily catch the wind, gliding and circling and waiting for
him to be dead enough to suit them. He'd swallowed the
last liquid in his canteen earlier and now the lack of
water had left him parched, his tongue swelling behind
dry, cracked lips.

He levered himself to a sitting position, his ribs
protesting as he suppressed a groan. A horned lizard
froze in its journey across the rock, flicking its tongue
out, investigating Charlie. *Thought I was dead, didn't
you?*

It was a hell of a note. He was safe enough from the
crawlers as long as he was breathing. On the other hand,
the birds overhead were already calling *firsts* on him.

Determined to make them wait on the meal, Charlie
resumed digging. Once, when he paused, wiping the
sweat from his eyes, he considered using his sharp knife
to hack off his leg. Old Mossy was gone and he couldn't

walk out on a stump, so he went back to work, dismissing the idea.

Sitting, he could see across the vast landscape to the mountains beyond. Lying down, he could see the sky or the inside of his hat. Not wanting to give the critters watching him any reason to doubt he still lived, he spent most of his time sitting.

When Charlie saw the horse and rider coming toward him, he thought he was hallucinating. The closer they got, the surer he was that he was seeing a mirage, a manifestation of Lozen's prophetic vision. The red dust and wavering figure were the same as his dreamwalk. But Old Mossy trotted to stand beneath the earth shelf where Charlie remained pinned and...

Naomi reached across the chasm of death to rescue me. Damned if his woman didn't stand up in the stirrups and toss a canteen of water to him. He must have looked in better shape than he felt because she started right in on her story, dismounting as she talked.

"I knew something was wrong when you didn't come back." Naomi talked, clambering up the boulders to reach him.

"Watch your footing," he tried to warn her, but his words came out a rough croak. He figured if it was a dream, it was a hell of a good one to go out on. He fumbled the water pouch open and filled his mouth, swishing the liquid over tongue and lips before swallowing.

"Help me get this damned rock off my leg." His voice wasn't much more than a raspy whisper but she understood.

"Charlie, Charlie, Charlie, what have you done to yourself? I swear, Mr. Wolf. I don't know how you managed before me." Naomi reached the plateau and climbed over the lip, crawling to his side where she crouched protectively, patting his shoulder, kissing his cheek and fussing.

"You'll make a good squaw yet," he teased her gruffly. "Go on back down and throw me the rope. You, me and Old Mossy ought to be able to get me out of this fix." A knot formed in his chest, strange emotions flooding him as his rescuer took charge and assured him he would live.

Naomi didn't waste time. She hurried down the rocky incline and, reaching the saddle, threw the end of the coiled rope to him. He tied it around the slab while she looped the other end around the pommel.

"I don't want to damage your leg more than it already is. When Old Mossy pulls, I'll help lift and push." She climbed back up to where he already had the rifle butt wedged and ready.

Old Mossy did his part as Charlie leaned on the pry bar. When the rock shifted upward, Naomi grabbed his leg and pulled it out from under the granite slab. Between the two of them they got him lowered to Old Mossy's back.

"Tie me on," he told her. He wasn't sure he was steady enough to ride without falling and his injured leg was swollen and sore, eliminating the possibility of gripping with it.

"No time for that," she said. "We need to get back to the girls." Instead of following his order, she climbed up behind him and wrapped her arms around his body, holding on to him tightly.

Charlie only remembered the arms that kept him safe on the ride back to the mountains. Had she not held on to him, he'd have fallen and died in the desert. Naomi clung to him for hours as Old Mossy carried them to the foothills and then up the incline to where the girls were hidden. He was in bad shape when the girls eased him from Old Mossy's back.

"Hell, woman, I might have knocked you out of the saddle. Then where would you have been?" he growled at Naomi the first moment he had sense. He rambled, trying to get his complaints lined up but finally gave up and just said, "What part of *stay put* don't you understand?"

"The part where you think I'd let you face danger alone. Hush while we fix this leg." Her words were tart but her tone gentle as she handled him. She and the Quince kid wrapped his ribs tight before Naomi bathed his leg, picking the grit and deerskin fibers out of the scraped flesh. His eyes were closed while they worked over him.

"It's got to be done. This is going to hurt, Mr. Wolf." He would have preferred to slide into oblivion but he was still holding on to consciousness when Naomi doused the gash with whiskey. As the pain slashed through him like a hot knife it was all he could do to keep from screaming like a child.

"I told my pa that the Sparrow Creek Young Ladies Academy was a waste of money, but he's determined I'll stay in Texas and my mama's just as determined I'll be a lady," the Quince girl talked to him while Naomi worked. The kid snorted at the idea of being a lady as she squinted down at Charlie's leg, assessing the damage.

"I'm going to be a doctor. Mama's not happy about the idea but she said she'll send me back East to medical school after I get *finished at* Sparrow Creek. Well, I'm here to tell her, I almost got finished for good." Charlie grunted, focusing on the kid's comments rather than the pain eating him alive. It seemed clear that being a lady wasn't high on her value list.

"You're already a lady. I 'spect you'll be a doctor someday too," he said gruffly, taking in the determined expression, steady hands and stubborn jaw.

"Really?" Brody searched his face to see if he was sincere.

"Yep."

The women fixed him up as best they could and covered him with a blanket. He went to sleep with Naomi assuring him she had everything in control.

He drifted in and out of fevered dreams. He remembered once telling Naomi to gag him if he started yelling.

"I hope that offer stands when you're well," she'd answered snidely. When he attempted to get up, she stopped him.

"I'm taking care of you now, Mr. Wolf. Rest easy," Naomi said. Somehow those words were enough. Charlie relaxed and slept, letting her strength wrap around him, keeping him safe while he mended.

The next day was rough. He was too weak to pay much attention to Naomi and her girls. Her constant presence soothed him and he rested, trusting her to stand guard. By the time the sun went down the second night after his rescue, he'd begun to feel almost capable of managing on his own. In the background, the girls finally quieted, their whispers changing to the sounds of sleep. He knew he should pry himself off the blanket and go check on things, but he didn't have the strength.

Charlie woke when he heard the giggle of young girls. It was an unfamiliar sound. He lay with eyes closed, analyzing what he heard—female whispers, the rustle of clothes and the sound of a horse lipping the meager strands of grass nearby.

He shifted his leg, flexing his bare toes, glad that he had feeling in his foot. She must have been watching him close enough to see his eyelids twitch, because Naomi laid her soft hand on his brow, checking his temperature.

"You're not as fevered as you were," she told him. "I wish I had medicine to use."

He'd been half awake earlier when the Quince girl had sniffed the wound, assuring Naomi it wasn't putrefying. There didn't appear to be any broken bones, but his flesh was torn and his knee and leg bruised and swollen.

"You make me proud to call you husband, Mr. Wolf." He must have drifted back to sleep because he was startled when Naomi bent over him, feathering a kiss across his cheek before whispering in his ear.

She left him alone for a moment and an ache of longing formed a knot in his chest. When she returned with a canteen, he spoke around emotion clogging his throat, "It's safer for you to call yourself Mrs. McCallister." His words came out stern, almost gruff.

"Naomi Parker McCallister—it sounds very important." She smiled at him. Then she tapped his nose for emphasis and added, "My name is your name, Mr. Wolf."

She moved away, leaving him to ponder her words. He closed his eyes mulling over a puzzle—how she'd become so important to him in the short time he'd known her.

He remembered back to their first meeting, picturing her in the alley, the barn, the trough—that brought a grin to his face. She must have been watching him because he soon felt her hovering presence.

"I've never seen you smile like that." Though his eyes were closed, he could feel her peering down at him. "What are you thinking about?"

He almost laughed out loud at her nosiness. He knew without looking she had her hands on her hips and her head tilted sideways, never doubting she had the right to demand an answer to a damn personal question.

"You, in a barn, in a trough, naked in my arms," he growled, popping one eye open. He opened both eyes in time to see the blush climb her neck and turn her cheeks bright red as she scurried away.

He slept most of the day and into the evening. When he woke this time, he reached out with all senses, straining to gather information. Something was wrong, something had awakened him. His eyes jerked open and he sat up so fast he banged his head on the rock shelf Naomi had tucked him under.

"Douse the fire," he ordered softly, struggling to get up and do it himself.

"You need to lie back down and keep that leg still." For once Naomi didn't question him. She kicked dirt on the small blaze of wood, smothering it quickly before hurrying to his side.

Charlie's head hurt like hell, he had to make water and he had nine females peering at him as though they'd never seen a man before.

"I need to take a piss—now." His crude words made Naomi's mouth prim up but she nodded, bending to help him stand. He pushed up against the rock, waving her off. "I can take care of this."

Damned if she didn't cross her arms and watch as he struggled to rise. When he was halfway inched up the rock and getting ready to straighten, she swooped down on him and tucked herself under his arm.

"Lean on me. I don't want you damaging your leg any more than you already have." She had him on the move toward the make-shift privy they'd devised before he could tender a response. She was so damn smug, he couldn't help rattling her a little. He had his hand braced on her arm. Deliberately, he brushed the side of her breast with his knuckles.

Her breath caught and beneath his vest, her nipples became stiff peaks. He rubbed harder, bending over her to murmur for her ears only, "You don't know how to mind, woman. My hand is itchin' to tan your fanny."

He rumbled his threat in her ear, smelled her hair and breathed the scent of his woman. The truth was, even laid up as he was, he wanted to run his hands all over her body again, claiming her and making sure she was real. Improbable as it seemed, Naomi had rescued him, completing the destiny he'd seen in his vision.

"Behave," she scolded, turning her head and brushing a kiss against his bare shoulder. Then she left him to his own devices, handing him a stick she'd fashioned into a make-shift crutch.

Charlie's headache was forgotten. He contemplated his good fortune as he emptied his bladder. He had a strong, courageous woman. She was a little too independent, but he would manage that out of her and she was young enough to have children so that would settle her down.

Another giggle floated to him—a son—he amended his thoughts. She was young enough to birth him a son. All the females swarming around the clearing made him uneasy. If he'd read the tracks right, the renegades were scouring the countryside looking for them. And instead of cowering quietly until they were rescued, the girls appeared to be enjoying themselves. He used his crutch to hop back to where Naomi was waiting.

"Those girls need to quiet down." Even as he spoke another soft laugh drifted on the wind. Naomi's smile instantly changed to concern.

"Can you manage?" Not waiting to see if he could, she hurried back to shush her young ladies.

Dammit, what the hell is the matter with me? As he watched the sway of her hips inside his borrowed pants, Charlie's cock tented his own buckskins. He set aside his lust and followed Naomi across the stony landscape intent on taking charge of the females from the Sparrow Creek Young Ladies Academy.

"There's a band of riders looking for signs out there," he motioned toward the arid desert below. "Might be sign of you they're hunting." He listed his orders. "No fires, no talk." Even Charlie recognized the impossibility of that, so amended his order to, "Whisper."

"We can't hide up here forever," Naomi frowned, murmuring doubtfully.

"We've got three horses, two guns and a couple of knives. What would be your plan this time, teacher?" Charlie answered gruffly.

"Well, there's no reason to be sarcastic, Mr. Wolf," she said, looking indignant.

CHAPTER TWENTY-ONE

C HARLIE LAY BESIDE the wagon two nights later. Naomi had gone to their makeshift privy and the girl they called Missy tiptoed over and looked down at him.

He snored loudly to reassure her they wouldn't be overheard and she crept back to her friends. After he'd refused their pleas for a fire and gruffly ordered them to get to bed, he'd feigned sleep. Apparently, the girls' gratitude for being rescued was quickly giving way to resentment. They planned a mutiny. He listened to them whispering in the dark.

"It's his fault we're stuck here," one of them said. "If we'd gone straight to Buffalo Creek, we'd be home by now." There was more than a hint of tears in her voice.

"We should leave without him. We can all go, ride double, maybe three up on the draft horse." Rebecca's plan was simple. Take the horses and leave with whoever wanted to go. He grinned to himself wondering how Old

Mossy would take to Rebecca's plan.

"Charlie Wolf's stallion isn't going to carry anyone but maybe Miss Parker and she's not going anywhere without Charlie Wolf." It was Brody Quince speaking.

He felt a tinge of disappointment at her disaffection until she added, "And I'm not going anywhere without her. So we might as well resign ourselves to being here a spell longer, because Charlie Wolf can't travel yet." She spoke as a doctor, setting conditions for his recovery.

The grumbling that followed dispelled the immediate need to guard the animals. Charlie waited until the girls had formed their usual rope circle and lay inside Brody's make-shift snake protection. Once they were bedded down, he stood up with his blanket and grabbed the crutch Naomi had fashioned from a broom handle she'd found in the peddler's wagon.

"The horses are there. Leave if you want. I reckon it'll be a sight easier getting one woman out safe than fooling with a pack of squalling brats." He knew they were awake and listening when he limped past.

Naomi had to have heard him stomping out of camp, but she stood with her blanket wrapped around her shoulders, gazing at the landscape below. He joined her on the wide stone ledge. It was a handy lookout post, with the wall behind and boulders scattered along the front leaving a space big enough for two people to share.

When Naomi leaned toward him and placed the back of her hand against his head, he caught it and pulled on her, wrapping her in a bear hug.

She came into his arms as if she'd been waiting for him to gather her close. He liked that. With eight sets of ears listening, there wasn't much canoodling to be done, but Naomi made a pallet with his blanket and he lowered himself to the ground, pulling her after him. He turned on his side, lying on his good leg, bringing her back against his chest with her rump against his groin.

Spooning together, one muscle relaxing at a time, Charlie molded his body to hers, surrounding Naomi with his being until they breathed as one. His rigid cock pushed insistently against her bottom. Her breath hitched and held when he slid his hands under the hem of her shirt, taking ownership of her breasts.

It wasn't his imagination when Naomi pressed backward, deliberately grinding against his ever-growing erection. He pinched her nipples and felt her jerk and arch, thrusting more of her flesh into his hands.

He buried his face in her hair to keep from groaning aloud as his hand snaked under the waistband of her pants, cupping her mound.

Her legs parted, letting his fingers relearn the soft petals of her womanhood. He kept one hand on her breast, continuing to knead her firm, sweet flesh, tweaking the nipple, pulling and rotating it and making her shiver.

Silently they caressed each other, waiting for quiet among the girls. Charlie played in her wet heat, nuzzling her ear and encouraging her wanton responses. She reached behind and fumbled his cock from his pants, stroking his swollen flesh up and down, pressing the crease of her rump against his length.

When he penetrated her with his finger, Naomi moaned and tightened her channel, asking for more. Charlie had his mouth on her neck, loving the taste of her and feeling her pulse race as they played. He kept her on the edge, teasing her body into frantic need and then soothing her into patient waiting.

His cock was so hard he could have pounded nails with it, her sex so wet his hand was slippery with her fluids and he hadn't yet let her come. Even as he seduced her passion from her, he listened to the night sounds and sleeping girls, waiting for the moment he and Naomi would have privacy. He wanted to be in her when she clenched and pulsed in ecstasy.

Covering them with her blanket, he ran his hand over her belly, stroking the flat planes of her stomach before grasping her waistband and shoving her pants down around her knees.

Charlie opened the slit in his pants and entered her from behind. He was too aroused for delicacy. All he could remember was the need for quiet as he hilted, thrusting inside her so deep his short curls brushed the crack between her rounded cheeks.

Naomi's back arched and a tiny moue of distress escaped her.

"*Mi corazón*," Charlie, whispered hugging her closer before dropping his hand lower, touching her pearl, swirling his fingers in her wet heat and returning to rotate the swollen nub at her apex. He thrust his cock again, feeling the drag of her channel around him and Naomi started her orgasm, her internal muscles squeezing his flesh as her release rippled through her body, unleashing his control.

Not a sound escaped either of them and the blanket muffled the soft slap of skin against skin as Charlie's pleasure spread upward from his toes, signaling his own imminent finish. A growl of pleasure rumbled in his throat and he stilled it behind clenched teeth. Naomi rotated her hips against his groin and when she shifted in his embrace, she inadvertently brushed his bad leg, sending a shard of pain cutting through him.

The avalanche of sensation overwhelmed him and he muffled his groan against her neck, his hips jerking in ecstasy, pumping seed into her feminine core, filling the deepest part of Naomi Parker with the essence of Charlie Wolf McCallister.

His knee and lower leg throbbed like a sonovabitch but it didn't matter. He left his cock inside her and rolled, rearranging them so her back rested on his chest, her bottom hugging his groin.

He caught his foot in her pants, kicking them off and leaving her naked but for her boots. Spreading her thighs, he rubbed his hand through her lower curls, teasing her pearl before rimming the place where his rod filled her entrance. He wanted to grunt, growl and roar. Each time he suppressed a sound, it intensified his arousal.

Charlie pulled Naomi's knees high and wide, planting her boots so they framed his hips. She swayed, arching her back and pushing her pelvis down, rotating her cunny, pressing against his finger pleasuring her nub. Her sex twitched and squeezed his cock and she reached between them, touching the place where they were joined.

When she rubbed the thick base of his shaft, scratching him there with her fingernail, he bucked upward, sinking farther into her sweet, sweet heat.

Nuzzling the spot where Naomi's shoulder joined her neck, he felt shivers race over her body, her skin pebbling with goose bumps. Leisurely, Charlie stroked her breast with one hand, toying with her nipple as he rubbed his nose behind her ear, landing a soft kiss there.

Naomi caught her breath, her sheath flexing hungrily around his shaft.

"Again," Charlie murmured, nuzzling her earlobe as he flexed his hips, sliding, fucking, nibbling, loving her until once again her climax unfurled. Naomi sprawled on him, limp and exhausted, her knees bent, her legs splayed wide accommodating his penetration.

Perspiration sealed them together and he licked a drop of sweat, savoring her salty flavor as she lay draped across his body. Her sheath rhythmically milked his cock. Lazily her hand brushed across his hip, her fingertips barely touching him. His half-aroused shaft thickened and once again became rigid, stretching her tight walls.

Patiently, he remained still, waiting for Naomi to catch her wind. When her breathing evened, Charlie pulled out of her long enough to reseat her, this time facing him.

She drooped above him, her hair tumbling over her shoulders in a curly mass and her shoulders slumped as she braced her hands against his chest. Charlie smiled. His schoolmarm was tired.

He drew her head down, plundering her mouth and flattening her breasts against his chest. His hand stroked her bottom, guiding her up and down movement as her cunny licked and kissed him. He should have been tired but he wasn't. Charlie wanted her with the fierceness of a wolf with his mate.

He couldn't get enough of the woman joined to his flesh, nipping her awake when she slipped into exhausted sleep and roughly pinching her nipples, demanding her attention, bringing her to release over and over. While the dark night gave them a private room and the young girls slept, Charlie Wolf claimed his bride and orchestrated their honeymoon.

"Good night," Naomi mumbled, finally pressing her lips against his forehead. After she'd closed her eyes and slept, he played with her hair, memorizing the moment.

His head was clear, he was more alert than he had been for days and his crazed courtship was settled.

She rested on his chest and he timed her sleeping, allowing a little longer before she had to pull on some clothes. He liked the feel of her skin on his. He stared up at the dark sky and grinned. He'd been like an animal in rut since he'd met her. The Indians named it the *mating dance*, when a young buck saw the woman he wanted and began wooing her. Inside, Charlie laughed at the past days of his driven pursuit.

When she'd left Flat Rock with his horse and clothes, he'd considered the possibility that his suit was being rejected—but he'd followed her. When she'd taken out on her own from Buffalo Creek, he'd followed her and sent Deacon tracking Jericho, which was before unheard of because tracking was Charlie's job. When she'd crawled into the outlaw camp, Charlie had been down on his belly shimmying in right behind.

He'd followed her into a hornet's nest in Flat Rock, knowing damn well it was a fool's mission. Charlie looked up at the stars and realized he'd been tied to this woman from the moment she'd answered, "Yes," when he'd asked," You trying to seduce me?"

I'd better come up with a plan dammed fast. As he lay holding her in his arms, listening to the sound of nine females sleeping, his expression became grim. When he could linger no longer, Charlie pulled the deerskin pants over Naomi's boots and up her legs, patting her awake.

"Wake up, *mi corazón*," he whispered in her ear. She lifted her head, her smile warming his heart in the dim half-light and chill of morning.

Rolling out of their cocoon to do sentry duty, he left her scurrying to pull on her clothes and tidy her hair.

Charlie used the crutch she'd made him to do a three-legged dance to the edge of the granite shelf that hid them from below. He sat on one of the boulders there watching the sun come up, waiting for the morning female flutters to begin.

It was a totally unexpected, excited cry from Naomi that brought him hopping across loose slate and shale. She was on her hands and knees, tugging at something under the wagon. Charlie just had time to admire her bottom sticking up when she sat back on her haunches and pointed at the box she'd found.

He hobbled to her side and looked down—rifles.

Eight girls ringed him, all looking down at the hidden cache of guns. There were three more boxes, each packed with twenty-five Winchester Model 1876 repeating rifles. One hundred Winchester carbines would feather Jericho's nest in Mexico very nicely. Or in the hands of marauding Indians a lot more blood would spill—on both sides.

"They're not going to quit looking for us, are they?" It was Missy Cotter showing more intelligence than usual. "I thought they'd get tired of looking for us and go catch some other girls." It was a pretty cold wish, but everyone understood her desperation.

"Well," Brody Quince offered her opinion, "I guess we'll have to shoot them if they find us. Any ammunition in those boxes?"

Charlie amended his earlier wish for a son. He'd take a daughter like the Quince girl as many times as Naomi gave him one.

"It's been over five days since my cousins left for Abilene. They were stopping in Eclipse to leave word that we're on our way. I expect some of your families will be wondering where we are," Charlie told them the truth.

Marnie nodded, Rebecca Johnson looked relieved and Brody Quince expectant. Naomi held up the shells that were packed in the bottom of each crate under the rifles.

Charlie gazed at the ammunition in Naomi's hand and wondered if she intended to fight the band of renegades with an army of twelve-year-olds. For an intelligent woman, he'd noticed that his schoolmarm didn't have a lick of common sense.

They couldn't practice shooting with live ammunition. The sound would bring every rider combing the desert looking for them right to their hideaway. But he made certain each girl knew how to use a weapon and had them loading and unloading too, hoping if the time ever came to defend themselves the girls would be able to point and shoot.

Naomi fumbled nervously whenever she handled a rifle. Brody Quince could probably shoot the eye out of a hawk in flight. Emily Erdman's eyesight, even with her glasses, was so poor, Charlie just hoped she could aim in the right direction if it was ever needed.

Marnie, Mary, Justine and Rebecca said they were as expert as Brody. Charlie doubted that the claim, but at least they knew how to shoot. Daisy proved willing to learn but unskilled and Missy seemed to be a complete washout.

"I can't do that. It's too heavy…" she'd whine. "My daddy tried to teach me once, but the noise is too loud…" The silly lisp that she affected became more intense and she puckered into tears. Charlie walked away from her.

"Can you load the guns?" Naomi persisted. Missy stopped bawling and found a job. She and Emily practiced loading the weapons and Naomi's students began working as a team, planning strategies to protect their stronghold.

"The canvas covering the peddler's wagon rolls up on one side. My mama says an ounce of surprise is worth a pound of skill. When we leave here and make a run for it we can keep it down until we're besieged…" Brody Quince said.

"That's a good idea. See if you can rig the other side of the tarp to roll up too," Charlie praised her gruffly.

Everyone including Charlie felt the chill of her words and he swallowed the bile rising in his throat.

Goddammit, innocent kids shouldn't have to face-off with a wild bunch.

The guns were bad news. If the weapons were already promised to the band of Indians that had escaped the reservation, the Apaches would be hunting them too.

Charlie took stock. The water barrel was less than half full even though they'd been rationing since the first day. The beans and peaches would last another two days, maybe three if they all sucked in their guts and ate less than the half rations they had already practiced.

He looked at the girls from the Sparrow Creek Young Ladies Academy with new eyes. For all their giggles and petty rebellions, he'd been with grown men who didn't act as well. He wanted to save them. Hell, he wanted to save himself. But most of all, he wanted to save his mate, Naomi Parker Wolf McCallister.

By tacit agreement, he and Naomi stayed apart. After their silent passion, it wasn't possible for him to keep his hands off her. Knowing what they faced made him want to bundle her on Old Mossy and go higher in the mountains where they could hunker down and survive until the danger was past. But he couldn't do that towing eight young'uns behind.

His heart ached with longing for more years with his woman. He'd just found her but they'd have to survive this mess if they were to grow old together. He felt her eyes on him when he hobbled around the camp and there was never a moment he didn't know her exact location.

CHAPTER TWENTY-TWO

NAOMI WATCHED CHARLIE and worried. Ever since they'd discovered the cache of guns, he'd become stoic, studying the sky, checking the weapons, instructing the girls and measuring the water several times during the day. She dreaded the moment they'd leave but understood they couldn't linger here any longer.

Charlie grasped her elbow and limped beside her to the overlook. It afforded them the privacy they needed to talk. Before he began speaking, he pulled her into his embrace, hugging her against him.

"I like the way you hold me." *I like everything about you, Mr. Wolf.* Naomi felt almost shy, which given their night time activity was ludicrous. She smiled up at him.

"You're pretty," he said gruffly, speaking low for her ears alone.

"You need to borrow Emily's spectacles, Charlie." It was true that in his arms, Naomi felt fragile, lovely and above all, cherished, but she rubbed her face against his chest and laughed.

"I say I have a pretty woman." He wrapped her tighter, lifting her up so her feet dangled above the ground, gazing at her sternly.

"I expect you need to tell me what we're going to do," she said, drawing a deep breath. Naomi slid her arms around his neck, burying her face against his shoulder, stifling tears. She wanted this time with him to last forever but she couldn't give into fear and become a burden instead of an asset. She had a hundred ideas churning, most of them impractical and born of desperation. She knew their survival relied on Charlie's knowledge and experience.

"It's time to get your students home. We're going to move them tonight, navigate by the stars. You're going to have to move away from here, traveling toward Buffalo Creek, pacing the draft horse as you go." He set her on one of the boulders and leaned against it, keeping his arm around her waist.

"All right." Naomi looked over at the sun already sliding below the horizon. Although it was still hot, she shivered. Dusk had arrived and they'd leave this place tonight. Naomi was ready to do something. Waiting worked against them with water running low and determined savages looking for guns.

"You'll ride the buckskin and keep a rifle in one arm and another sheathed and ready." Charlie said.

"I'm not very adept with a weapon, Charlie. Maybe we should tie the mare onto the back of the wagon and

I'll load guns too." Naomi frowned doubtfully.

"You're ramrodding this part, Naomi. If luck is with you, you'll run into a posse of citizens or a troop of soldiers coming for those girls and…" Charlie pulled her closer, hugging her close one last time.

"Stop." Naomi put her hand across his mouth. She bit her lower lip trying to keep from crying. "We are not going anywhere without you. Do not suggest other than that."

Patiently he explained his plan to stay behind. He'd destroy most of the rifles, holding a few back in case he needed them before he left. He'd wait and when he calculated Naomi had traveled far enough to have the wagon in the clear, he'd set fire to the guns, deliberately drawing attention away from the girls escaping in the night.

"No."

"Naomi Parker Wolf McCallister," he sternly pronounced her name. "Did you not hire me to save your students?"

"No … yes." She stopped and then added, "But not by killing yourself. There has to be another way."

He assured her there wasn't another way and walked her back to the wagon where the girls had dumped most of the peddler's wares, readying for travel. He nodded his approval and told them the plan in military precision.

"Two on the seat. If one goes down, the other picks up the reins. "

Naomi blanched and she swayed on her feet as she finally realized the enormity of the danger. She looked around at the girls ringing Charlie. Two of them would be exposed and vulnerable, the others hidden.

"I can't shoot worth anything and others can load guns, but I can manage a team of horses. I'm driving." Missy unexpectedly stepped forward.

"I'll sit up front too," Brody said quietly. "I can shoot and drive, so I'll cover Missy while she handles the reins." Time went fast and it seemed before Naomi could draw breath, Charlie said they were ready.

"Naomi, see those stars?" He walked them clear of the wagon and stood with his arm around her shoulders, pointing at the sky lit by a thousand lanterns showing the way. "Remember what I taught you about using them as your guide." He marked each spot, making her demonstrate her knowledge as he explained again how to navigate through the night using the pattern there to steer a course.

"Follow the bear…" He pointed at the constellation, murmuring the directions in her ear as he held her close. "You'll kick up too much dust during the day, camp when the sun comes up and travel from dusk to dawn. Travelling a steady pace, you'll hit the trail to Buffalo Creek morning after next. Keep driving and keep the sun at your back. When you get close, whip the draft horse into a run. You're not safe until you hit town."

"If you think you can get out of this marriage by

getting yourself killed, think again." Naomi turned and looked him, her heart in her eyes. "I expect you to catch up with us after you set your fires. If you don't, I'm not promising that I won't come back for you. I never thought to have a husband, but now that I've been exposed to the institution of marriage, I find that I am partial to the idea."

She pulled Charlie's head down, kissing him on the lips, the chin, the cheek and back on the lips, awkwardly placing each intimacy.

"I mean it, Charlie Wolf McCallister," she said again when he drew her closer and laughed, scraping his rough beard against her jaw.

"Yes ma'am," he answered gruffly. "Now let's get you loaded and on your way."

She called the girls together and told them the plan.

"Open those up, ladies." Charlie threw a box of cartridges to three of the girls, Becky Johnson, Brody Quince and Daisy Meadows. "I need a supply of gunpowder."

~~~∞~~~

"Why do you call your horse Old Mossy?" she asked, looking at the beautiful animal. She fed Charlie's horse some grass and fussed at the blanket covering him.

"Oyamossa," Charlie said slowly. He stopped tearing apart the rifle boxes and grinned.

"Oh, he has an Indian name," Naomi said, hearing the different cadence as Charlie pronounced the word. She paused and then corrected herself, "A Kiowa name. What does it mean?"

"It means 'fearless warrior' or close to that. The Indian language doesn't exactly match the English descriptions. Sam made the word into 'old mossy' so that he could remember how to say it. That stuck." As Charlie explained, a teasing look changed his grim expression.

"When we set up housekeeping, you'll have to teach me your other language," Naomi said firmly.

"I look forward to the lessons, teacher." Charlie stopped spilling the rifles onto the ground long enough to meet her gaze. Unspoken promises passed between them before he continued smashing the boxes and using them as kindling to start his fire. Finally, he turned to the stack of rifles and began methodically slamming the stocks against the ground, breaking each rifle before he threw it on the growing pile.

"Why are you destroying the weapons?" Naomi was shocked. He'd need the guns to protect himself.

"Army, Indian, outlaw?" he asked, giving her a bleak look.

Naomi could see the worlds he straddled. She picked up a gun and banged it on the rock, splintering the wooden stock.

"Can't let these fall into the hands of either the Apaches or the remnants of Jericho's band. And right now, both seem a mite closer than the army."

"I think you've made me stronger." She banged a second gun against a rock and felt the crack of wood under her hand. Her heart bumped harder and the breath stalled in her throat. Her fear overwhelmed her and she blurted, "I love you so much. Please don't get yourself killed."

Charlie's eyes changed, darkening to charcoal as he touched Naomi's jaw, sliding his finger across her mouth. But his expression remained stern.

"I'll use the gunpowder to get a little noise and light showing, priming the fire before piling on the guns. Then I'll lay a trail that leads up to it. I'm not lighting it 'til you've had plenty of time to get off the mountain and out of sight. Then I'll light the charge and ride like hell to join you."

"Can you ride now, with your bad knee?" It seemed she needed to remind him of his injury since he ignored it.

"I can ride. I'll belt my leg to the stirrup flap."

Harvey Collins' interesting items had yielded a stock of harness replacements. He pointed at the leather surcingle waiting to be strapped round his leg.

"Will that work?" Naomi asked doubtfully.

"Woman, I'm half Kiowa. I can ride a buffalo bareback if I have to." Charlie grinned.

"Well be that as it may, Mr. Wolf, make sure you hang on to the buffalo and stay safe so you can catch up to us fast," she told him tartly. She scolded him, drawing out their time together. As she talked, he moved her to the wagon, every step closer to the moment when they would have to part. Once there, Charlie delivered final instructions.

"Climb on board, girls. The wagon should travel fast, there's no cargo weighing it down now. You've got your box of rifles on board. I hope you don't have to use 'em."

The eight students from Sparrow Creek Ladies Academy looked solemnly at Charlie Wolf and then took up their positions.

Indifferent to the girls waiting to get started, he drew Naomi into his arms and kissed her, a deep, plundering tongue-tangling exchange leaving her breathless when it ended.

Charlie dropped his hands to her waist and lifted her onto her horse before she could cling to him. When a sob escaped her tight throat, he rubbed her thigh and growled, "Let the stars guide you, *mi corazón*. I'll find you on the other side."

What other side, how do you know I can find my way, what happens if I get lost, how do you plan to get away from the outlaws if they follow your lure? She wanted to pummel him with questions, delaying their separation.

Most of all, she wanted to know what name he'd just called her. He'd spoken it the night before and though she didn't know its meaning, the sound touched a place in her heart.

But Naomi didn't get to ask anything because Charlie limped over to Old Mossy before she could prolong the moment. He nudged his stallion's left shoulder and murmured a guttural-sounding command. Like a horse in a circus, Old Mossy bowed, lowering his withers for Charlie to grasp his mane and pull himself on, swinging his right leg over and sitting up.

The girls gaped at the show of equine mastery as Old Mossy stood, muscles rippling under his sleek skin while Charlie found his stirrups, adjusting them before buckling the strap around his leg.

"It's time. I'll ride in front and make sure the trail is clear until you're on flat ground. Naomi, take up your spot at the rear." He nodded at Missy, signaling they were ready.

Naomi rode the buckskin mare and stayed close as Missy drove the wagon down the side of the mountain. Every creak and groan of the old cart seemed magnified in the night. From the back of her horse, she studied the stars and memorized the path she'd follow to cross the desert under the night sky.

When they neared the bottom of the rocky terrain, Charlie rode beside her.

"Ride close to the wagon from here on," he said.

He started past her and she gasped, "Wait."

"Go now," Charlie said gruffly.

Naomi obeyed, looking over her shoulder to watch Old Mossy climbing the path they were leaving behind.

CHAPTER TWENTY-THREE

N O ONE SPOKE as the mountain receded into the distance. Hours passed until the shadowed rocks and cliffs no longer loomed behind them.

"Let's keep moving. The sooner we get to Buffalo Creek…"

"We'll pull over here. Miss Parker charted our course right." When Missy started to pass the spot Charlie had described, Brody Quince took the reins from her.

I'm Mrs. Wolf, Naomi silently corrected her student, grateful for Brody's intervention. She didn't want to argue with Missy. She knew all the girls would like nothing better than a frenzied ride toward their destination. But Charlie was counting on them following his plan.

Brody drove the rig toward a barely discernible slope but as Naomi watched, the top of the wagon disappeared. She followed, mystified until her mare trotted to the dry creek bed where Brody stopped. Naomi dismounted and tied the mare to the side of the wagon, loosening her girth but leaving her saddled. Smiling, she watched Brody take charge as Charlie would have.

"No fires, hoard the water, no moving around, no talk. We can't let a gully-washer catch us napping. When you're on guard, watch the sky and stay alert. I'll stand first watch."

Since it was impossible for her to sleep, Naomi kept watch with Brody while the other girls napped. Later in the day, she curled in the shade under the wagon and closed her eyes, but a vision of Charlie Wolf riding away filled her mind.

The afternoon dragged. They were anxiously waiting to resume their journey when the sun began to slip below the horizon. Rebecca watered the draft horse and pampered him as he stood patiently, still harnessed and hitched.

Naomi peered at the sky, willing it to fade from day into night. When once again stars displayed her map, she walked to the buckskin, tightened her cinch and mounted, signaling their start. Brody climbed on the wagon seat pulling Missy up beside her.

"Let's go home, ladies," she drawled, slapping the reins. They hadn't traveled far when fire flared high in the distance.

"Charlie set the rifles ablaze," Daisy's voice carried to Naomi.

"Quiet, ladies, or else Mr. Wolf's risk was for

naught." Naomi knew her voice was sharp but fear rode with her. Silence once again prevailed as they bumped across the rugged terrain.

At dawn, Naomi altered their course according to Charlie's instructions and found the trail leading to Buffalo Creek. Missy slapped the reins and sent the draft horse into a jarring run. It was midmorning when they drew close enough to smell scorched wood.

"Stop," Naomi said, riding close to the wagon.

"Mr. Wolf anticipated trouble. He said if we couldn't get to Buffalo Creek, bypass the town and head straight to Eclipse. It's farther away but big enough to offer safety." Fearing their would-be haven had been burned to the ground, Naomi turned their course away from the billowing black smoke, soothing their collective terror with Charlie's words.

Though the draft horse was covered in sweat and heaving in exhaustion, Missy urged him into a trot toward their new destination. They'd driven him at a hard run to Buffalo Creek and had no place to take refuge now that it was a wasteland.

"Check your weapons, make sure your rifles are loaded and get ready, girls. Missy, keep the wagon moving no matter what happens," Naomi said grimly, hearing the thunder of hooves approaching from the direction of the burning town. Recognizing their dire situation, Naomi faced the approaching rider, sighting down the barrel the way Charlie had instructed.

She gasped in relief when she recognized Old Mossy running toward them with Charlie, crouched low, gripping his horse with his thighs, his twisted knee and injured leg bound to the stirrup leathers. He skidded to a halt and pulled the buckskin mare to a stop, hauling Naomi from her seat, kissing her before setting her back atop her horse.

"Still my woman?" he growled.

"Well, of course and you're my man so don't forget it." Naomi blinked at him in astonishment, icicles of fear melting from her heart. Evidently satisfied with her answer, Charlie pointed at the devastation that had once been Buffalo Creek.

"Burned to the ground and still smoldering. You did good, Naomi. I came behind making sure you didn't have anyone following besides me. But I figured if they weren't behind, they might be waiting in the nearest town, Buffalo Creek. I scouted ahead. Glad I did." He paused to reach over and hug Naomi again before he looked at the wagon of girls. "I'll need help fetching water before we start out for Eclipse."

"Where's the water?" Relief poured over Naomi. Though the girls had hoarded every drop, the water barrel was empty. As soon as she'd seen the town in flames, she'd wondered what they'd drink until they reached Eclipse.

"We'll circle around the town. At the other end of Buffalo Creek there's a well. It's still fine. We'll fill the canteens and barrel and when we get close to Eclipse, dump the extra weight."

Brody Quince drove the wagon following Naomi and Charlie. Old Mossy snorted and danced nervously as he picked his way carefully to the smoldering wooden platform. Most of the buildings were already charred memories, a few toward this end of the street still burned, as though their fires had been set after the rest of the town was gone.

"Smart," Charlie nodded at the flames still flickering nearby. "Potter scooted most of the people out this end while his men held off the attack, then he set a firewall and ran like hell."

"He burned the town down?" Naomi stared at Charlie in astonishment.

"Looks like it," Charlie said, nodding at the burned buildings. "Good thing. Guess someone decided Collins stashed the rifles in Buffalo Creek. But while they were tearing this place apart it kept 'em away from you and the girls." He pointed her attention to the ground. "Bad thing, though. There's a hell of a lot more than twenty tracks. The new prints might be Apaches. If so, Eclipse is in a world of hurt because when the outlaws didn't find what they wanted here, they headed that way."

Naomi followed Charlie into the burning town on her skittish mare but the draft horse refused to budge, stopping at the edge of the smoke-filled area. Charlie didn't waste words. He unwound the ties binding his leg to the saddle and slid down. Limping to the draft horse, he unhooked the harness and backed Old Mossy into the traces.

Naomi dismounted and hurried over the scorched ground, stepping clear of burning debris. Before the wagon arrived, she had the first bucket of water waiting. The girls jumped down and formed a brigade, filling the barrel quickly. Nobody wanted to linger in the disaster area, but Charlie limped down the street, checking the scattered bodies for life. He returned wearing a grim expression.

"Nobody still breathing but not many dead from either side. Looks like most of the Buffalo Creek citizens made it out with the devils chasing their heels."

Naomi frowned at Charlie's leg. It was swollen again and his limp was pronounced as he walked beside Old Mossy pulling the wagon away from the well. His lips were drawn in a straight line and sweat beaded his forehead.

"First stop, you'll let me wrap your leg in wet cloths," Naomi told him, focusing on the pain he suffered rather than the ordeal they faced.

"You're a bossy woman." But Charlie's mouth curved into a smile as he chided her.

"Yes, I am. You'll have to adjust," she said tartly, emboldened by the laughter in his eyes.

"I suspect we'll both be doing that," he agreed, his expression changing to serious.

⫘⟶

They left the smoldering remains of Buffalo Creek and started for Eclipse. Charlie circled back, halting their progress from time to time, securing their rest in places he'd already deemed safe. It was a four-day trip by wagon to Eclipse. With Indians and outlaws both roaming the area, they were all conscious of the danger.

"We're going to travel fast the rest of the day and through the night. We'll rest the horses as needed, but we'll not stop to make a camp again." Charlie's orders made Naomi feel safer as he took charge again.

By the third day the girls eagerly pointed out things they recognized in the landscape as they traveled toward Eclipse. Since they'd begun their trek, they'd crossed outlaw tracks several times but had so far not run into them. Dreams of an easy ride home ended as they neared civilization. They heard the sound of gunfire coming from the direction of Eclipse. Charlie led them to a dense patch of cactus where they were to wait until he returned.

"I'll scout ahead and come back. Give the horses a little water, not much, and be ready to move when I get back."

"Don't get killed." Naomi had no time to say more than that before he was gone.

The girls checked the rifles, organized the ammunition and took their places, waiting tensely. It wasn't long before he returned, trotting Old Mossy to the wagon with his final instructions.

"We're gonna get close and then run the gauntlet. Outlaws have Eclipse under siege. Follow me."

Missy pushed the wagon horse into a steady trot, following Charlie in a wide swath around Eclipse, skirting the town and cutting through the desert to come in on the other side. They were close enough to hear the sounds of battle when they stopped one last time. Before dumping the water barrels to lighten their load, they all drank deeply, swallowing the tepid water as though it might be their last sip of life.

"Exemplary ladies face danger and master it with intelligent calm—as you have done and will again." Naomi clung to her mount, looking over her students. She wasn't sure if *Godey's* really said that or not, but it seemed fitting advice for the students of Sparrow Creek Ladies Academy. "You will survive this last challenge," she told them.

"Keep your heads low, aim straight and once we're attacked, keep shooting." Charlie's advice was more succinct.

"Ride beside the wagon horse when your girls start firing. Stay low and let the horse shield you until you see an open spot, then make a dead run for Eclipse." Charlie rode beside her, shielding her as they galloped toward Eclipse.

When the fast-moving wagon accompanied by two riders raced into battle, the surprised outlaws and Indians turned their weapons toward the girls and away from the embattled town. Yips and war whoops filled the air as both factions recognized the prize they'd sought.

Naomi could see Eclipse citizens scrambling to open a path through their barricade as the girls rolled up the tarp and let fire—eight daughters of Texas blasting their way home.

Charlie smacked the buckskin's rump and the mare went into a flat run closing the gap between Naomi and safety.

Suddenly a man popped up next to her, running by her side, reaching for her reins. Looking for Charlie, she kicked her horse, putting distance between her and the outlaw. A warrior wielding a lance and riding a spotted stallion bore down on her fast. Guiding Old Mossy with his knees, Charlie fought the other man in hand-to-hand combat, knife against lance.

A steady barrage of bullets ripped through the attackers before they could reach the wagon. Missy whipped the draft horse and Brody Quince fired steadily, rocking with the bounce and sway of the wagon as it raced to meet the Eclipse citizens coming to meet them.

Suddenly their escape was challenged as warriors rose from hidden trenches they'd burrowed in, spilling dirt and brush as they emerged and raced to capture the passing wagon. When one of the men climbed on the seat by Missy and grabbed the reins, Brody Quince shoved the other girl low and shot him point blank. He fell from the seat and she kept shooting, catching the leathers and tossing them back to Missy.

Naomi glanced at Charlie. Minus his hat, he crouched low on his horse's neck, his dark hair mixing with the midnight coat of Old Mossy.

He looks like one of the Indians. For the first time since their meeting, she saw him as others saw him—a wild savage to be feared. When Charlie circled Old Mossy, coming up by her side, she swerved her horse closer, throwing her arms around him.

Their mounts sped along stride for stride until bronze arms of steel lifted her from her mare and set her in front of him. All guns were trained on them when they raced behind the wagon through the barricade and into Eclipse.

"What in the name of hell did you think you were doing?" Charlie roared.

"Saving you," Naomi muttered, burying her face in his chest and wrapping her arms around his waist.

"That's three ass-beatins you've got coming," he whispered in her ear as they were surrounded by men ready to use their guns.

"Better quit canoodling and get inside the town, Charlie, although you two might not be any safer *in* than wherever you've been." It was Sam coming up on Old Mossy's left side. Deacon came up on his right.

"I'm very glad to see you are alive, cousins," Naomi said, beaming at her new relatives.

The McCallisters edged out the other riders, protecting as well as escorting Charlie and Naomi down the main street of Eclipse.

"We never made it to Abilene with the prisoners," Deacon explained. "Damn near got caught bringing 'em here."

"Wouldn't want anyone to think you're part of the Apache band, cousin." Sam handed him his Stetson and Charlie pulled it on, tucking his hair underneath.

Two men—one smiling and mild-mannered the other grimly suspicious, each wearing a star—rode beside the group, escorting Naomi, Charlie and the wagon loaded with girls to the town jail. The stern lawman kept his rifle aimed at Charlie.

"Point that gun elsewhere or I'll do it for you, Sheriff Wood," Deacon finally warned him.

"This is my town, McCallister. Don't get uppity."

"Your mouth is going to get you killed, Sheriff." Sam drawled. His calm tone didn't match the look he exchanged with Deacon. Both McCallisters edged their mounts nearer the lawman.

Naomi hugged Charlie, guarding him. Of course, his arms surrounded her doing their own protecting.

"I'll vouch for all three McCallisters, Hank. Now let's not get in a shoving match in the middle of the street." The second lawman, clearly the more level-headed, rode close, nudging the rifle in question aside before the McCallisters did more than threaten.

She relaxed, finally letting herself believe they'd be alright.

Chapter Twenty-Four

NAOMI VIEWED the second lawman curiously. He dwarfed the mean-spirited Hank Woods both in personality and size. When he put his mount between Charlie and the Eclipse sheriff, securing their safety as he accompanied them down the street, Naomi knew she liked him.

"Naomi, this is Hiram Potter, Buffalo Creek's sheriff." Charlie introduced the big man to her, then turned to the lawman. "Hiram," Charlie nodded at Naomi, "this is Naomi Parker—"

"Pleased to meet you Sheriff Potter and it's *Mrs.* Naomi Parker Wolf McCallister." As she corrected Charlie's introduction, Sheriff Wood gave her a disgusted look.

"You're a heroine in these parts now." Hiram Potter brushed aside Hank Wood's silent insult, tipping his hat and complimenting her. "We figured the girls were well on their way to Mexico. Reckon you saved their bacon."

"It was Mr. Wolf and his cousins who were

instrumental in the rescue. I simply aided them." She beamed at Charlie, glad to give him credit and pleased to have him safe beside her with no more bullets flying around. Then she thought it prudent to remind the men of the battle raging behind them.

"Should you not continue to fight the attackers?"

"Naw," Hiram Potter grinned. "The Indians were gone as soon as they saw you reach our barricade. The rest of the outlaws are on the run now. They've got nothing to gain by staying."

The Sparrow Creek ladies had wasted no time jumping from their war wagon, hugging each other once on the ground and dancing like wild Indians themselves.

"I'll be damned if that's not what the renegades are after. How'd you girls get possession of these guns?" Sheriff Wood asked, pointing at Marnie waving a Winchester in the air signaling their victory.

"Questions can be answered later, Hank," Hiram Potter said. He stepped in front of the other sheriff, tipping his hat in Naomi's direction and reaching a hand behind her to pat Brody Quince on the shoulder. "I know your folks will be glad to see you. Hamilton rode out to the ranch when the bastards..." He looked at the girls and his words stalled. "Begging your pardon, Hank. Just needed to welcome Lucy's girl home." Flustered, he took off his hat and rubbed a handkerchief across his brow before he added, "Please excuse my language, ladies. When the band of renegades burned us out of Buffalo

Creek, there wasn't but a few folks in town and most of us got out ahead of the wild bunch. If they hadn't been so bent on destroying everything there, they'd have caught us. Guess they thought Jericho was locked up in my jail.

"We got here just in time to warn Eclipse citizens that the outlaws were coming. Hamilton rode hell-bent for leather to the Double-Q before the renegades pinned us down. We hoped you'd stay put wherever you were." He scratched his head and put his hat back on, peering curiously at Naomi.

For the first time since the beginning of her adventure, she was acutely aware of Charlie's buckskins drooping and sagging on her form.

"Would this be the wagon Jericho is having a conniption fit over?" Sheriff Wood asked, taking charge again. One by one, the girls handed over their rifles and displayed the sixteen that were loaded and ready. No one mentioned the other three cases that Charlie had destroyed.

The men were immediately deep in conversation and the girls and their ordeal relegated to an unimportant event because they'd survived.

It would have been indelicate for anyone to mention the odor of skunk, dirt and sweat emanating from the young ladies but as soon as the wagon was unloaded, the girls and Naomi were hustled into the biggest building in Eclipse, the CQ Mercantile.

Before she walked through the doors, she felt the

pull of Charlie's glance and when she looked at him, he threw her the saddlebags.

"Use what you need, teacher."

She caught the toss, warmed by his need to care for her and his desire to protect her from the disapproval of the town.

"Thank you, Husband," she said firmly, loud enough for those on the boarded walkway to hear.

"It looks like she's not letting you weasel out of the contract, Chief." Sam McCallister laughed.

Naomi frowned at that. Did Charlie want out of the contract? Maybe he didn't want to acknowledge her as his wife. Marnie said an Indian squaw walked behind her husband. Naomi didn't see herself doing that, but maybe she could negotiate with him.

"Make yourself pretty for me, *mi corazón*," Charlie Wolf called loudly across the space separating them before she could spiral into complete doubt. Sheriff Wood ushered them into the establishment as if he owned it.

"You go ahead and pick out whatever you need, ladies." Then he cast a glance at Brody and added, "I'm sure under the circumstances the owner will approve your purchases. After that, there's rooms and a bath and such down at the end of the street at the CQ Boarding House."

"Whoever this CQ is," Daisy Meadows quipped, "looks like he owns half the town."

"Just about," Brody Quince answered. "That would be my aunt you're speaking of, my Uncle Hamilton's wife."

Although the store offered about anything they could want, the girls shopped quickly for essentials, more interested in bathing in a real tub and feeling the security of four walls.

The CQ Boarding House proved to be a respectable rooming house—for women only. The girls shared bedrooms, giving Naomi her own. The room was so elegant that she hesitated to sit on the side of the bed lest she mar the flounced and ruffled cover.

She paced, reluctant to undress, as if taking off Charlie's buckskins would in some intangible way break the connection between them. Finally, after all of the students had used the facility and retired to their rooms, primping and trying on their new clothes from the Mercantile, Naomi went to the bathing room across the hall and embraced luxury.

Staring at her reflection in the mirrored wall, she peeled off the buckskins and laid them next to the tub. After she drew water, she washed them out, wringing them by hand until all the excess moisture was gone. Then she hung Charlie's buckskins on a hook to drip on a towel and refilled the tub with bath water for her.

The earlier bathers had depleted the hot water supply, but it was still heaven. Naomi leaned against the back of the clawfooted tub, wishing it was Charlie cushioning her as he had in the trough.

My thoughts always seem to lead back to him. Marveling that it had been a fortnight since she'd been a spinster schoolteacher at Sparrow Creek Ladies Academy, Naomi examined her body, hoping it had changed during her two weeks of intimacy.

She counted her ribs, more prominent after the combination of too little to eat and rigorous activity. Sighing, she stood from the water and dried her legs, comparing their pale whiteness to Charlie's lovely bronze color.

Charlie said I should use his money. She pulled on the new undergarments, ignoring the twinge of shame over their cost. There had been plainer cotton drawers and certainly an abundance of muslin chemises that were less dear. But she'd taken guilty pleasure in choosing the fashionable chemisette with ruffles on the attached pantalettes.

Naomi fiddled with her new corset until the lacings were just right, then closed the front plackets, admiring the way it displayed the curve of her waist. Charlie had destroyed her old-fashioned wire contraption so she'd felt justified in replacing it.

The supple beauty enhancement she currently wore neither rubbed nor pinched. It cupped her breasts and tapered down to her waist, flaring out gently over her narrow hips. The whalebone inserts and padded material assured fashionable comfort.

Wishful thinking won't make them grow. They're just little. Naomi squinted down, assessing the small mounds Charlie cupped in his palms and suckled. Nevertheless, a tingle of excitement spread all the way to her core at the memory of his mouth on her.

She hadn't thought to buy a wrapper at the Mercantile so she ducked her head into the hall, making sure it was empty. Both backstairs and front were clear, so she scurried to her room and unearthed *the* dress.

Cornflowers—Mr. Wolf bought me a dress dotted with cornflowers after our first night together. She'd waited two weeks to don Charlie's gift. Nervously, she ironed the wrinkles from the outfit he'd bought for her in Flat Rock.

It wasn't at all like the somber attire in her usual wardrobe. Just looking at it made her feel young and pretty. Quivering with anticipation, she stepped into it, easily pulling it upward and on.

She frowned. It was long enough, but too big in the bodice and torso. Nevertheless, she ran her hands over the blue-flowered muslin, smoothing the flounced ruffles on each hip. Fisting a swatch of extra material in the front, she pulled the material taut and peered over her shoulder, ogling her behind in the mirror.

Pulled up this way, I like the way the dress makes my rump look. Silently she admitted Charlie's wicked influence had changed her forever.

She caught sight of herself smiling idiotically and

realized her eyes matched the color of blue in her dress. Ill-sized though it was, his choice had been thoughtfully considered.

I am a silly woman. Mr. Wolf probably doesn't even know what color my eyes are. He probably bought the only dress that appeared long enough to cover my knees. Her hair, free of the pomade she'd worn in the past to tame it, was a much lighter brown. Charlie liked to play with the curls after they coupled.

Now it's the color of dishwater. Naomi frowned at it in disgust. Just once in her life, she wanted to be elegantly attractive.

She shivered, wishing he would come and get her. She hadn't had much luck with people coming back for her and every moment spent separated from Charlie Wolf increased her doubt in their true union. Anxiously she relived each word spoken in a recent conversation between them.

She'd been relieved to find him still standing beside Sam in front of the sheriff's office when she'd emerged from the mercantile. Ignoring his smirking cousin, Naomi had returned Charlie's saddlebag and asked him again about the name he called her.

"*Mi corazón.* Is that your Indian word for me, like Old Mossy is for your horse? What does it mean?" she'd asked Charlie. Naomi grimaced remembering how Sam McCallister had let out a whoop and even Deacon had unbent enough to smile.

"It means sharp-tongued woman." Charlie's answer had been irritated. He'd scowled at both cousins and then back at her, chasing her away with his look.

She'd hurried up the street, joining her students and hoping she'd not embarrassed Mr. Wolf with her question. But, the words sounded so pretty delivered in his gruff tones, they made her heart catch. She wanted to know what they meant.

"*Mi corazón...* That doesn't sound like sharp-tongued woman," She frowned, determined that she'd find out what he really called her soon. But more important concerns intruded. *I need to wrap his leg. He's been hobbling around on it. I need him to...* She just needed him, period.

Naomi finished bundling her hair into a knot at the nape of her neck, swatting at the tendrils flying around her face. She bent toward the mirror, brushing at the stray locks, wishing that she had just a little pomade.

Down below, the front door slammed, signaling the arrival of some of the girls' relatives. She smoothed her palms on the dress, thankful she would meet parents in a skirt and not Charlie's buckskins.

Preparing for the coming introductions and greetings made her nervous. She was aware from Deacon's information that many of the girls were from affluent Texas families. She was determined to convey refined deportment, illustrating that, had she been allowed, Naomi would have been an excellent teacher for their daughters.

"Brody—Ambrosia Quince, come out here." The sound of pounding feet on the stairs accompanied two voices united in one purpose.

Naomi stepped out in time to see Brody fly into the arms of a big man who hugged her tight, threw in the air and said, "Damn, sugar plum, you had your mama scared half to death."

"Quincy, let me see my daughter." The woman next to the two cleared her throat and pulled on his arm.

"You can have her for a bit, Luce, but then I want her back. I'm not done huggin' on her yet." He squeezed Brody again, set her down and stepped back.

Naomi studied Lucy Quince, admiring her fashionable dress at the same time wishing her own fit better.

"Daughter, are you well?" Lucy asked, tipping Brody's chin up to inspect her.

"Mama, I was so scared." The budding doctor and brave student disappeared. As Naomi watched, Brody's lower lip quivered, she shuddered, tears brimmed from her eyes and she wrapped herself in her mother's arms.

The intimacy of the family's meeting made Naomi feel voyeuristic. She retreated, fumbling with the knob at her back but stopped before she could get the door open.

"Might you be Naomi Parker, teacher to these young'uns?" Brody's father asked.

"It's Mrs. McCallister, now. Miss Parker hired

Charlie Wolf to save us and then married him." Brody stopped crying to correct him. Lucy Quince looked startled.

"Would that be Rachel McCallister's son?" she asked Naomi.

"Yep." Before Naomi could answer, Brody forgot her tears and said proudly, "Best tracker in the state, maybe the whole country. He and Miss Parker saved us for sure."

Lucy Quince released her daughter and crossed to where Naomi stood. Before she knew what to expect, the small woman gave her a bear hug almost as rib cracking as Charlie's and then burst into tears, burying her face against Naomi's shoulder.

"When you get settled, come visit us and we'll throw a party celebrating your wedding to Mr. McCallister." Wiping her eyes and smiling, Lucy stepped away. All three Quinces insisted that Naomi come down to the sitting room where the housekeeper had laid out a table of food.

The students were rapidly consuming the meal when Naomi entered. Filling a plate, she seated herself on a chair at the side of the room and nibbled. Through the afternoon, Naomi greeted each set of parents with dignity, endeavoring to be gracious and ladylike, all the while wishing Charlie would come for her.

As soon as she could escape the reunions and happy tears, she eased out of the room and went back upstairs.

Shadows filled the corridor since it was too early for lamps to be lit. She was halfway to her room when two sounds—wheezing breath and the click of a gun hammer—made her freeze in her steps.

Naomi hoped someone in the room below would remember her. It hadn't taken the Quinces long to come round up their chick. That must mean the fighting was over and they thought all the outlaws were dead, run out of town or in jail. She looked at the one exception—a dirty old man, hunched over his weapon, ready to use it.

"Told you, you'd not seen the last of me," Harvey Collins snarled. "Walk down the back steps with me or I'll go down the front ones and shoot every whiny brat down there."

She didn't have a weapon or a way to refuse. Naomi walked to his side and the filthy miscreant grabbed her by the hair, shoving a gun against her head, cursing her and promising her speedy death if she didn't cooperate. She put up no resistance and it was unnecessary to manhandle her, but he seemed to enjoy dragging her down the steps by her hair in his fervor to get on with his business.

CHAPTER TWENTY-FIVE

C HARLIE GRITTED HIS TEETH and kept his calm. It had taken all afternoon to tell the two sheriffs—Buffalo Creek's Potter and the Eclipse man, Wood—about hiding the girls and then finding the guns. The sheriffs had inspected the stack of twenty-five remaining rifles and proclaimed them fine weapons.

"Good thing the rest didn't fall into the hands of the renegades," Hiram Potter said, decisively emphasizing the positive.

"How do we know the breed didn't sell the rest to the devils out there?"

There wasn't much to be done about Sheriff Wood viewing him as part of the enemy, but Hiram looked at the Eclipse Sheriff as if he wasn't quite bright.

"Hell, Hank, if that had been the case, they'd a not been outside your town looking for the guns, they'd a been in the streets shooting you with 'em."

"I broke the stocks on 'em and set fire to the lot," Charlie told them, figuring it was a good time to get in his story. In point of fact, using the gunpowder he'd salvaged, he'd blown the rifles to pieces.

Suffering Hank Wood's *hate anyone with red skin* attitude, Charlie was content he'd made the right decision. He resumed thinking about his woman. His mind was on getting her alone and in a real bed when Harvey Collins walked in, dragging Naomi by the hair and aiming a gun at her head.

"Turn loose those men you've got locked up back there." The old man shook Naomi by the scalp, emphasizing her stooped position as he pointed her head in the direction of the cells.

"All of them?" Hiram Potter drawled his question in an unruffled manner, distracting the outlaw as Charlie slowly stood.

Before Charlie could pounce, Harvey spotted the box of rifles on the floor. "I knew you'd found 'em when the girls blasted their way in." Keeping the gun at her temple, he hauled Naomi to the rifles. Though she said nothing, she turned her head and locked glances with Charlie.

Scared as he was for her, Charlie admitted he'd seen trapped catamounts that didn't look as fierce as Naomi. She wasn't frightened. She was furious.

"Give me the keys to the cell doors or I'll blow Naomi Parker's head off. I already want to do that, so it wouldn't be smart to give me additional incentive," Collins said.

"Who the hell are you to be giving me orders?" Woods asked.

"*I'm* the owner of those guns and *I'm* the man smart enough to ride right into town past your damn fool deputies with the rest of the Eclipse brigade." Collins sneered. "I'm here to reclaim my possessions and finish my business transaction with Jericho. Turn him loose, load the rifles back on the wagon and maybe I won't kill all of you."

"Well as to that, I wouldn't count on gratitude from Jericho 'twas it me. Ever since I got here, he's been pissing evil. Said he should have killed you when he had the chance."

Hiram tried to slow things down again. That seemed to jar the old man some and he looked scared for a moment. Before he could rethink his position, Hank Wood decided to take charge.

"I don't care if you shoot everyone in this room. I'm not turning loose the prisoners."

"Fine, we'll start with you." Just like that, the old man found a better target for his wrath than Naomi. Swinging the gun away from Naomi's temple, he shot Hank Wood in the head. Blood splattered back on them, more so than Harvey had apparently expected or planned for.

"Shit," he said, lifting the gun for a moment to wipe his brow.

As the men in the room stood stunned by the

slaughter, Naomi seized her opportunity and made her move—in the wrong direction, as usual. Instead of dropping to the floor and rolling, as he'd taught her, or gouging out Harvey Collins's eyes, as he'd suggested, Naomi screamed pure fury and knocked the gun from the old man's hand.

"Look what you did to my dress," she screeched.

Along with every other male in the room, Charlie looked at the blue cornflowers sprinkled with splotches of ruby red. Collins never had a chance.

Naomi towered over him, proving to be stronger also. She knocked him on his ass and pounced on him, straddling his arms, pinning them to his sides so that he couldn't muster any defense.

Although he'd shown her the move, Charlie was surprised she remembered it. As soon as she had the old man down, Naomi commenced banging his head against the floor, bent on ending his life, not escaping with her own.

Hiram Potter took the decision from her hands, rescuing Harvey and throwing him in jail before she could beat Collins' limited brains out.

"Got trouble in here?" Deacon poked his head inside and saw Hiram hauling Collins back to the cell as well as Hank Wood's gory remains.

"Nope." Charlie pulled Naomi into his arms.

"Naomi Parker is miss—" Hamilton Quince pushed past Deacon and charged into the sheriff's office, stopping his words in mid-sentence.

"Naomi Wolf McCallister is right here," Charlie corrected him, holding the woman in question in his arms while she clung to him and fussed about her dress instead of considering that she'd almost been killed.

"If I can't leave you in a woman's boarding house and know you're safe, where will I keep you?" He was doing his share of mumbling too.

"My beautiful dress is ruined. Turn me loose. If I get it off and soaking, I might be able to save it." Rather than struggle from his embrace though, she buried her face against his neck, all the while complaining. But her arms were wrapped around his waist and he crushed her to his chest, neither one of them breaking the hold on the other to worry about a little blood and brain matter caught between them.

Sheriff Potter came back into the room and picked up a stack of handbills, leafing through them instead of looking at Charlie and Naomi.

"Damn, Hiram, you'll have to take over here. We can't seem to keep a sheriff alive in Eclipse." Hamilton Quince disregarded them too, squatting next to what was left of Sheriff Wood.

"Not much of a recommendation. First Owen Bailey, now Hank Wood. A man would have to be a fool to take the Eclipse Sheriff's job." Hiram Potter continued leafing through the wanteds as he answered. He paused in his search, triumphantly pulling out a tattered handbill.

"Charlie, it looks like you've got a new bounty hunter in the family. Harvey Collins has a price on his head too." Hiram waved the wanted poster at them, as if giving them a wedding present.

"What did you say?" Naomi loosened her grip on Charlie's waist, turning to hear Hiram Potter better.

"The last sheriff of Eclipse turned to graft and corruption and it got him killed. Hank Wood was hired to take his place. I think you'll agree he didn't work out either," Hamilton Quince explained.

"No, before that—what did you say before that part, Sheriff Potter?"

"Harvey Collins is a dead-or-alive outlaw. You hit pay dirt." Hiram beamed and presented her with the handbill.

"Now, how do I redeem this?" Naomi murmured, taking the wanted poster. But then she frowned up at Charlie and asked, "Who was the last sheriff? What was the name Sheriff Potter called?"

The way Naomi's voice trembled, Charlie knew this was something important.

Hamilton Quince had been following the threads of the conversation as if it was a game of jump-in-when-you-can. He seized the moment.

"Owen Bailey, my wife's deceased husband, was the former sheriff of Eclipse." Hamilton scowled when he mentioned the man. "Why?"

Naomi trembled in Charlie's embrace. He felt a

surge of protective ownership as she stepped toward Hamilton Quince.

"I knew he was no good when I was eleven." Naomi held her hand out to him and when he grasped it looking puzzled, she added, "I guess that makes you my brother-in-law. I'm Naomi Parker, Comfort Parker Bailey's sister. I told her when she decided to marry Owen Bailey that he was an undesirable. But she didn't listen to me."

Charlie watched the importance of Quince's words get past her need to congratulate herself on being right. Her expression changed from astonishment and doubt to one of hope.

"Could you take me to her? Can I see Comfort, please?" she whispered. Then the shock of too much excitement, tragedy and worry must have weighed upon her, because Naomi, his warrior woman, began to cry.

~~~

Naomi composed herself and returned to the boarding house, looking at it with fresh eyes. Comfort Quince had done quite well for herself. Hamilton had announced his intent to bring his wife back to town in the morning. Meanwhile, Naomi was left wondering why her sister hadn't shared her obvious good fortune.

The thought depressed her spirits. She was glad to have Charlie Wolf by her side. Hamilton had directed her to make herself at home, so, she did. When she and

Charlie started up the steps to her bedroom and the bathing area, Mrs. Carmichael, the housekeeper interfered.

"He can't go up," she declared.

"I'm sure my sister will welcome my husband. He is a hero, you know." Bristling with hostility and ready to quarrel, Naomi shielded Charlie behind her. Charlie paused on the stairs, leaving the altercation to her.

"Don't matter him bein' a hero or a devil—he's a he—and Comfort don't allow no males up those stairs. She says she's runnin' a respectable boarding house not a bordello." Mrs. Carmichael stood hands on hips, staring up at them.

Naomi blinked at her speechlessly for a moment, then cleared her throat.

"Neither my sister nor her husband are here to make the decision so I am giving my approval," she said carefully. Naomi returned the housekeeper's stare. Suddenly the housekeeper let out a cackle and slapped her leg.

"Seems right to me. Guess Comfort can sort it out with you when she gets here in the morning." She shrugged, starting for the kitchen then stopped and turned back to speak to Charlie.

"I helped birth Brody Quince. Much obliged for what you did." To Naomi she said, "Bring that dress down here when you get the chance and I'll work on the blood stains. I reckon if he's a hero that makes you a heroine."

Blushing at the unexpected praise, Naomi took Charlie's arm and hurried them both up the steps before they ran into more interference. She immediately hustled him into the bathing room, apologizing for the absence of hot water.

He snorted at the lack and let her fuss as she filled the tub for him.

"You need to soak your leg. It's been days since we doctored it."

"They dry yet?" He pointed at his buckskins hanging from the hook. He tested them and decided. "Close enough."

"Better take that off." Charlie nodded at her dress and said gruffly, "Don't want to let the blood get set in it."

Much as Naomi would have enjoyed climbing into the tub with him, their days of liberated behavior on the trail were at an end. Her students were sequestered in a room for the night as they waited for parents to collect them. Also, evidently Comfort had one permanent boarder who worked at the Mercantile and lived here too.

"I bathed earlier," she told him. "You soak. I'll sponge off in the bedroom."

Hurriedly, before he could tempt her into wanton behavior, she exited to the room across the hall. Once there, she shimmied out of her dress, shuddering as she used the water in the pitcher to sponge off her face and arms. For a moment, her breath caught remembering the danger she'd just faced.

I might as well get used to it. Charlie is a bounty hunter and he... Her thoughts piddled to a stop. She was married to a man who would always be gone. Her mood was lightened when Charlie, bare-chested, wearing only his damp buckskins, came through the bedroom door. Although she'd been intimate with him many times, she blushed as his gaze traveled slowly over her, studying her new under garments. He shrugged on his vest and pointed at her dress.

"I'll take that downstairs for you when I see if I can beg some food." Dress in hand, he started through the door and then paused, turning back for a last order. "Don't change your get-up."

CHAPTER TWENTY-SIX

NAOMI STILL WORE her fancy underwear when Charlie came back through the door carrying a tray of food in his hand. Taking in her worried expression, he decided to distract her and nodded at the velvet chair across the room.

"Saw one like that in a Mexican bordello not long ago," he said slyly, teasing Naomi as he reminded her of the housekeeper's earlier disclaimer.

Clearly outraged at his comment, she studied the piece of furniture closely before turning her gaze back on him. Her expression changed to calculating. He had an uneasy feeling his joke had gone wrong.

He thought he'd better set his conversational foray straight, lest it come back in the future and bite him on the ass.

"I had to go across the border to bring back a wanted. He was staying at the prettiest place I've ever seen. There were these white frilly curtains at the windows and the furniture was bright, happy colors.

Made you feel good to be there."

She lifted an eyebrow.

"I don't bed whores," Charlie continued doggedly.

"You'll burn in hell for lying," she declared.

Charlie had gone from a joke about Juarez to frying in Hades in half a conversation. He figured he'd do better quiet.

She gave him one of her quelling looks that didn't even work on twelve-year-olds. He expected to get chastised for comparing her sister's furniture to that of a flop house or for visiting a brothel. She surprised him again.

"I would like to see places like that," Naomi said as if they'd been discussing it. "I've decided that I'll travel with you—like a squaw."

He wasn't ready for this conversation. As he watched, Naomi folded her arms and sat on the edge of the mattress ready to talk. By the set of her jaw, he could see whatever was on her mind, she'd prepared her argument.

"I don't want to be left behind. I've been left behind by people all my life—my pa, my brother, my sister, the Lancasters."

"You said the Lancasters died," Charlie corrected her. Naomi waved her hand as if that was a minor detail.

"I don't want you to leave me behind. I can travel with you."

"I live a rough life, Naomi." He didn't tell her it

wasn't fit for her. They both already knew that.

"Rougher than the past three weeks?" she asked, her eyebrows rising in wonder.

Well, she had him there. All things considered…

"If I can't be with you, I would ask that you not consort with other women," she continued when he didn't answer.

"Likewise," he agreed. "I don't want you foolin' around with other men."

That appeared to startle her. She even blushed a little as if she hadn't considered the possibility of other men hanging around her when he was gone. He had. And he didn't like the idea or anything else about the notion of being apart.

"We'll stay together," he said.

"Hold out your hands," she ordered him. She walked over to the table where he'd left his knife and pulled the weapon from its sheath. Carrying it, she crossed to where he stood. Charlie wasn't sure what she had in mind until she cut a thin line on his palm and one on her own, slapping their hands together like he'd once done on the night they'd mated.

"We have an agreement," she announced.

"Naomi, our hands are going to get scarred up to some extent if we have to mix blood every time we reach an accord."

"I just want this to be real." Her bottom lip trembled as she whispered her words, making Charlie's heart beat harder and his breath catch in his throat.

"You think I'm ever going to let go of you, woman?" he growled. "For a schoolmarm, wife, you don't have a lot of sense. You're my woman forever."

"And you belong to me now, Mr. Wolf." She poked his chest with her finger. "Don't forget that, if you have to visit fancy houses in the future." Then, having told him who was boss, she ran to the bed and jumped on it, bouncing as though she were a kid.

"Come here," she ordered him.

He was a quick student. Teacher didn't have to tell him twice. He crossed to the bed and peeled down her drawers, focusing on what he revealed rather than what he removed.

"Do you like my new undergarments?"

Charlie paused, inspecting the lacy ruffles on the bloomers.

"Good," he grunted, dropping them on the floor.

"I think they're love—" The rest of her thoughts on ruffled pants cut off in a shriek when he parted her thighs, lifted her by the rump and set his mouth on her sex.

He tasted the velvet-soft folds inside her cleft, stroking her with his tongue. She writhed in his hands, arching into his intimate caress. He wanted to consume her, breathe her essence into his body, anchor her spirit to his.

"You could have been killed today," he said, looking

up from his feast long enough to reprimand her for having been in danger.

"Charlie," she gasped. "Not now."

"Yes ma'am." He flashed a grin at her and resumed his attentions, kissing his way from her thigh to her nubbin of pleasure, stopping there long enough to suck. He penetrated her with two fingers, lapping her liquid heat as she came with a shriek.

"Best hush," he teased, settling her under him on the bed and muffling her cry with his lips. "Can't be sounding like a bordello up here."

He entered her with a thrust, enjoying the pulsing ripples of her orgasm before he began stroking in and out.

Charlie took her hard and fast the first time, venting his fear, lust and need. Just as fiercely, Naomi wrapped her legs around his waist, writhing under him and taking him deeper than he'd ever been.

When they collapsed together, he tried to roll off her, knowing his weight too great for her to bear. She slid her arms around his neck and kept him from moving.

He leaned far enough away to study her, frowning at the scrape marks his whiskers had left on her porcelain skin.

Her hair spread on the pillow beneath her head in a halo of light brown curls. He buried his face in them, loving her scent. It occurred to him that his bounty hunting days were over. As much as she wanted to be with him, he wanted to be with her more. And he would not ever put her in a position of danger again. He didn't know exactly how to explain how much he needed her. He tried.

"When that crazy bastard pressed his gun to your head today, Naomi, I—*I was scared, I thought I'd die if you died, I didn't want to ever be without you again*—I was concerned."

"Well, I wasn't," she said, blinking up at him. "I had it all planned out how—"

Charlie took her lips with his kiss before he released her and rolled from the bed.

"We need to work on your fighting skills," he said gruffly, smiling down with pride at the other half of his heart. Her stomach rumbled and he nodded agreement.

"Let's eat." Charlie set the tray on the mattress and Naomi wrapped a sheet around her, laying out the feast he'd carried up from the boardinghouse kitchen.

"You cook?" he asked Naomi as they split the last biscuit. Though they'd been living on the trail together, there hadn't been any chance for her to fix a meal for him. Naomi shook her head.

"Do you?" she asked hopefully.

"Nope, not unless you count opening beans."

"Who cares?" Wiping her fingers exuberantly on the white napkin Mrs. Carmichael had included on the tray, Naomi flung herself backward on the bed and stared up at him. "We're alive."

They started the night on the bed until Naomi shifted restlessly and decided she was moving.

"I'm used to sleeping on the ground now. This mattress is too soft."

Charlie agreed and moved them to the rug on the floor, curling around her protectively.

"Do you think my sister will remember me?" she whispered.

"Woman," he told her, hugging her close, "of course she remembers you. Naomi Parker is unforgettable."

As if his opinion mattered more to her than anything else in the world, she beamed at him and fell asleep.

Naomi wanted to cling to Charlie the next day. He sat with her in the porch swing, waiting for her reunion with Comfort. It had been seventeen years since she'd seen her sister and over ten since she'd gotten a letter. She was afraid Comfort had simply forgotten all about her.

"Maybe this is bad idea, Charlie."

"I'll scalp her for you if she's mean." He slid his arm around her shoulders and hugged her. Naomi swatted him, giggling at his offer.

"She had long black hair like yours when we were girls. Comfort was the pretty one."

"You have a beautiful soul, Naomi." Charlie cupped

her face and looked at her sternly.

She smiled her thanks, wishing that even if his opinion was true, it would be nice if the beauty of her soul would spread to her face and form.

His cousins loitered near the hitching post or lounged on the steps talking business with Charlie while they waited. Mrs. Carmichael brought food out to the porch and fed the McCallisters, lingering to talk to Charlie's cousins.

"I knew your grandma. Nice woman," she said. Rather than seeming intimidated when they just stared at her, she added, "Knew your grandpa too. Jonas McCallister was a devil. You boys take after him?"

"They are courageous men bringing justice to this land." Naomi got flinty-eyed, all set on defending her new relatives.

Charlie squeezed her arm and she looked over in time to see a smile flicker across his face before he gazed at the housekeeper and resumed his stoic expression. Mrs. Carmichael departed.

"Damn, Naomi. Glad you set her straight. I was afraid she was going to take the food back," Sam drawled.

Deacon mopped up the gravy on his plate with a roll and ate the last crumbs before he joined the conversation. "Much obliged, cousin. Good to know we have an educated woman ready to speak well of us."

Not certain whether Deacon mocked or complimented her, Naomi didn't know how to answer him. It proved unnecessary, though. Apparently convinced that the McCallisters were worthy, Mrs. Carmichael came back with slices of pie and loitered some more. She leaned against the doorframe studying Charlie.

"Bring your Mama into town for a visit sometime," she finally said. "I knew her before she got carried off."

Charlie grunted noncommittally. Naomi was saved from answering for him when an elegant carriage pulled up in front of the house and Hamilton Quince jumped down before lifting his wife to the ground.

Naomi stood and faced her. When she'd been a girl, Comfort had been pretty. Now she was the most beautiful woman Naomi had ever seen. Smoothing her hands over the cornflowers in her dress as if drawing courage from Charlie's gift, Naomi admired her sister's everything.

The costume Comfort wore sported a small bustle, the black piping on the gray material making her eyes appear even darker and more mysterious than Naomi remembered. The clothing covering her sister's lovely figure couldn't be described a mere dress—it was a gown, the white ruffled neckline accenting Comfort's glossy black hair coiled at her nape in an intricate twist.

Naomi blinked, measuring the sophisticated image of her sister against the fashion plates pictured in *Godey's Lady's Book*. Nervously, she patted her own flyaway curls.

"Remember what I said about her hair. If she disrespects you, it'll look good on our lodge-pole." Charlie's whisper caressed her nape with an almost kiss before he straightened and took her hand in his.

"Behave," she scolded softly. "I'm trying to make a good impression." Though she pretended to be scandalized at his threat her heart warmed at his offer. Now that her sister stood before her, Naomi clung to Charlie's hand for support.

Chapter Twenty-Seven

T HE LADIES OF THE ACADEMY were all safe and journeying home under the protection of their families, no one besides Hank Wood had been killed in the outlaw attack, and two long separated sisters were reunited.

Naomi should have been ecstatic. For the first time in her life she had money to spend and a store where to spend it, her sister's CQ Mercantile being a pleasure to visit.

But instead of appreciating the blessings surrounding her Naomi spent every moment of each day waiting for Charlie's return. She judged his behavior harshly. As soon as he'd witnessed her reunion with Comfort, he'd left with his cousins.

"Visit with your sister now that you've found each other. Relax, spend some of this money. I'll be back." He'd stuffed a few greenbacks in his shirt pocket and thrust the rest at her. "Here, use what you need."

He'd looked happy to go. She feared he'd re-embrace a solitary life unfettered by a wife. He'd said he'd be back soon, but she went to sleep at night worrying and every moment she spent alone in Eclipse, a kernel of hope that had sprouted in her soul withered a little more.

The first afternoon after Charlie's defection, the two women so long separated sat together in the sunroom. An awkward silence grew between them when they were alone. Comfort, being more of a social creature than Naomi, seemed impelled to open the conversation.

"My circumstances with Owen Bailey didn't allow for my sending for you." Comfort looked miserable and ashamed.

So many times, Naomi had had this conversation pretending both sides, questioning her absent sister about why she'd abandoned her, and making up excuses Comfort might offer. Now the questions and answers seemed pointless.

"I memorized *Godey's Lady's Book* and advertised myself as a teacher of deportment. I fared well and saw a piece of the world. I had an adventure," Naomi told her. "The past doesn't matter. We're here now." Her words rang true. Charlie Wolf wasn't here now, that was what made her feel soulful and lonely.

Comfort seemed bewildered by the answer, evidently expecting recriminations rather than acceptance. Naomi didn't really attend most of Comfort's conversation until she started asking questions about Charlie Wolf and their future plans. It was a subject on Naomi's mind too.

"Where does he live?" Comfort asked.

"I don't know." Naomi swallowed, feeling miserable.

"Does he own property?"

"We didn't speak of it." She didn't know that either.

"Who are his people? I mean besides those strange cousins of his. Truly, Naomi, I know that *Godey's Lady's Book* cautioned about speaking ill of anyone..." She paused.

"A young lady should be very guarded indeed about speaking evil of anyone and equally so of how she repeats the disparaging remarks of another," Naomi chanted in her most scholarly tone.

For a moment Comfort stared at her then convulsed in tears and laughter. She swooped across the room and grabbed Naomi from her chair, dancing her around in a circle as she hugged her.

"My God, Naomi, we did it. We both escaped that godforsaken place and—"

"We found each other." Naomi hung on to her sister and finished her sentence.

Comfort stepped back and wiped her eyes. "Well, actually you found me. But we're together again."

Naomi's misery lightened under her sister's ecstatic welcome but she returned to her favorite topic, Charlie.

"He left with his cousins and I don't know when

he'll return." *When not if. Stay positive, Naomi. He said you were his woman.*

"Those two are odd, Naomi. I hope it doesn't run in the family. It's a terrible truth that a woman may have to work hard to win her husband, but she gets the crazy relatives for free." Comfort concluded her earlier discussion of the McCallisters with her opinion of Charlie's cousins.

"Old Jonas McCallister was mean as the day is long. Good thing yer man don't take after 'im," Comfort's ever-present housekeeper, eavesdropped shamelessly and shouted comments from the kitchen when she wanted to voice her opinion on any topic.

"My friend, Hiram Potter, vouches for the McCallisters so I know they're good men." Roberta Harris, seamstress and permanent roomer at the boarding house, welcomed Naomi also. Instead of feeling an outsider, Comfort's friends introduced Naomi to Eclipse and fashion.

Naomi denied their urging to order a dozen gowns, but she did ask Miss Harris to alter Charlie's gift to better fit her. The cornflowers on the dress had always made it pretty but once Roberta tucked, pinned and stitched, the dress draped and molded on her figure as it should.

After Comfort's continued coaxing, Naomi ordered more clothes from Roberta because being taped and measured as though Ma Lancaster had her again, filled the long hours without Charlie.

It wasn't hard for the sisters to resume a friendship that had been interrupted seventeen years before. Naomi smiled a lot, supported Comfort's business venture by spending Charlie's money, and, after the first week, plastered on a weak smile as hope died within—he wasn't coming back.

"What is wrong with you?" Comfort finally demanded, pouncing on her listless behavior.

Grimly, Naomi confessed her doubts.

"Of course he's coming back," her sister scoffed. "You've got his saddlebags. Men don't leave their personal items with someone they're not planning to see again. Besides that, you have his money." Then, apparently remembering the last shopping excursion she'd used to cheer Naomi, she amended, "Well, you have some of his money."

Naomi knew these things in her head, but her heart waited for his return, more frightened each day of his absence.

Comfort insisted that they visit the Double-Q ranch and since it was a way to get her mind off missing Charlie, although she did miss him there as well, she spent two nights visiting with Brody Quince and getting to know Brody's mother, Lucy.

Brody had already demonstrated many times over her storytelling ability, but repeated the events of the Sparrow Creek students' rescue for anyone who would listen. Naomi became a permanent part of each audience, hearing the event told by another, one whose opinion was as strongly admiring of Charlie as her own. Listening to Brody comforted Naomi as she mourned his loss.

Which was why, when they returned to Eclipse, trotting down the street in the Quince buggy—and she saw Old Mossy tied in front of the CQ Boarding House—Naomi's head went up, her spine straightened and her nostrils flared, preparing for the moment when she would tear a strip of hide off Charlie Wolf McCallister for leaving her alone so long.

Charlie traveled to Fort Stockton, accompanying Hiram Potter, his McCallister cousins, and the U.S. Army as they herded the outlaws to jail. It had been decided that Jericho would remain under federal custody and all interested parties had to travel with the prisoner to settle up claims.

He hated leaving Naomi. When he'd told her he was going, she'd been thumbing through her instruction manual on wifely duties. She'd folded her hands in that old-maid pious manner of hers but she'd remained uncomplaining, although he could see the words fighting to bust loose from her tight lips.

"What's your *know-all book* have to say?" he'd asked to distract her, wondering not for the first time what she found inside her book that could be so important.

"The correct manner in which a wife should behave within marriage." She'd carried *Godey's* with her through trials and troubles, continuing to consult it once she was safe.

"And?" Charlie had hidden his grin.

"It advises that a wife should be silent and respectful, comporting herself in ways he finds pleasing while remaining an example of chaste womanhood."

He'd stepped close to her, plucked the book from her hands and pulled her into his embrace.

"I like the way you comport yourself just fine." Charlie had to stifle his growl of lust, thinking about how before he'd left, they'd taken to sleeping on the floor, so when she was comporting herself as a wife they didn't squeak the bedsprings in Comfort's four-poster.

Since Naomi seemed determined to follow the advice of her book on the role of wife, including docile obedience, Charlie didn't figure it would hurt her to read up on it. It was clear to him she didn't have the natural bent for it on her own.

All in all, he was pretty sure Naomi's venture in minding her husband would be a brief affair. It was a shame he'd missed it. He couldn't wait to return to her and see if it had been more than a momentary episode in their married life.

After finishing their business at the fort, he and his cousins swung over to the MC3 to inform his mother about his new marriage. Rachel immediately declared herself ready to meet his bride and accompanied him back to Eclipse only to discover Naomi gone.

Rachel didn't seem to be concerned at all. She waited in the parlor of Comfort's boarding house and visited with Mrs. Carmichael. Charlie paced the front porch, irritated that Naomi wasn't where he'd left her.

Sam and Deak added their nickel's worth of deviling, declaring Naomi was out on a bounty hunt without him. Finally, accompanied by his mother, the housekeeper stepped outside and wagged her finger at him.

"Naomi moped around here looking like a lost pup after you were gone. After they spent most of the money you left in that saddlebag of yours, Comfort took her off to the Quinces."

He'd about decided to ride out to the Double-Q and fetch her when Comfort and Naomi came trotting up the street in a fancy rig belonging to Hamilton Quince.

Charlie felt the cut on his palm begin to itch, whether to remind him of his bond or because he wanted his hands on her ass he couldn't say. Before the horse was tied off or the ladies ready to step down, he stood next to the carriage waiting for his wife.

"What is it about 'stay put' that you don't understand?" He set his sister-in-law on the ground, speaking past her to Naomi.

"What took you so long?" Naomi launched herself out of the seat and straight into his arms. She followed her first question with seventeen more before she slowed down to notice him.

He'd been without her too long to hold back and, relatives watching or not, he hoisted her into his arms and kissed her. He didn't much care and apparently, neither did Naomi. The rest of Eclipse had disappeared some time before, at least as far as they were concerned. When they finally came up for air, Naomi pulled his hat off.

"You cut your hair." Her words were plaintive, shocked.

"Yep." He'd sat on a stool in his mother's kitchen and let her cut it. He touched his neck self-consciously, feeling bare. "What kind of man has prettier hair than his woman?" he repeated her question to him from sometime before.

When he'd been crouched Indian-style riding into Eclipse and she'd swerved to protect him from guns held in the hands of white men, he'd made some hard decisions. He now also wore white men's denims, boots and Sam had bought him a fancy Stetson with some of their Jericho bounty. He had a feeling the boots weren't going to last, but he was willing to break 'em in and see.

But none of that mattered at the moment. There would be time for telling later. Right now, he needed a room and two or three hours of uninterrupted showing of how much he'd missed her.

"*Mi corazón*," Charlie murmured into her ear, holding her closer than decency allowed. "I missed you." He kissed her again, his tongue penetrating her lips, savoring her taste.

"I missed you too." Naomi's kiss slid from lips to jaw before she wrapped her arm around his waist, hugging him. In honeyed tones unlike her usual self, she asked, "*Mi corazón*—what did you say that means?"

Her question appeared casual as she walked beside him, as if the answer was unimportant. Charlie knew from her change in manner though, that she hoped to trap him into divulging a secret.

"Chattering badger," Charlie answered. When Naomi's lips pursed and her face primmed all up, he grinned, ready for the next skirmish.

"My Kiowa name is Chattering Badger?" Her voice rose indignantly. "The last time you said the words, you claimed they meant sharp-tongued woman. You can't keep your stories straight, Mr. Wolf. I will expect better of you in the future."

Whatever else she might have said he silenced with his kiss.

Two women stood watching from the porch of the CQ Boarding House.

"What does he keep calling her?" Comfort Quince asked.

"Gray Wolf, Charlie's father, called me the same," Rachel McCallister murmured, smiling at her memories.

"*Mi corazón* means, *my heart.*"

Included free with this book, please enjoy

McCallister Bounty Hunters

Destiny's Dream

In 1866, three McCallister youths set out on a quest to
find and spy on Lozen, the Apache warrior priestess. The
seer has captured Charlie Wolf, the half-Kiowa
McCallister's imagination and he's determined to share
this adventure with his white cousins, Robert and Sam.
The boys are half-grown striplings when they leave the
McCallister ranch. After their encounter with destiny,
they are men.

This short story is a non-erotic companion read to *Wolf's
Tender*, *Five Card Stud*, and *Trouble in Disguise*. Prior
familiarity with those books is not necessary.

Destiny's Dream

GEM SIVAD

DESTINY'S DREAM
McCallister Bounty Hunters

ISBN 978-1-62622-903-7
Copyright © 2013 Gem Sivad
Published by Gem Sivad LLC

Manufactured in the United States of America.

COVER DESIGN

Michael Hart

CHAPTER ONE
The McCallisters, 1866 Indian Territory

R OBERT MCCALLISTER RODE between his brother, Sam and his cousin, Charlie Wolf. His gut twisted in anxiety and he stretched in the saddle, more to release his tension than to ease his muscles. Even for striplings calloused by hard work, it had been a rough trip. Charlie had made a quiet visit to the ranch during the night, climbed to the porch roof, and then through Rob's window.

At his insistence, they'd wakened Sam and crept from the house. After leaving the ranch at sunup, they'd traveled all day at a fast pace, only stopping to give their horses a breather when needed.

Rob clenched his jaw to keep from voicing his worry. Now that they'd reached this place of cliffs and secret canyons, his companions were energized, as if their adventure had just begun. He, on the other hand, was filled with dread.

He studied Charlie Wolf and winced at the scar on his left cheek marking his copper skin with a pattern of tiny stitches. The savaged face was the result of an attack on him by their grandfather, Jonas McCallister. The stitches had been sewn by Aunt Rachel before she'd sent Charlie away.

Rob's dark-skinned, half-Kiowa cousin was Aunt Rachel's son. After her Indian husband, Gray Wolf, had been killed in battle, Charlie had returned her to her white home as his father had directed.

After Jonas had made short work of brutally driving his daughter's child from the ranch, Charlie had returned to his father's people to live with his Kiowa relatives. But, he kept in touch with his mother, sneaking back onto the McCallister ranch to see her when he could.

She'd named her son Charles after her brother—Sam and Robert's father—and Wolf, after her Kiowa husband. The first part of his name was as deep as white went with Charlie Wolf.

Rob and Sam had become adept at hiding him and distracting the old man so that Rachel could visit with Charlie when he came. But this time he'd come to talk to his cousins, inviting them to ride along with him to see the Apache mystic the Indians revered and the whites feared.

So here they were instead of back at the ranch.

They'd been gone a whole day and by this time, the old man had already planned every stroke of the whipping he'd deliver on Sam when he caught up with him.

That was the nature of the beast they lived with. Jonas had made it clear from the beginning that Sam was expendable. Robert, being the older and made in the old man's image, he coddled and spoiled as much as a tyrant could. Rob had tried rebellion but that didn't work but once. The old man had punished his sins on Sam's back.

Since Charlie Wolf wore buckskins and a loincloth, dressing like his Indian kin, Rob figured his cousin might actually survive if they were caught during this dumbass escapade. He wasn't nearly as sanguine about his brother's chances.

Sam's mane of gold would look real pretty on an Apache lodge pole. The Indians would favor his hair just as much as the ladies of ill-repute did at the Eclipse Golden Nugget. Though the kid was still shy of fifteen, he already regularly visited the saloon looking for a game of cards and Rob knew his brother had followed more than one of the Nugget's ladies upstairs for a mattress dance.

"You plannin' on marrying Annie?" Sam had asked him not long ago.

"If she'll have me," Robert had answered. He'd been courting Annie Ross and liked everything about her. She made a better future seem possible.

"You ever kiss her?" Sam drawled.

"If I had, I wouldn't say. A man doesn't talk about his…" Robert knew his face was red and he'd sounded like a pompous ass. He had kissed Anne, though it hadn't been more than a brush of his lips against hers.

Sam had suddenly seemed older and wiser than Robert. "Loving is good, brother. You should marry her and get the hell away from this ranch."

Sam bore more than his share or scars from the old man, though not all of them were visible. As soon as it became clear that the young boy couldn't learn to read, Jonas McCallister had labeled him an idiot.

"You'll weaken our strain. Better if you'd died when you were birthed." It was Jonas's constant message and the nature of the unfair and cruel treatment in which their grandfather gloried.

Aside from the reading part, Sam was adept. He could tie knots, follow a trail, cypher numbers and calculate in his head. But he could barely sign his name, and though the old man had beaten him for his failure, he couldn't put letters together and make words.

It was a puzzle Robert didn't understand. But he knew his brother wasn't weak minded. The kid could play a game of cards and tell just by watching the play what was left in the deck and what everyone held in their hands. He was canny in more ways than that. Hell, he spoke three Indian dialects as well as Charlie Wolf.

Robert's ruminations ended when Charlie Wolf reined his mount to a halt and slid to the ground.

"No talk from here on," his cousin's murmur was a bare whisper as he led his horse to a copse of scrub pines. Robert and Sam tied their mounts and followed their cousin.

Rob nodded when his brother tapped his nose, mouthing the word *smoke.* The scent of burning sage drifted in the air. His cousin crouched low and then dropped to his stomach; Rob and his brother did too, belly crawling to the edge of the cliff. Once there, they lay side-by-side, peering at the Apache camp below.

White men weren't supposed to know this place, but Charlie Wolf had ridden with his Indian relatives for three full seasons and they'd trusted him to keep tribal secrets. Rob felt both flattered and uneasy that his cousin had shared his knowledge with his white cousins.

From their vantage point, Rob recognized the markings that distinguished the braves as Mescaleros, Arapaho, Chiricahua and Kiowa. He counted at least four war chiefs and estimated that there were over a hundred Apache braves attending the powwow.

The person inside the circle appeared to be a male warrior. Rob stared down at the figure, trying to decide if *it* was a *she* and the reason they'd come to spy. With great care, he turned his head to face Charlie, arching his brow in silent question. *Lozen?*

Charlie nodded and Rob's teeth clenched. They were prying into secret Indian business. Regardless of the figure's appearance, they were gazing at Victorio's sister, said to be a witch, healer, and spiritual guide for her people. Charlie claimed she was a woman of magic.

Rob didn't believe in magic but if the McCallisters lived to tell about this day's foolishness, he'd agree that some kind of divine intervention must be at work. If they were caught, no doubt, the men of four Apache nations would be happy to slit both white and Kiowa McCallister throats.

He could feel ground heat through the barrier of his clothes, but chill bumps skated up and down his arms. Repressing a shudder he thought fleetingly about a predatory bird that could molt the huge White Owl feather the Indian priestess waved across the fire.

Suddenly she leaned closer to the blaze and fanned the fire into flames, sending gusts of smoke drifting upward. The threads of white and gray twisted into strange shapes, eerily clear against the backdrop of the midnight sky. Robert was as mesmerized as the Indians.

As one of the chiefs leaned close to hear her words, Rob teetered precariously on the edge of the cliff and strained to hear too. Next to him Sam remained focused on the ceremony. Charlie hadn't said why he'd been determined to see the tribal mystic but once Sam had heard his plans, there'd been no stopping him either.

Rob lay flat on his belly, disapproval making him rigid and tense. He'd argued against the foray into Indian Territory. After being unable to dissuade Sam from the trespass into forbidden lands, Robert had come along to protect the other two.

But Robert forgot the danger as he became enthralled by the sight of the Apache woman commanding the attention of so many warriors. His gaze was so intent he missed the stealthy approach of the Indian braves slipping soundlessly through the night.

CHAPTER TWO

B Y THE TIME Robert realized they'd been found, two braves had jerked Charlie and him to their feet and an Arapaho warrior was straddling Sam, holding a knife at his throat, and fisting a handful of hair. Rob knew enough Apache to understand the message the Indian crowed, jerking on Sam's blond mane.

"This will look fine hanging in my lodge."

"Black Hawk, cease." The guttural rebuke came from the brave holding Charlie Wolf. "Lozen wants these watchers brought to her alive."

"Cousins, we've come to parlay," Charlie said in Kiowa, greeting the Indians as kin and ignoring the precarious fix the McCallisters were in.

"Sharp knife you got there," Sam muttered in Apache. The only answer to Sam's overture was a trickle of blood running down his neck.

Rob swallowed a groan. Knowing his brother wouldn't want to appear a coward left Robert dreading what next might come out of Sam's mouth.

Evidently the brave named Black Hawk was intent on being first with his prize. He hauled Sam to his feet and pushed him toward the camp below. Robert clenched his fists, watching for the moment he and Charlie could break loose and...

Charlie was as docile as a sheep going to slaughter. Robert didn't understand what was happening, but he controlled his desire to lash out at the Apache shoving him toward sure doom.

"For God's sake keep your mouth shut, Sam," he muttered as his captor brought him alongside his brother.

None of them had a chance to make a move before they were pushed in front of the witch woman. In a moment of utter stillness, the night and sounds receded, leaving only them, the flickering flames, and Lozen.

*Boom...boom...boom...*Robert swayed on his feet, the pounding of his heart steadying to match the low throb of sound at the periphery of his senses. Funny he hadn't heard the drum from the cliff above. But now the pulsing beat smothered his clamoring thoughts about how the hell they were going to get out of this fix.

"Release them," Lozen ordered. The braves stepped away leaving the McCallisters to face her alone.

Though Apaches surrounded them, they were less frightening than the sturdy, grim-faced warrior of indeterminate gender he faced. As Robert watched, her form wavered, becoming almost transparent. *Am I hallucinating?*

He tried to breathe shallow, afraid the air was laced with a drug more powerful than the laudanum his mother used every day.

"Why do you come here?" she asked Charlie Wolf.

"I've come to barter for a woman."

Charlie tried to remain relaxed. It seemed a good answer, more explainable than his need to see Lozen. No doubt their Apache interrogator would recognize a lie. On the other hand, Charlie Wolf did want a woman and planned on taking a Kiowa wife as soon as he acquired enough Indian ponies for a trade.

Releasing a rich, husky sound that floated through the night, the witch laughed, inviting the men of four tribes to share her mirth at Charlie's excuse for spying on her.

"You brought white eyes to our sacred place. Why should I not kill you where you stand?"

"I brought blood of my blood to bride hunt with me," he answered. In retrospect, it didn't seem like such a good idea. Last night he'd foolishly tried to blend his two worlds. She was a living legend he'd wanted to see and share with his white cousins.

"Gray Wolf set his feet on the path to your destiny when he took the white squaw from her tribe. There will be no Apache woman for their son."

Charlie Wolf showed the witch no emotion. Nevertheless, her soft spoken words resounded around the campfire, an edict among the people of four nations. If they survived tonight, Charlie's bride hunting had been curtailed before it got a good start.

Lozen moved down the line and stood in front of Sam.

~~~~

Sam listened intently as Lozen began the interrogation with Charlie. He was glad that she hadn't started with Rob. Sam's brother had a way of peering down at people, being as he was taller already than any man that Sam had seen in the territory.

He was worried that Rob would go all pious and sour or worse yet start a brawl. Best thing his brother could do was tell the truth. He'd come along to look out for the fools who'd decided to get nosey.

Charlie said he was bride hunting and claimed them as his relatives to excuse their presence. As usual, his cousin was cool under fire but Sam didn't think the woman bought the bride hunt story.

Lozen moved away from Charlie to stand in front of Sam.

"Do you claim Gray Wolf's son as blood of your blood?"

"Damn straight." Sam didn't want to show the witch woman any disrespect and gave her the same smile he shared with the whores at the Golden Nugget. He figured Lozen had the old man topped for dangerous, but even so, Sam had a hard time focusing on her. The wind, which hadn't been there a moment before, gusted over the fire and sent smoke clouds drifting to twine around him.

CHAPTER THREE

LOZEN'S SPIRIT GUIDE had sent her to this gathering place of the ancients. She'd drawn together the leaders of four Apache nations to name a guardian for the sacred cave hidden inside the sandstone cliff.

But the ritual had barely begun when she'd detected the presence of the spies. Gray Wolf's son she knew by story. He'd ridden with his father at the Sand Creek Massacre and fought to rescue the Indians under attack. She had no quarrel with the Kiowa half-blood though she'd brought the boys to the Indian meeting, expecting to anoint the sacred place with their blood.

She moved from the son of Gray Wolf to the next boy in line. When she met the blond youth's gaze, Lozen's lips curled in a half smile.

The handsome boy flashed an easy grin at her, his expression suggesting that great mischief lurked within. The warmth of his smile didn't reach his eyes and his gaze remained as cold as a frozen lake in winter.

Lozen admired the playful expression decorating the sculpted features of the youth not yet a man. She expected to find fear lurking within when she probed his mind. Instead, she found violence. Before he could strike, she dusted the fire with powder, sending new tendrils of smoke twining around him, binding his will.

Ayeeee...... Lozen shook her head to clear her sight, startled by the old soul peering at her through the eyes of the white boy. The smoke tendrils coalesced into one, then two, then many faces hovering protectively over his shoulder.

The seer didn't like what she saw. She wanted the caves to be guarded by an Apache warrior. The *chosen one* was a pale faced boy. She pulled her knife, enraged by the idea of entrusting the young viper before her with this place of dreams. But she couldn't strike. The will of the ancients forbade it, securing their future, the cave's secrets and the boy's destiny as one.

"And you?" Her question snarled from her, almost a hiss as her anger spilled over the clearing, infecting the other warriors. "Did you also come for a woman?"

"Heard you were magic." He spoke in English, his speech slurred as he pointed at the tendrils weaving in front of him as if he saw what she saw and that explained everything.

Lozen's hostility melted when he smiled wryly and paid her homage in her native tongue. "Thought you might be able to make me smart as the wolf," he motioned at Gray Wolf's son, "or pure of spirit," he nodded at the young warrior with red hair.

Lozen clutched the white boy's chin and locked gazes with him as the ancients swirled in the air above, favoring him with their presence. Behind them, the drumbeat grew louder, echoing off the canyon walls as a gust of wind sent sparks skittering into the air. Finally, she released his jaw, and stepped back from the trio.

Her vision wavered for a moment as she approached the last of the intruders. He was tall and burly in stature, his shaggy hair reminding her of the grizzly bears hunting in the high country. She had no reason to spare his life. He would make a good sacrifice to seal the guardian's spirits to this place.

She called upon the ancients, her nasal song a plea accompanying the rhythmic drum beating in the background. The white boy's eyes widened in shock as Lozen grew larger until she gazed across at him, daring him to tell a mistruth.

He remained outwardly calm when she touched the fiery red thatch on his head and grasped a lock of hair, measuring the strength of the future warrior he might become if she didn't kill him this night.

～∞～

As Rob stared at the witch, behind her flames leapt high, crackling and sending sparks into the dark sky. A puff of smoke twined around her figure, changing her image until he beheld an Indian maiden of great beauty.

He focused on her gaze, ignoring the hand that stroked his head as if measuring the worth of his scalp before taking it. Rob shuddered at the force of her nature as their locked stares fought for dominance.

"And you, do you also seek an Apache woman?" Her voice rolled over him, her question carrying a mighty wave of power. The witch woman studied his face, her expression pensive.

"No, ma'am, I'm not bride hunting. I came with Charlie Wolf and my brother to make sure they keep their hair during this visit."

Robert shook his head, trying to clear his senses. When he looked at Lozen again, the Indian maiden was gone and he beheld the sturdy warrior. Specter or real, there was no doubt in his mind that the McCallisters would live or die by Lozen's decree.

After an eternity that might have been mere seconds, she turned from Rob and walked to the side of the camp where the contents of a black kettle steamed in the air.

After scooping the brew into three bowls, Lozen carried one to each boy. When they all stood holding the noxious smelling liquid, she spoke. "Drink and know your dreams."

Charlie considered Lozen as if trying to read her intent, Robert hesitated, sniffing the mixture for the scent of poison, but before he could caution his brother, Sam downed his in one gulp.

"Come on, boys, the party's just begun." The kid's laughter taunted death, Lozen, and the rest of the watchers as his legs buckled and he went to his knees.

Lozen tilted her head imperiously, waiting for Charlie and Robert to drink, also.

Charlie tipped the contents into his mouth, swallowed, and collapsed next to Sam, his will robbed from him. Robert drank the brew but being the biggest, his body resisted the effects the longest.

"So you've killed us?" he muttered as he lost his battle to resist the concoction and began his descent into oblivion. Rob was awake long enough to hear Lozen's promise.

"I've given you your futures. What you make of them is yet to be seen."

Drink and know your dreams... Lozen's words whispered in his mind as the tendrils of smoke wrapped around Robert and he went down.

He was propelled into a world of bitter cold, where deep snow blanketed the landscape and frozen shards of ice rained from the sky. He staggered forward, straining to hear the beckoning sound that called to him over the howling storm. As he stumbled through the blizzard, for a moment the wind calmed enough to reveal the source—a baby's piercing cries guided him through the torrent of chaos surrounding them.

Robert scooped the toddler in his arms, shielding the child with his body as he carried the baby toward the light beckoning in the distance.

He fell more than once and had the little one not wrapped its arms around his neck, Robert might have stayed down. Instead, as the infant hugged tight to him, he struggled to his feet and staggered through the storm. When he reached the light, he hammered on the door until he felt his knuckles split. "Open up," he yelled over the blizzard wind. When at last the door opened, he set the child on its feet and pushed it toward warmth and safety.

CHAPTER FOUR

B LACK HAWK HAD FOLLOWED the seer's orders and helped capture the spies. Now, he intended to claim the honor of killing them. He looked to Chief Nana for permission but the old chief stayed his hand, waiting on Lozen for direction.

With the three captives sprawled on the ground unconscious, the young brave was anxious to claim their scalps. He unsheathed his knife but Lozen grabbed him and took his blade.

"This one," she nudged Gray Wolf's son, "though of two bloods will be true in spirit to the Apache."

"He brought the enemy to our camp," Black Hawk dared to argue.

"He followed the path set for him by the ancients," she answered, shrugging away his complaint.

She moved to the red haired giant and looked hard at him, as though undecided about his fate. Then her face relaxed.

"Fire burns in this warrior's belly. His life will be filled with pain. We will leave him in the hands of *Ussen*," she declared.

Black Hawk's rage simmered. He'd be glad to send the intruders to the land of the Great Spirit. Lozen demanded obedience he didn't want to give.

"This one walks with the ancients. Do not touch him," she warned Black Hawk as she hovered over the third spy, as if admiring his exotic features.

Black Hawk itched to separate the pretty yellow hair from the youth's head. He searched the unconscious boy's face for evidence of his connection to the old ones and saw none.

Arrogantly, disregarding her words, he reached to draw the knife that Lozen had tucked into her belt. Before he could grasp it, she grabbed him by the throat, squeezing until he panted for air.

Black Hawk felt the power of the old ones surging through Lozen as he dangled from her one hand, struggling to breathe in the crushing grip. When his sight began to fade and his chest burned with pain, he understood that Lozen was as strong as the strongest warrior and it was a kindness to the young brave that she didn't snap his neck. Instead she answered him with wisdom.

"As I grasp your fate in my hand, so their souls hold our destiny in their own. Leave them. They will bring no harm to our people."

The fact that they were alive to see the sun rise the next morning surprised Robert. The ground was cold, but shouldn't have caused the chills that wracked his body. He attributed it to the after-effects of the noxious liquid he'd downed and not the savage blizzard in his dream. Cautiously he opened his eyes and turned his head. The campfire was dead and there was no sign left of the Indians.

The groans of Sam and Charlie told him they too had survived. Sam rose first and stirred the ashes of the dead campfire.

"Guess we still have our scalps." Charlie sat up next, rubbing his head.

"Since we're alive to see morning, wake up, brother." Sam nudged Rob with the toe of his boot until he gave into the prod and stood.

"Where the hell did you find that?" Robert growled, nodding at the knife Sam held.

"Found it stuck in the ground by my head. If I'd rolled over just right, I'd a cut my own throat." Sam experimented with his grip, holding it blade out and crouching Indian style.

"Lozen left you a gift and a warning," Charlie Wolf cautioned.

"I got the message. Won't be man or beast sneakin' up on me again," Sam muttered grimly.

"You'd never know there were over a hundred Indians here last night." Rob looked away from his brother and cousin. Regardless of the fact that the morning sun was already hot enough to fry an egg on a rock, he shivered.

Sam put fingers to mouth and blasted a shrill whistle. It took a spell, but his horse came trotting into the canyon, followed by the other two mounts.

The horses had been stripped of gear and turned loose to wander away or save their owners' hides. Charlie said it was another test of their worthiness fashioned by Lozen.

Rob kept his mouth clamped shut lest his teeth chatter as he made a rough nose halter from his belt and climbed on his mount to head home.

"Lozen took us spirit walking in the otherworld to find the threads of who we'll be." Charlie said but Rob hoped to hell he was wrong.

There will be no Apache woman... The message Lozen had given Charlie left his future a bleak prospect since white women sure as hell wouldn't be wedding the half-Kiowa McCallister.

Though he remembered his own dream with uncanny clarity, Rob didn't volunteer to share his vision.

His throat felt raw and throbbed painfully, his knuckles were inexplicably bruised, and he couldn't shake off the chill of a cold that hadn't been real.

"This is sacred place. It belongs to the *ancients* not to man," Charlie Wolf warned them before they left.

Before they rode from the box canyon, Sam made them wait while he paced around the interior, inspecting the cliff walls and boulders. He finally stopped by the dead campfire and stared at the ashes. As he fingered the knife at his belt he asked, "You fellas see those smoke snakes twining around me last night?"

He didn't mount up until he'd memorized the landscape, assuring both Charlie and Rob that he intended to return. "I like this place. Haunted or not, I reckon I'll be coming back here someday." Sam sheathed Lozen's gift as his glance played one more time over the terrain.

"It's all yours," Robert said gruffly, frowning at the idea of his brother returning alone.

As they rode back to the McCallister ranch, if each of the boys thought about the dreamwalk he'd taken with Lozen, none volunteered to share his vision. The incident was buried, but not forgotten as the McCallisters grew into men.

The End

MORE BOOKS YOU MAY ENJOY

ECLIPSE HEAT

McCallister Clan

Destiny's Dream
Wolf's Tender
Five Card Stud
Trouble in Disguise

Quince

The Journal of Lucy Quince
Quincy's Woman
Perfect Strangers

Hawks

Breed True
Whispering Grace (coming soon)

UNLIKELY GENTLEMEN

River's Edge
Unlikely Gentlemen
Cerise Amour

BITTER CREEK HOLLER

Call Me Miz
Miz Spelled
Ursus Horribilis
Miz Behavin' (coming soon)

JINX

Cat Nip
Blood Stoned (coming soon)

SINGLE SHOTS

Pinch of Naughty
A Staged Affair

 ABOUT GEM

Gem and her family live in a rural area where wild turkey, bear, and deer wander the country roads. Watching them is inspiration for her muse. She enjoys writing all genres but has a particular passion for steamy historical romance and twisted paranormal tales.

Although she has hermit tendencies, she loves hearing from fans. For updates (or if you're an avid *Words With Friends* junkie) follow her at any of these places:

GEM'S WEBSITE
GemSivad.com

NEWSLETTER
GemSivad.com/Dreamcatcher

FACEBOOK
Facebook.com/GemSivadAuthor

TWITTER
Twitter.com/GemSivad

TSU
Tsu.co/GemSivad

www.ingramcontent.com/pod-product-compliance
Lightning Source LLC
Chambersburg PA
CBHW031506210626
46816CB00019B/1565